"Don't you touch me. Don't ever touch me again."

She glared and he saw how much she despised him. "You lost that right when you left me behind."

"You'd be better off dead than with those savages." Thomas crossed his arms to keep himself from reaching out to her. "It was for the best."

"Don't tell me what's best. You don't know—you can't know. They have my daughter. I want her back, and you're going to help me."

Her chest heaved as she stood before him, the picture of a mother defending her cub.

"I hear you're some kind of a bigwig in this town. Maybe you can get the army to send troops, because they sure as hell won't listen to me."

"When did you get so bossy?" he asked.

"The day I reached my last hope and realized it was you...!"

* * *

High Plains Bride
Harlequin® Historical #847—May 2007

D0638227

Praise for Jenna Kernan

The Trapper
"Kernan's engaging characters [and]
a colorful backdrop… make this classic
western romance something special."
—*RomanticTimes BOOKreviews*

Turner's Woman
"Makes for tip-top reading."
—*Romantic Times BOOKreviews*

Winter Woman
"Presents a fascinating portrait of the early days
of the West and the extraordinary men and women who
traveled and settled the area…. Kernan has a knack for
writing a solid western with likable characters."
—*Romantic Times BOOKreviews*

"*Winter Woman* is an exciting, no-holds-barred
story with unforgettable characters.
Ms. Kernan's first novel is a winner!"
—*Rendezvous*

"With this strong debut, Jenna Kernan puts her name
on the list of writers to watch for and *Winter Woman*
may just be the start of a long career."
—*The Romance Reader*

High Plains Bride

JENNA KERNAN

HARLEQUIN®

TORONTO • NEW YORK • LONDON
AMSTERDAM • PARIS • SYDNEY • HAMBURG
STOCKHOLM • ATHENS • TOKYO • MILAN • MADRID
PRAGUE • WARSAW • BUDAPEST • AUCKLAND

If you purchased this book without a cover you should be aware
that this book is stolen property. It was reported as "unsold and
destroyed" to the publisher, and neither the author nor the
publisher has received any payment for this "stripped book."

ISBN-13: 978-0-373-29447-3
ISBN-10:   0-373-29447-6

HIGH PLAINS BRIDE

Copyright © 2007 by Jeannette H. Monaco

All rights reserved. Except for use in any review, the reproduction or
utilization of this work in whole or in part in any form by any electronic,
mechanical or other means, now known or hereafter invented, including
xerography, photocopying and recording, or in any information storage
or retrieval system, is forbidden without the written permission of the
publisher, Harlequin Enterprises Limited, 225 Duncan Mill Road,
Don Mills, Ontario, Canada M3B 3K9.

This is a work of fiction. Names, characters, places and incidents are
either the product of the author's imagination or are used fictitiously,
and any resemblance to actual persons, living or dead, business
establishments, events or locales is entirely coincidental.

This edition published by arrangement with Harlequin Books S.A.

® and TM are trademarks of the publisher. Trademarks indicated with
® are registered in the United States Patent and Trademark Office, the
Canadian Trade Marks Office and in other countries.

www.eHarlequin.com

Printed in U.S.A.

Twelve years ago, when I told my mother-in-law, Terry, I had completed a manuscript, she neither laughed nor rolled her eyes, but instead offered to read my first work in progress all the way from miserable start to dubious finish. Only a true friend could have done that and offer nothing but praise and encouragement. Thanks, Terry, for being a mountain of support.

Chapter One

I leaned my back up against an oak,
Thinking it was a trusty tree;
But first it bent and then it broke;
Thus did my love prove false to me.
        The River is Wide, American folk song

California, 1864

"Turn around, you son of a bitch."

Thomas West heard the emphasizing click of the pistol cocking. The woman's voice was not familiar. He lowered the razor pressed to his throat and lifted the towel, wiping off the remaining suds with measured strokes as he hoped that she would not plant a bullet in his kidney.

He turned to the woman, trying to place her. Full green skirts and a deerskin jacket revealed little about her age or shape. The wide-brimmed hat cast her face in deep shadow, showing only the stubborn set of her chin and the thin, grim line of her pressed lips.

She looked prepared to kill him. In his mind he'd given no woman cause. Though one had given cause.

"Sarah?"

The corner of her mouth quirked, and she lifted her chin to reveal familiar gray eyes. His breath caught. Time had stolen the round face, replacing soft features with high cheekbones and a pointed chin. Faint lines engraved the fine skin at her eyes—her beauty no longer pliant, but etched in granite.

"Mrs. West now," she said, rubbing his nose in it.

He gritted his teeth, refusing to acknowledge her marriage. Fourteen years, and the pain was as fresh as the day he had first heard the news.

"You promised to come back," she said, keeping the gun level.

"And you promised to wait."

A flicker of emotion changed her expression from steel to sorrow. She blinked, and the muzzle dipped. Recovering quickly, she focused and aimed. Thomas braced for the bullet.

"I need your help," she said.

"Funny way to ask, creeping up on a man and pointing a gun at his guts."

"Just wanted to ensure your attention."

He swabbed the towel over his cheek again, removing the sweat with the remaining soap. "You have it."

She released the hammer. "The Indians took my daughter. You're going to help me get her back."

He scowled. "You want help? You'd best ask the girl's father."

A vicious smile widened her full lips. "You *are* her father, Thomas."

The razor slipped from his hand, clattering off the planking. He scraped against the rough cedar shingles as he sat with a thud on the wooden porch. Somehow Sarah had shot him without ever pulling the trigger.

His ears rang with the thunder rolling through his brain, as her words echoed like a rifle shot through a box canyon. Her father—you are—father. The faithless woman who could not wait for his return had borne him a child. The possibility of it sank its teeth into the marrow of his bones. But Samuel had told him…Sarah's words butted against his brother's as he tried to understand what was happening.

Memories flashed through his mind. The air had been scented with pine when Sarah crawled through his bedroom window that last night before he headed for the goldfields. She came to him and loved him and promised to wait forever.

A few months later she had wed.

He sat motionless as Sarah squatted before him, the smile gone as she stared at him with fierce intensity.

"You hear me?"

Thomas nodded.

She holstered her pistol and strode across the porch to the water barrel, returning with a dipperful. She held the offering to his lips. He swallowed the warm water as he gazed at the face that had not left him for so much as a day in fourteen long years.

Had she tracked him all the way from Illinois?

Water dribbled down his chin, soaking the front of his shirt. She righted the dipper and flung the dregs out into the yard. He watched the water arc and fall, changing the dry dirt into droplets of mud. For the first time, he noted a freckled gelding, saddled and packed for the trail, resting a hind hoof as it stood beneath the old cedar.

Thomas met Sarah's gaze, searching the face he had once hoped to see every morning for the rest of his life, back in the days when he believed women could be faithful. Before Sarah tore his heart from his chest and threw it in the dirt like the water dregs.

When he found his voice, he didn't recognize the strangled thing it had become. "You sure she's mine?"

She snorted. The ladle swung from her fingers as she headed back to the rain barrel, taking her time, as if counting to ten.

"When we find her, you can judge for yourself."

She stopped at a safe distance, far enough that he couldn't see the blue flecks in her eyes. He staggered to his feet, making it to the upright beam supporting the porch roof. His stomach heaved, poised to expel the contents of his breakfast. He kept it down by force of will, refusing to humiliate himself before her.

Sarah closed the distance to a few paces, then hesitated, pinning him with a wary gaze. He studied her, searching in vain for a strand of silver in her thick chestnut braid. His red-gold hair had faded at his temples before he hit thirty. More white crept into his crown, stealing its former radiance. She retained her rich hair color—though the innocence was gone from her eyes, along with the hope. In their place shone grim determination.

"They have my daughter. I want her back, and you're going to help me."

Her chest heaved as she stood before him, the picture of a mother defending her cub.

"I hear you're some kind of bigwig in this town. Maybe you can get the army to send troops, because they sure as hell won't listen to me."

"When did you get so bossy?" he asked.

"The day I reached my last hope and realized it was you."

He absorbed the verbal kick. He knew her well enough to know that it was true, that she would have asked each friend, called in every favor and begged for help from complete strangers before turning to him.

He wouldn't have thought it possible for her to hurt him any more, but she did. The woman was nothing but one big hurt from start to finish. Pain could not describe the scramble his gut had become. Sarah's arrival hit the dead spot in the center of his chest and tore open a fresh wound.

"You have some explaining to do," he said.

She challenged. "I have? That's a hoot, because I never did see your face after you left town. Still searching for your fortune, Thomas?" She settled a fist upon her hip. "Still planning to come back to me?"

The resentment rang in her voice. She sounded as if she hated him, as if *she* had been the one betrayed. He frowned at her as he considered what her words implied.

He *had* made his fortune in California, mining miners instead of ore, for all the good it had done him. Selling hardware to all those men had given him wealth. But money could not buy what he had lost. And now she stood on the porch scowling like a woman scorned.

"I wrote Samuel," he said.

Uncertainty flickered in her eyes. Confusion knit her brow as she leaned forward, leading with her stubborn chin. Damn him if he didn't want to kiss her still. He must be insane. He gritted his teeth, forcing hot air into his lungs through flaring nostrils until the urge to touch her faded somewhat, but not completely. No—never completely.

"When?" she asked.

"Soon as I was able. Damn you and him both."

Now it was Sarah's turn to drop hard and sit on the porch step. She stared at the empty yard, muttering to herself.

"Letter. I never saw a letter. Why didn't he show me?" She glared up at him. "You never wrote me."

The accusation struck home and he shifted his attention, unable to meet the condemnation glowing in her eyes. He wouldn't tell her about the darkness or the sorrow when he realized that all he could ever be to her was a burden. How could he have known he would recover?

"Why, Thomas?"

He longed to tell her but couldn't. "Samuel said you were married."

She buried her face in her hands. "I had no choice."

"You had a choice. Why him?"

"For the baby," she choked.

Thomas recalled his grief at discovering this second betrayal. He had been willing to give her up, but she had given him up first. Even her unfaithfulness hadn't made him stop loving her. It had only served to increase the pain at discovering she bore Samuel's child. But now she said it wasn't his brother's.

"I can't blame you." But it wasn't true. He did blame her, but not as much as he blamed himself. He cleared his throat. "Samuel was the better man."

Their gazes met, and he read his pain echoed in her face.

"Was it the injuries, Sarah, that made you change your mind?"

She cocked her head. "Change my mind? I don't understand what happened out there, Thomas. What injuries?"

She didn't know. He stiffened, remembering the attack. Seeing Apache raiders rushing forward with short, thick clubs. Waking in the desert, feeling the sun, but seeing nothing. Hearing the screams and realizing they were his brother Hyatt's.

He couldn't breathe. He forced down the memories, locking them back into their cave. He wouldn't remember that time. Sarah's voice drew him to her again and he looked down at her lovely face.

"I knew something happened. But they wouldn't say. Finally, Samuel told me about the Indian attack."

So she married him.

"He said you both died. Is Hyatt alive, too?"

A quick shake of his head was the only acknowledgment that Hyatt was gone. "But you were already wed by then."

Her eyes rounded for just an instant. "No, I wasn't."

He heard her but did not understand. It was wrong, this version of events, so he corrected her. "You married two months after I left."

She straightened, her posture a clear warning of an impending storm. "Thomas, I did not marry until after the letter arrived from Commander Russell."

He recognized the name he had fabricated all those years ago as a means of releasing her from a promise she should never have had to keep. Freeing her from him, or what was left of him after that terrible day. In many ways, every part of him that mattered had died in that desert.

All that had been left was his love for Sarah and his guilt over Hyatt. He didn't know where to turn. Certainly not to his father, who had condemned him for luring Hyatt to the gold fields when the family needed him at home, and not to his mother, who had made him swear to look after her baby boy.

So he had turned to Samuel, the responsible elder brother, who would know what must be done. Could it be possible that the person he had trusted most had betrayed him?

His head sank. Perhaps it was no less punishment than he deserved.

Sarah still stood rigid, waiting. "Who told you I was married?"

"Samuel."

She cried into her hands now, as he inched closer. Acting on impulse, he rested a palm on her shoulder. Instead of crumbling against him as she once had, she leapt to her feet, spinning about like a cornered badger.

"Don't you touch me. Don't ever touch me again." Her eyes glittered with a feral hatred. "You lost that right when you left me behind."

"Those Apache would have…would have…" The words lodged in his throat and he could not finish. "You'd be better off dead than with those savages."

"I've been dead for fourteen years." She dashed the tears from her cheeks with a quick scrape of her knuckles.

Thomas crossed his arms to keep himself from reaching out to her. "It was for the best."

"Don't tell me what's best. You wrote Samuel, but not me!"

"You didn't write at all."

"Because they told me you were missing! They all lied to me." She tore at her hair. "To keep me there. They knew, they knew I'd follow you if they'd told me. I wanted to search, but Samuel said I needed to protect the baby."

Her ranting rattled him badly. "Sarah?"

At the sound of his voice she seemed to remember herself. She leveled an accusing stare on him.

"When did you write Samuel?"

"Late June, maybe." But he hadn't done the writing. Dictation, that was all he could manage back then.

Sarah stared out across the yard, thinking back.

As unexpectedly as lightning flashing from a clear blue sky, she launched herself at him and beat her fists against his chest until he captured her wrists and held her fast. Tears streaked her cheeks as she struggled against him, against herself.

"Why didn't you come for me? Why didn't you write?"

"You married Samuel."

"Because I thought you were dead."

He gripped her arms and gave a hard shake and she stilled. "He said the baby was his, Sarah. He claimed the child."

"What?" Her eyes rounded in horror and then narrowed in an instant. Her voice rang with accusation. "And you believed him."

Guilt flashed through him as the wall of certainty, built over fourteen long years, cracked. He said nothing in his defense and she nodded her understanding.

"You should have written to me. I would have told you the truth."

"I couldn't."

"Why?"

He shook his head.

They stared at each other in silence.

He dropped his voice to a coaxing tone. "Come inside, Sarah."

Her shoulders drooped a moment. Then she drew herself up and mounted his front steps.

He opened the door to the home he'd built on three acres, big enough to give him the privacy he needed, but too small to farm. He never planned to farm anything again as long as he lived, because farms reminded him of Sarah chasing chickens in the April sunshine and of Hyatt milking cows.

She swung past him and he caught her scent. With it came another belly punch as the memories swept in, bittersweet and broken all to hell.

She'd thought him dead and turned to his brother. The simple explanation didn't dull the pain; if anything it made it worse, far worse to know that she'd loved him once. That she had acted from desperation. How much easier it had been to believe in her betrayal and blame her for it.

But why, of all the men in Illinois, had she chosen his brother?

"When did you find out I was alive?"

She paused halfway down the hall, turning slowly to face him. "You remember Ben Harris?"

He did, had happened upon the man in San Francisco years ago and given him enough money to get back to Illinois where he belonged.

"He saw you in a fish market. He told us you were alive. By then your mother and father were gone."

Another bit of his heart crumbled to dust. There would be no forgiveness from that front, not that he deserved any.

"You broke your ma's heart as well. Why didn't you at least write to her?"

He had no answer, no words to convey his grief and guilt and weight of his failure. He had not kept Hyatt safe, nor had he brought him home. He lived it, but he would not speak of it. Not even to Sarah.

"I don't understand any of this. First I hear you are missing and then dead. I receive no word from you. Who is Russell and how could he have thought you were dead?"

He lowered his head in shame. "I'm Russell. I had that letter written after Samuel's…. After he said you carried his child."

"Oh, Thomas, no."

She sobbed, and her knees gave way. He guided her to the narrow carpet runner and then released her wrists. He knew not to offer comfort this time. Instead, he crouched on his boot heels with his back to the wall. At last she raised her head.

"He's dead, Tom. Samuel died of cholera heading out here, two weeks before they took Lucie."

All the air left his lungs as this news hit him like a body blow.

An instant later, a wave of regret struck as he recognized the possibility of ever setting things right between them had died with his elder brother. He sank onto the carpet. "When?"

"May."

So, the daughter he did not know existed had been taken by savages and the older brother he had idolized and envied had betrayed him and was now buried along some lonely wagon trail.

"My God," he muttered.

She blinked the tears from her eyes. "God won't help me. But you will. Do you understand, Tom? I want my daughter back."

Chapter Two

Sarah clutched her horse's reins and followed Thomas to the water trough. Their first meeting had gone badly, even after she had readied herself to see him. She had expected lies, rejection, even pity. Nothing could have prepared her for this.

Could it be that he had not abandoned her?

The possibility rocked her. Her life now seemed a series of misunderstandings and mistakes, heaped one upon the other like torn clothing in her mending basket.

She studied his back as he opened the corral gate. The wiry, eager boy she once loved had matured into this stranger before her. Her gaze roved, freed by his inattention. His broad shoulders stretched the blue cotton of his work shirt as he slid back the two poles.

Her stomach twitched as she pushed back the memories of long ago. They did nothing but tear at her with tiny claws. One night of bliss followed by fourteen years of anguish. Now, after an eternity, just a glimpse of him made her tremble.

He wore no hat, and the sunlight showed that the bright flame of his strawberry hair now lay salted with white. The effect was flattering, making him more handsome than he had been in her memories.

He turned, waiting for her. She tugged at the lead line and her horse, Freckles, followed obediently, anxious for water. As she passed Thomas, she realized that only his blue eyes remained unaltered by time. His look held hers an instant before he returned his attention to securing the gate.

Freckles lowered his head to drink. The Appaloosa gelding slurped noisily for a time. She loosened his girth and waited.

Thomas brought a grain bucket and then dropped a half bale of hay on the dry ground. Sarah drew off her gelding's bridle and hooked it on the nearest post. For a time, she busied herself grooming Freckles. With that done, the awkwardness between them grew again, broken only by the munching sound of Freckles finishing his first course before turning to the next.

Thomas leaned against a sturdy crossbar of the rail fence. "Sarah, you're gonna have to tell me what happened out there so I know what's what."

She nodded, already dreading the ordeal of the telling. If it were not for her daughter, she would never speak of it to anyone. The memories were too terrible to endure a second time. But for Lucie she would face the devil himself.

Thomas watched her gaze drift upward to the top of the fir trees. He knew she was looking back in time to the nightmares only she could see and he knew that she had more courage than he.

"*Three months ago, May 25.* That was the day they took her. There were so many trains of wagons on that trail. Why ours?"

He knew about such unanswerable questions. They dug into your soul and festered.

"Emigrants by the score. We could have traveled in larger numbers, but everyone told us there was no danger. We had only four wagons and could make better time, so we went on ahead. The sun was so hot. No breeze. I remember looking forward to the day's end when we could stop and rest."

Her hand went to her breastbone.

"They came upon us so swiftly, it liked to stop my heart. Two hundred Ogallala Sioux circling as we struggled to bring the wagons together. The devils. Their leader made signs of friendship. I did not trust them, but Mr. Stanley stepped forward to shake hands. Soon they had our sugar. They came in such numbers. I dared not refuse even when they asked for the flour. They dumped it on the ground and took only the sacks. Pillaging in the guise of trade. They even stole the blue star quilt that Lucie and I had made together.

"When they offered to share dinner with us, I wanted to take Lucie and run, for that is what my heart told me to do. But we followed like lambs to the slaughter. The men perceived the villains' true intent as they led us to a rocky glen and halted, refusing to go on.

Sarah pressed her palm tightly to her mouth. Her eyes squeezed closed for a moment before continuing. "The chief insisted and when Mr. Stanley refused, he grew insolent. Stanley would not be moved into an ambush and called for camp to be set on the spot. I meant to run from camp, so I took Lucie into the treeline on the premise of gathering wood.

"The Indians waited until the men set aside their weapons to see to the animals. Then they attacked.

"From the brush I saw an arrow pass through Mr. Wheaton's leg, pinning him to his wagon. The Indians used him as a living target. I held my hand across Lucie's mouth to keep her from screaming as they hacked at him with tomahawks."

Sarah swallowed her distaste before continuing. "When they finished their butchery, they came for us, walking fifty across. I stumbled upon a shallow den of some animal and forced Lucie beneath the craggy stone. I told her to stay there until I came back. I meant to lead them away." Sarah pressed her palms over her eyes. "Why did I leave her?"

Thomas reached for her but hesitated, remembering the reception he had received the last time he tried to comfort her. He made a fist and let his hand drop to his side. Sarah's grief-stricken expression cut him to the core.

He knew this anguish—had lived with it day by day throughout the years. He tried to focus on her words, but his mind flashed back to Hyatt, hiding in the wagon. Stay in the wagon. Hide. Quiet. Hyatt's blue eyes staring, looking to Thomas for reassurance as Thomas threw the canvas sacks over him. His burial shroud.

"Thomas?"

He blinked at her, suddenly remembering his surroundings. "What happened next?"

Sarah reached out, but not to him. Blinded by tears, she groped until her hand met with the fence rail and clutched it as a drowning swimmer grasps a log. Her voice trembled as she continued. "I shook the bushes and heard them shout. But they were not distracted from their line."

Tears streaked Sarah's face. "When they reached the place where I'd left Lucie and passed by, I thought they had missed her. Then a miracle happened. To my left came a rattle. The Indians paused not five feet before me, afraid of the snake, my savior. They turned back. I was so happy we had escaped. I waited in twilight while the Indians packed what they could carry and burned the rest."

Thomas gagged as he recalled another wagon ablaze. The smoke had scorched his nostrils as he clawed blindly at the canvas.

He wanted to shout at Sarah to stop. But he didn't. Instead he stood paralyzed, remembering as Sarah's voice continued.

"When night came, I crept toward the place where Lucie waited, but in the darkness I could not find it."

Sarah lifted her tortured gaze and Thomas felt bile rise in his throat.

"I pictured her alone and frightened not ten feet from me, and the Indians just beyond. I couldn't call out to her.

"They departed by torchlight. Still, I waited in the darkest hours before dawn, fearful some Indians remained to kill any survivors."

She wept and Thomas extended his handkerchief. Sarah pressed it to the fountain of her tears.

"At dawn, I…empty."

"They took her."

She nodded and wrapped her arms about herself as if clutching Lucie, and her voice jumped to a wail that tore at his heart. "I found her shoe."

Sarah squeezed her hands over her eyes and wept. Thomas ventured to touch her, and this time she did not shake him off. He patted her as he did his horses when quieting them for the blacksmith. Sarah's shoulders jumped beneath his hand. At last she hiccuped and lifted her head.

Her hair stuck out in all directions and her nose shone pink as a wild rose.

"No one would help me. Not the wagons that came after or the captain at Deer Creek or the major at Fort Laramie." She pounded a fist upon the rail. "They were all like turtles, tucking in their heads at the first sign of danger."

"They refused to search?" He could not quite believe it.

"They sent a unit to retrieve the dead but wouldn't give chase. No jurisdiction—Indian territory, undermanned." She choked his handkerchief in her fist and shook it. "How I hate them."

He imagined pummeling the commander's face to a bloody pulp as Sarah drew a breath.

"Did they take any other captives?"

"A young bride, Kathryn Jackson." Sarah wiped her nose. "They butchered her husband.

"I carried the money for our family and offered all I had for Lucie's return. I tried, in vain, to shame the army into taking some action. They leave their fort only to ride the wagon trail and never venture into the prairie. In the end I thought of you."

Her watery gaze pinned him with a look of such desperation, he knew he would travel to hell itself to recover their daughter.

"I lost you. I lost Samuel. I will not lose my child, as well."

He nodded. She'd been through the mill but loved Lucie enough to go back to the plains to find her. He silently vowed to protect and provide for Sarah on this dangerous journey. If

High Plains Bride

she'd allow it, he'd even try to comfort her, but that possibility seemed remote at best. He sighed and pushed off the fence rail. "You rest here. I have business in town."

She set her jaw.

"Do you need anything for traveling, Sarah?"

She hesitated, then broke eye contact, and he knew that her pride prevented her from asking.

"What?"

"Nothing."

"Nothing from me, you mean."

She frowned at him, showing he had hit the mark. Not one woman on this earth could rile him faster than Sarah Talbet.

But it wasn't Sarah Talbet anymore. It was West. Mrs. Samuel West.

"How much of that money do you have left?"

"None of your business."

"I'm bringing your horse to the smithy for new shoes."

She did not object. He turned and headed to the barn to saddle his buckskin, leaving her standing in the corral beside her trail-weary Appaloosa.

Why had Samuel come west? He had the farm and a family. Why make such a foolhardy journey?

Had Samuel spent those long years missing the company of his little brother as much as Thomas had missed him?

Sarah said Samuel had lied. Could it be? One of them had. Either Sarah married soon after Thomas's departure or she had wed only when he was reported dead. Who did he believe? Up until a few minutes ago, he'd trusted his brother completely. Now, he didn't know.

The air about him grew heavy. The sweet odor of molasses and leather made his stomach heave. He sat upon a hay bale, cradling his head in his hands as he realized he believed Sarah.

"Oh, Samuel—why?"

Sarah had been the love of his life. Samuel knew it. He thought back, recalling that his brother had taken a shine to

Sarah early, but Thomas had won the battle for Sarah's heart. Thomas had won at most everything they had fought over. His brother had not been as fast at running or as talented with numbers, but he had been the eldest and they looked to him when trouble came. Had Samuel loved Sarah enough to do anything to have her—even if that meant driving off his own brother? The betrayal burned him like a firebrand.

If Thomas had not written that letter faking his death, would Sarah have married?

The possibilities tumbled together, crashing like boulders in an avalanche. How could he have known about the child?

An answer came like a condemnation. You could have written to Sarah.

He made a quick rebuttal to himself. "I couldn't. I was blind and broke." And heartsick at Hyatt's death.

How could he write her? She was an honorable woman and likely would have still taken him. But he could not burden her with a blind husband and could not stomach the thought of her pity.

All Samuel had done was pick up the treasure he had cast aside. It was his own fault.

As for his brother's part—if placed in Samuel's position, what would he have done to keep her?

His thoughts were tangled up like an unbroken horse wound in its lead line.

Thomas rose on weary legs and then bridled his horse and cinched the saddle. When he reached the open barn door he found Sarah standing beside her bridled gelding. He reached for the reins. "I'll make preparations in town."

Sarah kept custody of the reins. "We."

"What?"

"*We* will make preparations in town."

Sarah stared him down. He looked as if he wanted to order her to stay behind, but he didn't—couldn't, really, as she was not his. He hesitated a moment before nodding.

Together, they mounted and he led the way south to Bakersfield.

Sarah kept her own counsel on the ride, trying to ignore the pulsing pain in her lower back. She had ridden ten miles already today. At last they reached their destination.

She did as he asked at the Indian Affairs office, waiting impatiently while Thomas spoke with the man in charge. When he returned, his red face told her he had received no satisfaction.

"They're not going to do a damn thing!"

She pressed her lips together as she followed him, scurrying to keep up with his long strides. He did no better with the local marshal, who offered sympathies but nothing more. The fruitless meetings ate away the afternoon.

Thomas glanced up the street. "You want to stay in town?"

She hesitated. Having spent nearly everything on trying to shame the army into taking up her cause, offering rewards for information that proved useless and then searching for Thomas, her funds were low. She didn't want to appear a pauper, but neither did she want the entire town talking about her staying at his place.

"For how long?"

"Just the night. We'll head for Sacramento tomorrow."

One night. She likely had that much silver.

"Fine."

"I'll get you situated and then be back in the morning."

They walked the horses over to the boarding house but found the place full up.

"All that's left are the rooms above the saloons, but you can't stay there." Thomas glanced across the dirt road, considering the establishments in question. "I could try a friend of mine. He's married."

She stared at her feet. "We'll be going tomorrow. Perhaps I could stay with you."

It hurt her pride to say it, but she did not want to impose on strangers.

"Guess that'd be all right." He leaned in, and she smelled coffee and leather. "Seeing how we're family."

Sarcasm? She studied his inscrutable face but could not tell. All that was clear was the hurt in his eyes. Weariness now ached deep in her bones. The thought of the mile-long ride to his place nearly made her groan aloud.

By the time they reached his property, twilight was stealing across the yard. Her horse stopped without her urging and Sarah swayed with fatigue. Thomas slipped smoothly out of his saddle and dropped the reins. Buck nudged him, obviously expecting some recompense for his labors. Thomas scratched the horse's ears and then turned to Sarah, reaching up to help her dismount. She hesitated and he waited, hands outstretched.

With a sigh of defeat, she threw a leg over the saddle horn and released her foot from the opposite stirrup. She slid from warm leather into his arms. Strong hands gripped her waist as he eased her down. She held his shoulders to steady her descent before he set her gently on her feet. There he paused, as if reluctant to let her go. His familiar scent surrounded her. She grew dizzy with the fragrance of this man, changed from the boy she had loved. He gazed down at her from the deep shadow of the brim of his hat. Even here she could see the grim set of his lips, as if he fought against something painful. What had happened to him?

The heat of his palm crept through her thin deerskin coat, through the blouse and the shift beneath. Familiar hands, unfamiliar hands. Her heart raced as his warm breath fanned her cheek. For one instant she thought he meant to kiss her.

Reality crashed upon her. What once had been now lay broken by years. She stepped back.

He cleared his throat. "Lantern and matches are inside to the right. I'll see to the horses."

He seized both sets of reins and disappeared into the barn. Sarah stood trembling. Coming here had been a mistake, a terrible mistake.

Why was she putting herself through this torture?

The answer came in one word—Lucie. For her daughter's sake she would stay with this man, her last hope—her only love, her mortal wound.

She turned toward the house and staggered up the steps to the front door on weary legs. The latch lifted with a click and Sarah stepped into darkness. Groping, she found the kerosene lantern and the cold cast-iron matchbox hanging on the wall. A strike against the iron box and the match flared blinding white. Sulfur burned her nostrils as she lifted the glass to light the wick.

Even in the cheery yellow glow, the house seemed hollow. She gazed about with a critical eye. Thomas obviously prospered here. The imported runner leading back to the kitchen, glass lanterns and sturdy furniture all spoke of wealth. His two-story clapboard home looked neat and clean but a feeling of emptiness pervaded it. Why?

She glanced into the living room, noting the bare walls and stark unadorned windows. The tabletop beside the single armchair lay empty, except for a pipe and bowl of ash. A rifle and shotgun hung above the mantel as grim décor.

Minutes ticked by in her head, for no clock graced the parlor. A bear hide lay before the hearth. Should she go to the kitchen and put on a kettle?

She hesitated, knowing she was intruding in his home—in his life. He had not asked her here. But here she was, as welcome as a skunk under his porch.

Finally, there came the click of the latch. He carried her bags over his shoulder with one hand as if they weighed next to nothing. She recalled the trouble she had just lifting them onto the horse's rump and stood in silent appreciation of his strength.

"Well, don't stand there like a hat rack, head for the kitchen."

He took possession of the lantern and led the way, depositing her gear beside the table and then stirring the coals in the woodstove. She stood just inside the door, uncertain as a stray dog at the back step. In a few minutes a fire chased off the chill.

"Coffee?"

She recalled he made terrible coffee. "No, thank you."

His expression turned stormy again. "Is it the coffee you hate, or just me?"

She made no answer.

His face colored. He rubbed his neck as he searched for something else to offer her. "I don't have any tea or milk. Never have company. Don't suppose you drink whiskey."

She chuckled and he stared at her in seeming astonishment. Was it from hearing her laugh? She tried to remember the last time she'd laughed and could not. Melancholy settled in her bones at the reminder of something else she'd lost with Thomas's leaving—her joy. Lucie had brought some of that back into her life. She did not plan to lose it again.

How much like him was his daughter. On her, the bright strawberry curls looked lovely. Somehow God had seen fit to give her his blue eyes, as well. The freckles, unfortunately, came from her, as did the dimples, though Sarah had not had cause to show her dimples in years.

Samuel's dark hair and Lucie's bright curls had made the truth obvious to all. Many saw Samuel's marrying her under such circumstances as a noble act, though she was cast as soiled goods by most. When news reached the gossips that Thomas lived, overnight Samuel went from a man to be respected to one who had been hoodwinked. He overlooked the gossip and kept his own counsel on the matter instead of blaming her for his lot. Sarah found the situation harder to ignore. Her friends abandoned her and their vicious little offspring teased Lucie mercilessly. Living outside the circle of society had changed them all and Sarah was determined never to cross the line of social propriety again. Yet here she stood, alone with the man who had once caused her to forget all consequences.

"Come sit." He indicated a chair at his table.

Sarah crept forward and slipped into the place he indicated, knowing she should have stayed in town. He poured himself a cup of coffee and sat across from her.

Sarah glanced about the huge kitchen. Why was there no woman here? She saw no evidence one had ever occupied this space.

What women had he known in the long stretch of years that lay between their parting and this joyless reunion? She had no rights to him, but that in fact did not lessen her jealousy.

"Did you marry, Tom?"

He cast her a look. Color crept up his neck, but whether it was from embarrassment or shame, she could not tell.

"No."

No, because he loved her, or no, because he hated her?

His eyes flicked up. "But I was engaged once."

He meant to her.

She placed her hands upon the smooth surface of his empty table, preparing to rise. "Perhaps I'd best go."

"No, you'll stay."

Sarah stood. They faced off across the pine table as uncertainty pressed heavily upon her weary shoulders. "I'll just set my bedroll on the porch, then."

"You won't." Indignation rang in his voice. "You'll have my bed."

The thought of sleeping in his bed sent an expected thrill of excitement dancing up her spine. Shame followed immediately. He had merely offered her a bed out of hospitality. Thomas was now her brother-in-law, but he still gave her chills.

"No, I couldn't. I'll rest by the fire."

He rubbed his neck again. "This is my home and I say you sleep in my bed."

The double meaning of his words obviously occurred to him too late, for his face flamed scarlet. He broke their gaze.

"Tom, I am not sleeping in your bed."

He shifted from side to side as he considered her.

"You did once."

She spun away. Damn him for bringing up what hung unspoken between them. She reached the back door. Thinking only of escape, she pulled it open a crack before his hand forced it shut.

Sarah whirled to face him.

"That night was the worst mistake of my life." She tossed the words at him and watched as they struck like a bucket of icy water hurled at his face. It wasn't true, but she couldn't take it back. So she stood with tears filling her eyes, making his shocked expression swim before her.

He gaped, and her stomach tightened with regret. But how could she tell him the truth? That one night was all that had kept her alive these many loveless years. It had also been the moment when everything changed for the worse. No, that wasn't true—not everything. The one great gift in her life, her child, had come as a result of her impulsiveness. Lucie was all Sarah had left of her love for this man.

Thomas leaned in, forcing her to press herself back against the door.

"You didn't think so at the time."

She stood tall in a show of bravery that she did not feel.

He hovered as if deciding what to do with her, the strength of his body reminding her that the decision was his to make. Her body pulsed with longing.

He lifted his hand, giving her time to dart away, but she stayed like a beaten dog, yearning for its master's touch.

His knuckles grazed her cheek and her eyes drifted closed to savor the contact. Her knees went weak, and she was glad for the strong support of the solid oak behind her.

Tom's whisper brushed against her skin like a butterfly's wing. "Still beautiful as ever."

He stroked her throat. Pleasure issued from his fingertips, rolling through her like ripples from a stone cast into still waters. How could he move her after all these years? Only *his* touch did this to her.

She remembered his kisses and craved them again. She also remembered him leaving her behind. Her desire for him warred with her fear of repeating past mistakes. After so many years, did they know each other at all?

"Thomas." Her voice sounded strange to her ears. "I'm not the girl you once loved. We've changed."

His hand faltered, then slipped away. She recognized the desire and watched his scorching gaze cool to ice. The flush on his cheeks and flaring nostrils told her that he struggled with himself. He still wanted her, but now he held himself in check. She needed to look away, but his fierce stare held her mesmerized.

"Why did you marry him?"

"For the baby."

He gripped her arms. "I'm not asking why you married. But you could have had anyone. Why him?"

She met the challenge in his eyes. "To give your child your name."

His hands slipped away, leaving her cold and hollow. His eyes darted about as if searching for a way out. But there was no way out for either of them. Not any more.

The tears she had held in check now streamed down her face as she whispered the truth, that secret she had not even admitted to herself. "I couldn't have you, so I took the one you loved best."

His chin lifted. "I loved you best."

Chapter Three

The kick to her hip woke Lucie. She blinked in confusion, surprised not by the kick but rather by the total darkness inside the teepee.

Following Calf barked orders and Lucie scrambled to comply. After three months of hearing nothing but this strange savage language, she understood enough of the words shouted at her that most days she managed to get by without a beating.

"Up, lazy girl. Up."

Lucie pushed the errant strand of hair from her face and quickly found a stick to stir the coals to life. Following Calf roused her husband, Running Horse, with more kindness. The brave ducked out to relieve himself, the sound of his urine stream just beyond the buffalo hide making his wife chuckle as she retrieved the remains of the antelope from last night's dinner.

Seeming to remember Lucie, she rolled her eyes and motioned. "Your hair."

Once, Lucie's strawberry blond hair had been a source of great pride. Now it was the bane of her life, attracting unwanted attention by being so different from everyone else's. Wavy instead of straight, red instead of black, fine instead of thick. Some of the children had dubbed her Frightened Fox and the name had stuck.

For the first time since Lucie's arrival, Following Calf seemed ready to remedy Lucie's lack of a conventional hairstyle. She forced Lucie to sit before her and gathered the wild snarl of her hair.

"I will need a knife to cut through these tangles."

Lucie resisted the urge to pull away from the tugging fingers. Using an ivory comb stolen from the Wests' wagon, her captor attacked Lucie's mane.

Memories of her mother's gentle ministrations collided with the rough abuse she now suffered under the same comb. She had not cried in months—thought herself no longer capable of the luxury—but found her throat closing at the sight of her mother's prized possession. She swallowed and squeezed her eyes shut, refusing to surrender to despair.

Running Horse ducked back inside the teepee and seemed to note nothing unusual about his wife's sudden interest in Lucie's appearance.

He thrust the bowl of meat at Lucie. She hesitated, suspecting a trick. Never had she eaten first.

Something was happening. Her heart whispered hope. Had her mother arranged for her release?

The possibility rose within her, like a seedling breaking through the soil. That would explain the sudden interest in her welfare.

Her scalp ached by the time Following Calf laid aside the comb and lifted the bowl of grease. Lucie's confidence faltered. Why make her look like an Indian?

It made no sense.

She ached to ask, but feared both the answer and the cuffing her curiosity generally gleaned. Following Calf scooped a generous dollop of grease and smeared it into Lucie's hair. In a few minutes, two straight shiny braids lay upon her shoulders.

"Fetch water," ordered her mistress.

Lucie sprang to her feet, clasped the rope handle tied to the buffalo bladders and darted out into the gray gloom that preceded dawn. A single lark called into the darkness. The wet grass froze her bare feet. September already and no shoes. Again she mourned their loss.

She dallied by the river, listening to the growing cacophony of bird songs. She paused, inhaling the crisp morning air, delaying as long as she dared, before hurrying back up the bank, sorry to leave behind the only peaceful moments of her day.

Back in the lodge, Following Calf forced her to kneel as she stripped Lucie out of the ragged blue dress. Lucie's cheeks burned in shame. Over the last few months, her body had become strange and embarrassing. Her nipples had begun to swell into ever-enlarging painful disks. She glanced at Running Horse, who paid her no heed but instead rubbed his tired eyes and then retrieved the platter of cold meat.

Following Calf poured icy river water into a wooden trencher and soaked a bit of tanned leather, twisting it to remove the excess. Then she scrubbed Lucie's face, arms and hands more harshly than necessary to accomplish the task. Moving behind Lucie, she roughly washed her neck, ears and back, then swabbed the leather over her chest. The contact with the sensitive skin of her nipples caused Lucie to bite her lip to keep from crying out.

"Dress."

Lucie scrambled to comply, tugging on her petticoat and wishing she had a needle and thread to repair the torn shoulder and ragged hem. Her moment's assessment of her attire cost her a vicious pinch to the sensitive skin inside her upper arm. She stood trembling as the couple ignored her once more, speaking together so rapidly she could only make out a word or two. Horses, blanket. That was all.

Following Calf took the one additional step of scraping the dirt from beneath Lucie's fingernails with a knife.

The woman turned to Running Horse. "She is ready."

Ready for what? Lucie's mouth went so dry she could not speak. Her tongue seemed huge in her mouth as she tried to form a question. Running Horse hauled her to her feet.

"Follow," he said.

"Where?" whispered Lucie.

He scowled, then ducked through the portal without condescending to speak to his captive.

Outside, blue smoke curled from the tops of teepees, dogs sniffed about for scraps and girls carried water for their mothers.

What was her mother doing right now?

As always, the instant she thought of her old life, a melancholy too deep to name descended upon her. Running Horse gripped her wrist and strode purposefully along, leaving Lucie to dance behind in an effort to keep up or be dragged. He halted at the chief's tent and Lucie trembled, staring at the open flap. They were expected.

Whatever had happened, it merited the chief's attention. Did they mean to kill her at last?

Gall rose in her throat and she choked, forcing it back. Running Horse called out and then waited for his host to bid him welcome. Lucie hesitated until her master called for Frightened Fox and then she ducked into the rabbit hole, as she considered these round gaps in the hide. She thought of her lovely warm farmhouse in Illinois, and her spirits flagged.

From experience, she knew not to sit with the men. Instead, she huddled as far from the warmth of the fire as the leather walls allowed. As the lowest member of the assembly, she merited only the place nearest the drafty entrance. She dreaded the cold nights to come. How would she survive January's bite?

The men smoked and conversed as she struggled to understand. They seemed to speak of buffalo and hunting.

Why was she here?

Finally, someone mentioned Frightened Fox and then some other word with fox and the men all laughed. Her cheeks heated, knowing they mocked her and wondering why she still cared. At least she could not understand this latest humiliation.

She glanced about the group and noticed an unfamiliar face. The man beside the chief did not live in the village, but she had seen him before. Where?

The answer struck like lightning. On the dreadful march with the warriors—that was where she had seen him. When she would not eat the raw meat they offered, this man correctly guessed the reason and boiled the elk. She still had not wished to eat, but feared him. He would not leave her until she had consumed the entire portion.

That food saved her life.

Although after the last three months of misery, she did not know if she should thank him.

He lifted three wool blankets, and Lucie's eyes narrowed. Had he obtained his wealth through trade or by killing a family of settlers?

When he extended the bounty to Running Horse, her heart seemed to lodge in her throat. Suspicion tightened her innards, squeezing the breath from her.

Running Horse smiled and nodded his thanks. The man glanced at her, meeting her gaze, and a bolt of fear passed through Lucie.

Had he bought her?

She puffed like a winded pony, resisting the urge to flee. Running Horse pointed at her.

"You go with Eagle Dancer."

Lucie's stomach dropped, as confirmation arrived like a brick in her belly. She hated Following Calf. Running Horse, though never exactly kind, at least ignored her.

This warrior could do far worse than beat her.

She thought of Julia Cassidy, the older girl she had walked with through Kansas. Her companion had vowed she would kill herself before allowing a savage to touch her. That was the only thing to do, according to Julia. Lucie found that she did not have the courage to end her life, miserable though it was. Would her family really expect it of her?

Eagle Dancer stood, his dark eyes meeting hers with that same fierce, unfathomable expression. She trembled as he motioned for her to follow him from the teepee.

Why did he buy her? The worst possibility arrived first. Would he rape her? She had expected that from the first minute of her capture. It was all her friends in Illinois could talk about when they'd learned of her family's plans to travel west.

That was why she was thoroughly surprised that, although she was regularly cuffed and kicked, no one had molested her in that way. She stared at Eagle Dancer's back. He was a full-grown man, with a stubbly chin. What could he want with a skinny girl who did not even reach his shoulder? Her mother said she was all knees and elbows, and this was never more true than now, thanks to the scant food she had been receiving.

She reached his side and somehow found the courage to speak. Lucie clung to hope as she posed her question.

"You bring me to my mother?"

He paused and his brow knit in confusion, then he looked away. When his gaze met hers again, the scowl remained firmly in place. He shook his head, sinking the knife of certainty into her heart.

Her legs gave way. He caught her arm, easily holding her up. His strength frightened her more than his scowl. He waited until she tried to draw away and then released her and turned to go. She glanced back to the chief's tent and to Eagle Dancer, and then followed her new master as he retrieved his pinto and said his farewells. Lucie noted that Running Horse held the reins of a new bay mustang.

Three blankets and a pony, the price of a slave.

She searched in vain for some means of rescue from this fate and found only the stern faces of the elders.

The fierce warrior leapt onto the pinto's back and pressed his bare heels to his mount's wooly sides. Lucie, wearing only a cotton dress, envied the creature her fine winter coat as she fell into step behind the man. Her legs seemed carved of wood, and she did not know what kept her upright.

Following Calf stood before her tent as they paraded by. Lucie refused to look at her, lifting her chin as she stepped past her former nemesis. It was the best she could do to show the woman how little she cared about leaving. Tonight Following Calf would sleep under a new blanket, but tomorrow she would fetch her own water.

The unknown loomed before Lucie, but she would not give Following Calf the satisfaction of seeing her fear.

Behind her, Following Calf's hiss was unintelligible, but Lucie understood. Her mother would say there was "no love lost" between them.

Dancing Eagle's pinto walked on and Lucie followed along the river as children who once threw stones and sticks now hurled only insults. Lucie didn't care. Their words did not bruise her skin or bring her to her scabby knees.

Finally, the most persistent of the boys retreated along with the barking dogs.

Lucie filled her lungs with cool morning air. As unexpectedly as she had arrived, she left the village. Yesterday, she had not an inkling of the changes this day would bring, just as she had had no warning on the day of the attack. Day after day she had walked beside the wagon. Each week had flowed into the next and in one instant everything had changed. Her life seemed either monotony or mayhem.

How long until the next upheaval?

The river flowed away from her path, and she wondered where it would lead. The urge to run tempted her. There was only one man to elude now. But he had a horse and she did not know how to find her people. She glanced at the trees to her right, and considered dashing into the heavy brush.

What was best to do—run or wait?

Lucie's mother had told her to wait and she would come back for her. But the Indians took her first. What would her mother say to do? She tried to listen to her words, picturing her here beside her.

Should I run before he takes me?

The silence was broken only by the pony's tail swishing away the flies.

Would her mother still want her back if this man forced himself on her or would she want her to follow Julia Cassidy's dramatic vow to die before allowing dishonor? Lucie pictured plunging a knife into her breast and shuddered. She did not wish to dishonor her family, but neither did she wish to die.

Lucie was so consumed with her own thoughts, she did not notice that Eagle Dancer had halted his pony until she ran into the creature's hind quarters, bouncing backwards like a rubber ball. The pinto flicked his tail and glanced back as if to ask how Lucie could be so clumsy.

Eagle Dancer extended the water skin to her. She accepted the offer, drinking heavily. From experience, she knew not to expect to be fed or watered regularly and took advantage whenever food or drink was given. Horses got better treatment than the slaves here—far better.

The man waited as she drank first. Twice today she had received sustenance before her captors. She did not understand, and this worried her.

The warrior tucked away the skin and leaned toward her, seeming to loom. He offered his hand and Lucie backed up.

"Take it," he said.

She did not want to but could think of no way to avoid following his order, so she reached out.

His fingers clasped her forearm in an iron grip and swung her behind him. The last time she had ridden a horse, she had been trussed up like a turkey. The day of her capture played in her mind as she winced at the gruesome memories.

Kathryn Jackson had wept inconsolably over her husband's murder. She refused to walk and so they slit her throat and left her naked body on the prairie, like a slaughtered doe. Lucie gave her captors no trouble after that, doing exactly as she was told.

Eagle Dancer rode on with Lucie clinging to his back like a

possum. Late in the afternoon, he stopped to water his horse and eat. Lucie smiled when she realized she would eat as well.

Her smile vanished an hour later when he laid out one sleeping skin, and she understood she would lie alone beside this strange, fierce man.

Chapter Four

Thomas stripped the sheets from his bed and replaced them with fresh linen. Finally, he draped his Hudson Bay blanket and the quilt he'd bought from Mrs. Clarkson over the sheets. Up until now, everything he needed from a woman he had purchased—clean laundry, meals and company.

Years ago he'd sought women who resembled Sarah. One had the same color eyes. Another mimicked her walk. Once in bed, he'd close his eyes and imagine Sarah, young and lithe beneath him once more. But when he opened his eyes he was with a stranger in a foul little room above some saloon. Lately that kind of company had brought him only disgust. Better to see to his needs alone than to take a whore.

For reasons he never thought on for too long, sleeping with such women tarnished the bright memories of Sarah in his bed. But she didn't seem to feel the same. For her, the night that he had cherished as his fondest memory had been the worst mistake of her life. He hung his head in grief.

Sarah had said they had changed. If she only knew how much. His brother's blood stained his hands. His father had accused Thomas of luring Hyatt away. No doubt Thomas's stories of gold and glory had done just that. His parents were right to blame him for the death of their youngest boy, for he blamed himself. He had lacked the courage to face them and so he had lost Sarah, as well. He was unworthy of her now, in so many ways.

When his eyes came back into focus, he found himself staring at the log cabin quilt and picturing Sarah writhing, moaning beneath his brother Samuel.

His fist slammed into the pillow, leaving it bowed.

Embarrassed by his outburst, he reined in his rage and fluffed the down again.

Sarah was in this house. She would undress beside his bed, slip between clean sheets and lay her head on his pillow. And he would be downstairs sleeping alone on a bearskin rug.

"Damn it."

He was all mixed up inside. She needed his help. That much he knew. Their daughter needed his help.

Thomas sat heavily upon the bed.

Lucie.

That's what Sarah had named his daughter, in honor of his mother, in honor of Samuel's mother. He placed his hands over his face and wept. He cried for his parents, now dead and gone, and for Samuel, who'd taken Thomas's place in the life he'd thrown away to chase a dream. He wept for Hyatt, who Thomas had led not to riches, but to his death. Finally, when the sobs grew raw and painful, he cried for the daughter he didn't know, half-grown and now in peril. When he finished, he had no tears left to mourn his pitiful mistakes. The bits of his life seemed shattered like a dropped mirror, and he could think of no way to fuse the jagged fragments back into one whole piece.

All his family was gone.

No—not all. Lucie was family. His family.

"Damned if I'll lose her, too."

He stood. He swallowed past the lump that had lodged in his throat like a wishbone ever since Sarah had appeared on his doorstep. He glanced at his reflection in the mirror. His eyes looked worse than the morning after Sarah's birthday. Each

October on the sixteenth, he made a tradition of getting so drunk he couldn't think about her. Now he felt as though it were the morning after, although he hadn't touched a drop. How to face her again?

Had he almost kissed her?

Why, in the name of God, would he think he had the right? But her skin was still so soft and she smelled of chamomile blossoms and fresh ginger. The combination was invigorating and unique, like no other woman.

He tipped his head back and groaned, studying the plastered ceiling. He had pictured her in this room too many times to count.

But always she came contrite and willing. She'd beg for his kisses and fall hungrily into his arms. He'd make her wait before surrendering to her pleas.

The ferocious badger waiting in his parlor little resembled his vision. No, not at all. The reality surpassed the fantasy.

"Damn it!"

He splashed water on his face, discarding the waste out the window, and then righted the pitcher and bowl. Finally, he turned a slow circle, seeing the room as she might. Everything in order. He glanced at the top drawer of his bureau, and he saw its contents in his mind. He swept across the room, yanked open the drawer and scooped out the daguerreotype hidden at the back. She'd never know he'd kept her image all these years.

Sliding the precious keepsake into his pocket, he headed downstairs. A light showed in the kitchen. He turned to the foyer, scooping up her saddlebags and toting them back upstairs, delaying their meeting a few more minutes.

Back in the hall, he listened but heard nothing. Finally, he drew himself up and stepped into the kitchen.

Prepared for anything, he faltered to see Sarah sitting at his table asleep upon her forearm beside a cold, untouched mug of coffee.

In sleep, her innocence returned. Her earlier anguish fell away, leaving the girl he remembered. His Sarah.

Would she ever be his again?

He studied her features, peaceful in sleep. Motionless, he drank her in, savoring each gentle breath.

She didn't know what had happened back then. Samuel had never told her, and Thomas lacked the strength to watch the horror of the truth break across her features. She had regrets too; he understood that part of her, having lived with his own for years. The shame and sense of failure had nearly killed him. If only Hyatt had lived, he could have written her. Even without his sight he might still have reached out, but now he was not worthy of any woman, let alone his Sarah.

His failure to rescue Hyatt and his weakness with Sarah were the two failures he could not change.

How long would he have to pay for his sins?

"Sarah?" He nudged her arm.

She started and righted, flashing her confused gaze about the unfamiliar kitchen. Her arm stretched out, and the cup of untouched coffee tipped, sending brown liquid streaming across the tabletop.

"Oh, look what I've done."

They both reached for the rag, fingers connecting as his hand enveloped hers. A familiar ache sparked in his groin from the mere brushing of their fingers. The power of their connection startled her as well, judging from her round-eyed stare and gaping mouth. He drew back first.

Her white knuckles choked the cloth. Then she drew a breath and returned to mop up the mess, before wringing out the rag in the stone sink.

"I'm so clumsy." She laid out the cloth to dry.

Graceful as an antelope, he thought, but said, "Come on, I'll get you settled."

He carried the lantern up the stairs, marching slowly, as if to the gallows. He paused in the hall, opening the door for her. She hesitated.

"I don't feel right about taking your room."

"I insist."

Sarah lingered in the doorway, turning to face him once more.

"Thomas?" She paused to bite her lip, causing a pulsing pressure in his groin. "What happened to Hyatt?"

Ice water flooded his veins. He stepped back, retreating from those searching eyes. She didn't hate him now, but she would once she knew.

Thomas shook his head, refusing to speak, refusing to break this fragile and uncertain start with the awful truths that marked his soul.

He handed her the lantern. "Privy's out back. Call if you need anything."

By some miracle he managed to descend the stairs to the bottom step before his knees gave way. How he had got this far, he had no notion.

Memories of Hyatt rose in his mind. Thomas had told his brother to hide in that wagon, robbing him of a chance to fight and, in so doing, robbing him of his life. He pressed his palms to his forehead in despair.

Above him, Sarah moved about. She paused, and then her light step came again. Another pause, longer this time. When next she crossed the room, no tap of her boot heels accompanied her stride as she padded on his flooring on bare feet. Did she wear her nightgown? He pictured her drawing back the covers to lie down on his clean sheets.

He crept halfway up the stairs, a thief in his own home, and paused at eye level with the light spilling across the wide planking. Desperate for a glimpse of her, he sagged upon the staircase again. He had never noticed the two-inch gap beneath the bedroom door until this moment. Now he focused on the small portal to her world like a hungry child with his nose pressed to a bakeshop window.

A rustling sound reached him as she drew back the blankets and sheets and then pulled them back over herself. Then came a sigh, clear as the call of a lark. The next sound confused him for a moment. It reminded him of a hound rooting for a scent. Then a high whine joined the mix and he recognized it.

Sarah was crying.

Thomas slipped down the stairs, retreating from Sarah's anguish. Her grief tore at his heart. He had not the right to comfort her nor the courage to listen. In the living room, he shook out a blanket and spread it over the rug before the fire.

He drew off his boots and belt, then lay in the quiet room, listening to the coals crackle as flames consumed the last log, leaving only the orange glow of a dying fire. He rolled to his side, landing upon the hard edge of the picture case. Thomas drew out the likeness of Sarah's younger self and studied it by the waning light of the fire.

The faint image on tin still showed her lovely smile as she sat full of promise and expectation in the year before that night, before he took her and left her, before she bore him a child. Regret rose so deep it threatened to drown him. He hated his part in killing the hope in her eyes. He couldn't go back and make things right, not for Hyatt, not for any of them. All he could do was what she bid and find their girl.

He closed the case, not strong enough to gaze on her image an instant longer. As the fire died away, he rolled from one side to the next, tugging at the blanket as if engaged in a death match.

Thomas had certainly slept in worse places—damp, uneven places. But for some reason this dry, warm room and this soft fur mattress now seemed the most uncomfortable bed of his life.

"Well, hell."

He threw off the blanket and stormed outside into the evening breeze. Leaning on the porch rail, he gazed up at the stars scattered like fireflies across the night sky.

"Are you looking up, Lucie?" he whispered. "I'll be coming for you directly and I won't quit until they kill me or I bring you home safe."

Chapter Five

Somehow Thomas readied the wagon, tied the saddle horses to the back and headed out.

As he crossed the yard, he felt Sarah staring at him from within his house. He flicked his gaze to the windows. A shadowy outline disappeared the moment he turned his head.

She watched. He always knew when her eyes were upon him. He felt it on his neck like her warm breath.

By the time he reached the road, the sensation had passed. In town, he dropped off the horses at the livery and then he spoke to his clerk about taking over for a while. The man's shock quickly passed when Thomas offered him ten percent of all sales in his absence in addition to his salary if he would oversee the entire operation. His clerk's wife would check on his place, and their married daughter would go on cleaning it for him. That took care of his home and business.

"Oh, and bring my stock to the livery," said Thomas.

"No need to pay," said Bill Hauer. "I'll just keep them with mine."

"Appreciate it."

"How long you figure to be gone, Tom?"

Thomas shook his head. "No telling."

He selected what he needed at his hardware store, visited the bank and then headed to the grocer.

After negotiating a trade for most of his supplies, he turned his attention to an area of the store that he rarely even spared a glance. The women's clothing and other assorted female niceties had had no place in his austere life until today. He lifted a bar of lavender soap and sniffed. Then he tried the rose.

With one bar in each hand, he raised his gaze to find Mr. Jenson regarding him with a lopsided grin.

"So you have a visitor," he said.

His tone did not judge.

"Says who?" asked Thomas, struggling to keep the resentment from his voice.

"That little lady stopped here yesterday for directions. I pointed her your way, so I hope you don't owe her money."

Thomas lowered his guard.

"She's…" Thomas hesitated. It was hard to say his sister-in-law, when once he'd planned to call her wife. "She's my brother's wife."

"Oh, that puts a different spin on it."

"My brother passed."

"Oh, Tom, I'm surely sorry. She come with the news, did she?"

"Yes." He wondered if telling Jenson and thereby the whole town was a mistake. He couldn't see that it would be, so he went on. "Samuel had the cholera on the trail."

"Terrible shame."

"That isn't the half. The Sioux attacked their wagon and they took…their daughter." Thomas paused, realizing how near he came to saying *his* daughter. That would be difficult to explain. He didn't give a hang what folks thought, but Sarah had always set great store by the opinion of strangers. So he chose his words with care. "We're heading to Sacramento, then east to the plains. Appreciate it if you'll keep an eye on my place."

"You got Billy running her?"

"Yeah, he'll do fine. Just check in. He might need help on occasion."

"Glad to."

"And we'll be traveling. I need to pick up some gear for Sarah."

Thomas looked at the unfamiliar female goods then back to Jenson in desperation. "Can you help me?"

"What's she need?"

"That's the thing. The woman is stubborn as all get-out. But she's my responsibility now." Thomas admitted to himself that having some say over her life pleased him.

"Well, her boots showed some wear and her coat isn't suitable for winter. Noticed she don't have a sunbonnet."

"We'll be trail riding. Her hat will do."

"All right then." Jenson started collecting items. "Stockings wear out fast and yarn to darn them."

"What's this for?" Thomas lifted a pretty scrap of lace.

Jenson grinned, poking the rosebud made of pink ribbon in the center of the oddity dangling from Thomas's finger. "That's a New York garter to hold up a woman's stockings. But Thomas, I got them for Henry's gals over at the Blue Buck."

Thomas let the ribbon and lace slip from his hand.

"Most proper women don't wear those, but I've seen them show an interest. I think Miss Calhoun would have bought a pair if she could have done it without nobody seeing."

Thomas chose a pair with blue ribbons. He studied the tiny glittering beads sewn to the lace and admired the artificial rosebuds. "They wear them with woolens?"

"Now, Thomas, you seen the stockings them gals wear, ain't ya? They're silk."

"You got any?"

His eyebrows lifted. "Sure do, but they're not sturdy enough for traveling and they're dear."

Thomas shrugged.

In the end he bought boots, a small leather coat lined with

fleece, two heavy blouses, a wool skirt, one wool dress, lavender scented soap, woolens, a scarf, calfskin gloves and a pair of silk stockings with fancy New York garters.

He left the goods with Jenson and went to collect his horses and wagon. Then he loaded up his purchases, now neatly wrapped in brown paper. He tied the newly shod horses to the back and headed for home.

Sarah waited on the porch, descending the steps to help him unload. She smelled of fresh mint.

He squinted at her. "You been in my kitchen?"

He'd told her earlier that he made all meals and to keep clear of his things. She hadn't been happy but had nodded her consent.

"I made tea and sandwiches." Her voice sounded defensive.

He suppressed a smile.

She picked up a box of hardtack and carried it up the steps. He followed with an armful of packages. She helped relieve him of the parcels, laying them beside the hardtack. Her hand brushed his arm, and he savored the sweetness of her touch. He'd tried to forget her so many times he'd lost count. Now he understood why he never could. The woman was unforgettable.

He studied her face, noting her red-rimmed eyes.

"Sleep well?" he asked, knowing the answer.

"Very well, thank you."

That stopped him. He scowled.

"So that's how it going to be."

She narrowed her eyes. "I'm afraid you have me at a loss."

"Yeah, loss of sleep, you mean."

The stubborn slant of her jaw remained a moment longer and then she dropped her gaze.

"Is it so obvious?"

"To me it is."

Their gazes met and held.

How long had she been staring at him with that quizzical expression? More importantly, how long had he been making calf eyes at her?

"Come here," he said. "I want to show you something."

She followed him to the rear of the wagon, where her freckled horse stood.

He lifted the Appaloosa's rear right leg. "Look at that."

She studied the new shoe and freshly clipped hoof.

"Beautiful. Thank you, Thomas."

The way she said his name, kindly, with none of her earlier venom, made his stomach jump. He dropped the hoof.

"I got you some things."

The frown returned, forcing the smile from her lips. "I told you, I don't need anything."

He straightened, folding his arms across his chest. "Whether you like it or not, you're my responsibility now."

She matched his stance, standing with him toe-to-toe. "Well, I won't have it."

The woman was as unreasonable as a freshly branded mule.

He drummed his fingers slowly on his upper arm. "So you want me to drop everything and leave my business to help you, but you don't want me to buy you any gear. That about it?"

Her scowl wavered as the illogic of her position hit home. At last her shoulders sagged.

"I don't want to be in your debt."

"And I don't want you riding to the Black Hills and back without a proper coat."

Her eyes relayed defeat, but still she kept her mouth clamped shut.

He dropped the resentment from his voice. Instead he spoke softly, as he used to when discussing important matters with her. "Sooner we leave, sooner we're on her trail."

Her head dropped, and he knew he'd won this round before she opened her mouth. "All right then, but I can use your kitchen. You keeping me out of the one place I feel at home is just stubbornness, Thomas, and you know it."

He rubbed his nose as he fought the urge to deny her request. "Only if you'll accept what I offer."

Her gaze flashed to the wagon and the neatly tied parcels.

"I just said I would."

"All of it."

"Yes, very well."

He grinned and handed over six large packages, then carried the remaining bundles to the porch.

"I'll see to the horses. And we'll head out after lunch." He led the team to the barn.

He took a minute to check the bridles for wear and inspected the rest of his tack. When all the horses were happily munching hay, he left, wondering if Sarah had yet opened one particular bundle containing two New York garters and silk stockings.

His mouth went dry as a thrill of excitement rolled through him. He remembered her perfect leg and thought that silk could not be softer than her skin. A stirring of his flesh forced him to hesitate before leaving the barn. His gelding lifted his head, casting his big brown eyes upon him.

"It's not like she'll let me touch her leg again anyway."

The horse dropped his head to grab another hank of hay, then returned his attention to his master.

"But I can imagine, can't I?"

Chapter Six

Lucie trembled in her thin cotton dress. The warrior set no fire against night. He held out pemmican to her. She recognized this combination of dried crushed berries and powdered buffalo jerky, since she had been responsible for making most of Following Calf's winter supply.

She never refused food now and devoured two pemmican biscuits. Eagle Dancer sat upon his buffalo rope, chewing as he stared boldly at her. She grew so nervous under his perusal she could barely swallow.

The sun crept low over the horizon. Soon she would be alone in the darkness with this man. She feared him and what he might do to her person. What chance did she have against a warrior?

None.

For some reason, she glanced about them—searching for what, she did not know. Rescue? Her mother? There was nothing but the waving grass and empty prairie. The cottonwood by the river now stood tall and frightening in silhouette. At last her gaze fell on him again and she met his intent stare. Her breath caught.

"Don't hurt me," she begged.

He frowned. "I will not."

But she knew it hurt to lay with a man and that his words were lies.

"What will you do?"

His slow sensual smile froze her blood.

"I am only twelve winters."

Actually she'd turned thirteen in August, but she would not tell him that.

He frowned.

"I am a child."

"Then listen, child. You sleep beside me this night. You rest here." He placed his open palm against his ribs, beneath his extended arm.

Did he really mean sleep or did he mean to fall upon her? Her time with Following Calf had taught her caution.

"Why did you buy me?"

She bit her lip, hoping that he would say his sister needed a slave or his mother had lost a daughter. But he only stared at her with wide dark eyes.

"I wanted you."

She gulped and he laughed at the sound she made in her throat.

It was like being told you'd hang, but not right away. The sentence hung over her head as he lay down in the pocket of his furs and motioned for her to follow.

"Come," he said, holding open the flap.

The night air grew cool, but she hesitated.

"Obey me," he said.

She did not dare defy him, and so she slunk forward like a whipped dog, inching into the place he made for her. The great hide descended, enveloping them together.

She had never slept beside anyone but her mother. Following Calf had given Lucie her own hide. Now she lay still as a chunk of wood as the scent of leather and of the man beside her mingled with the musty smell of buffalo. He drew her close, to the place he said she would rest—beside his heart.

She felt it beating steadily as her own heartbeat pounded like the hooves of a jogging pony. After a few minutes of inactivity, he stroked her head. She shivered with trepidation. This is when it would happen. She would be soiled and no decent man would have her.

She sniffed, afraid to weep.

"Rest."

His arm slipped from her hair to drape across her middle. The weight of it pressed uncomfortably against her stomach, but she dared not move.

The warrior's breath puffed against her head, and she knew he slept. She exhaled her relief and allowed her own eyes to close. Before sleep took her, she thanked God for sparing her innocence .

When she woke, she lay curled in his arms like his pet cat. She tried to escape, but he roused at her wiggling effort to slip from his embrace. His grip tightened. One eye opened and he frowned.

She said nothing, only stared up mutely, waiting.

His arm lifted like the drawbridge to a castle and she escaped. He did not touch her again that morning.

They journeyed six days along an unknown river and across open plains. Each night he held her close but never violated her person, if you didn't count his stroking her hair or cheek.

Far off, shining blue and purple, rose the Rocky Mountains. Lucie glanced back over her shoulder for the hundredth time that day.

How would her mother ever find her in this wilderness? She had seen no whites since the first night of their capture and spoken no English since that day.

When her mother came, would Lucie even remember how to speak?

A voice in her head, the evil voice that always whispered fearful things, spoke. She won't find you. You'll live with these savages forever unless they kill you.

She scowled, wishing the voice would go away and bother someone else. Her mother would find her, was trying right now. The last thing she'd said to Lucie was to stay put and she'd be back for her.

But what if they had killed her?

That voice again. Lucie straightened, her long neck craning to see behind her. Her mother had been only a few feet from her. Lucie thought that meant she had escaped. Now doubt whispered in her ear. Perhaps they had killed her like they'd killed Kathryn Jackson. She trembled at the possibilities.

Eagle Dancer drew in the horse and turned to look at her. The expression she once thought fierce now seemed more concerned. He threw his bare leg over the horse's neck and slid off, pulling her down by the arm an instant later.

He pointed at the tears on her cheek.

"No," he said.

She nodded and he wiped her face.

At the river, he motioned Lucie to follow and she did, grateful for an opportunity to drink. She dug a small hole in the sandy bank and waited while water filled the gap, then she scooped the clear liquid into her palm and drank.

Replete at last, she turned to see Eagle Dancer wash himself. He stood naked in the river, and Lucie turned away, but not before seeing his lean, muscular shank.

She waited on the bank until he returned and drew out his killing shirt. That was what Lucie called it, one of the brightly dyed shirts the men wore for war and entering villages. His buckskin looked blood red and bore a hideous tasseled fringe of human hair. If she understood correctly, these long strands were the trophies of war, enemies killed in battle.

Lucie searched the front for an auburn strand but found none. Eagle Dancer put on his leggings for the first time and combed out his long dark hair.

She straightened as the meaning of his actions became clear. They neared the journey's end.

She feared what would come. Would the women and children of this village taunt and torment her like the last?

The warrior confirmed her suspicion a moment later when he braided his hair, adding feathers to the ends, and painted the forelegs of his horse with red stripes.

Wherever he was taking her, they had arrived. She searched the hills about them, but saw no smoke, heard no dogs and smelled no horses.

After he finished preening, he turned to her. A cold shiver of dread inched up her spine. Eagle Dancer's big hands gripped the tangle her hair had become.

He pressed a firm hand on her shoulder, forcing her to sit before him. He lifted a brush of porcupine quills and set to work tugging first at the ends and then moving steadily upward toward her scalp. He took no extra measures to hurt her as Following Calf often had. Lucie lifted her skirt above her knee to inspect the progress of the bruises left from the stick the woman had last beat her with. Who would own her next?

She shivered and Eagle Dancer laid a hand on her shoulder, but whether to still or reassure her, she could not guess.

When the knots were all pulled out, he divided Lucie's hair and added grease before braiding two plaits. He finished his ministrations by placing a ring of blue and gray feathers upon her head.

Thus made presentable by the standards of the savages, she was again commanded to walk behind her captor's horse. She wondered if she had made a grave error by not escaping in the night as he slept. The urge to flee became more desperate with each passing step. Under cover of dark she could have eluded him, even stolen his horse. They had slit Kathryn's throat for refusing to walk. What would they do to a runaway slave?

She shuddered as possibilities danced in her mind.

But where would she go? The way back to the wagon trail tangled in her mind like a ball of yarn. Even if she escaped recapture and found the trail, how would she find her mother?

She hunched behind the warrior. Fear kept her from escaping. Her yearning to be free did not overwhelm her desire to stay alive. During these three harsh months of captivity, the fright had settled into a constant wariness, like the soldiers on guard duty at the forts. She saw no immediate danger but was always ready for it to present itself.

Perhaps she was not his slave, but some kind of sacrifice. Once she had watched in horror as Following Calf had butchered the family dog. They ate the meat in a barbaric feast. If they could so easily kill their dog, how much simpler would it be to kill an enemy slave?

Her terrors echoed in her mind. She had not the courage to ask Eagle Dancer about the fate awaiting her. He seemed to have forgotten her now. His horse's ears pricked, and Lucie listened. It was several minutes before she heard the shouts of children. A lone guard stood on a hilltop beside the river. He waved, and Eagle Dancer waved back.

A cry came from the sentinel. The call roused the village. Soon they streamed over the hill, children first, running on firm brown legs. Next came the women, lining the path, waving and calling in something like a yodel.

Lucie resisted the urge to cover her ears as they paraded down the Sioux version of Main Street, stopping before a teepee of white leather. Scalps fluttered from the hide and grotesque, crudely drawn figures danced along the leather canvas.

Eagle Dancer slid down to greet two women. The similarity of their features made Lucie think they were mother and daughter. They crossed their forearms and placed open palms upon Eagle Dancer's chest in a salutation with which Lucie was now familiar. This was his family. A wife and mother?

She hoped so.

The women turned to her with poorly disguised curiosity. Lucie's stomach clenched, and the rapid beat of her heart made her breathing quicken.

It was all she could do not to grip the horse's tail to keep him from pulling her into the crowd of strangers.

The women tugged at her faded calico dress and lifted her braids. Despite Eagle Dancer's trouble, her new style did not keep the forest belles from marveling at the color of her red-gold hair.

She glanced back to Eagle Dancer, hopeful he would intervene before the women smothered her, but he drifted toward the men and finally disappeared.

Lucie could not breathe. The women pushed and shoved to get a look at her. Spots danced before her eyes, and she feared she would faint.

The woman who had greeted Eagle Dancer first grasped Lucie's arm and pulled her through the crowd, drawing her into the large central tent.

There, Eagle Dancer waited wearing a somber expression, which only made him look more dangerous. Her body went cold as if dipped in ice water as she stood between the wall of women behind her and the ring of warriors before her.

Chapter Seven

In Sacramento, Thomas arranged an appointment with Colonel Jessup of the U.S. Army. Sarah included herself in the meeting.

"How long has your girl been missing?" He directed his questions to Thomas, having ignored Sarah since the introductions.

"Since May twenty-fifth." Three and a half months already. Sarah knit her hands to keep from fussing.

The man spun the end of his full mustache, curving it until it resembled a fishhook.

"And thirteen, you say? She's likely dead. If she's not dead, well…" He gave the mustache another twist. "You'd best presume her dead. After those savages have had at her, you won't want her back."

Sarah's rage bubbled over; at the center was her own failure to keep her daughter safe. The day they'd taken Lucie had been the second time in her life she'd wanted to die, and both times her daughter had kept her alive. Now she rose from her seat beside the door and stepped forward, her boots reporting like gunfire on the wooden planking. Jessup had time only to lift an eyebrow.

"Well, I *do* want her back, Colonel."

His tone dripped with condescension. "Mrs. West, I met that Oatman girl, Olive. What's a gal like that going to do? She's ruined. My opinion, they should have left her in that desert."

"I've had quite enough of your opinion," said Sarah. "If I had my way, we'd leave *you* in the desert. Come, Thomas, we'll do better without this bigoted, impotent little bureaucrat."

Jessup surged to his feet roaring like a buffalo. "If you were a man, I'd make you answer for that."

Sarah made a face. "But I'm not a man, just a woman who is best forgotten—like my daughter."

The colonel turned to Thomas. "You'll get yourself killed."

Tired of being ignored, Sarah jabbed a finger at the navy wool covering his chest. "I will not abandon her."

"If you go into the Black Hills, they'll take you, too."

"Good day, Colonel," said Thomas, ending the discussion. He clasped Sarah's elbow and steered her out into the street.

There in the bright sunshine, Sarah still shook with rage.

"It's the same everywhere I go," she said. "Why do I continue to hope someone will help me?"

Thomas's stern look stopped her in midstride.

"I'm helping you."

All the fight drained from her, and she landed hard on a crate before a druggist's. Thomas leaned against the wall as he watched a cart drawn by a lame mule rattle by, then turned his attention on Sarah.

"Question is—what now?" he said. "We can't ride into the Black Hills alone. We can try the army out there, of course, but if Jessup is any indication, that route is a box canyon."

"They should be ashamed."

"Reward?"

"I tried that."

"For how much?"

"One hundred dollars for return, fifteen for information."

He lifted his eyebrows but said nothing.

"What?"

Thomas pushed the brim of his hat up, giving her a clear look at his eyes. "Not much money, is all."

She scowled, folding her arms before her like a shield. "It's all I had."

He nodded, and then his gaze left her to study the street again. She recognized the long pauses that often occurred when Thomas put his mind to a problem.

At last he said, "I'll offer considerably more."

It took great restraint not to leap to her feet and throw her arms about him. Instead, she clasped her hands before her in thanks.

"Could you, Thomas?"

"But I think you were right about shaming them. Folks on the wagon trains and those back east, they have a right to know the army won't aid them if they run into trouble."

"How do you propose to alert them?" she asked.

He pointed, and she followed the direction of his finger to the newspaper office.

"You want to advertise?"

"You heard of that paper?"

She shook her head.

"Run by a fellow named McClatchy. The year he took over, he ran our state treasurer out of office for embezzlement. McClatchy's pen caused the man's impeachment. Newsmen live on scandals. He'll find it real interesting that the army failed to order even a cursory search for Lucie."

Hope surged into her with the next breath.

"McClatchy can get more attention with a printing press than an entire artillery unit with cannons blazing. He'll stir things up, maybe even embarrass them into action."

Sarah stood, preparing to grab the bull by the horns.

Thomas stayed her with a hand. "Let's plan this. What we say will determine how this plays out. We need to feed them all the details that will sell papers and change policies."

Faced with the importance of the task, Sarah sank back into

her seat. She listened to Thomas's advice and added details of outrageous behavior, like the ball that the officers at Fort Laramie held even as the wounded and dying survivors of the wretched attack were brought under their ambivalent care.

"The wife of an army captain even offered me a dress. Can you imagine? They did not even venture out to recover the bodies until the next day."

"McClatchy will eat that up. Let's go."

He offered his hand and she took it, releasing him with reluctance as she stood.

Sarah and Thomas crossed the dusty street side by side, united in a common purpose. The door of the *Daily Bee* struck a bell, and the jangle alerted the man behind the counter to their arrival.

The interview took much of the afternoon. When McClatchy finally laid down his pen, Sarah felt as wrung out as a wet dishtowel twisted dry. When she stood to leave, she found her joints stiff.

Without her uttering a word about her bone weariness, Thomas responded, clasping her elbow and guiding her out into the street. An afternoon shower had turned the road into a quagmire, and she lifted her skirts to keep her hem from the mud.

She kept her attention on the ruts and manure as Thomas moved them safely through the maze of wagons and riders. Together they crossed the road to the wide plank sidewalk.

"That was a hell of a story, Sarah. You were damned lucky to survive it," said Thomas.

She glanced at him, seeing compassion for her terrible journey, and welcomed this small offering.

"Part of me didn't survive it."

"You did the best you could for Lucie."

"If I hadn't told her to hide, she'd be here with me today."

"If we could see into the future and know how things worked out, I'd have done lots of things different."

She slowed her pace as possibilities stirred. "Name one."

His first thought was that he never would have left her. But to say so would be to give her great power over him. Her appearance and revelations had already torn him to ribbons. He could not risk his tattered heart further.

"I would have locked my window that night."

She halted, looking as if he had kicked her in the stomach. At first she paled, but in a moment that changed, as the shock ebbed and her cheeks burned with color.

"That is one thing I would *not* change. You don't know her, Thomas, but Lucie is a wonder. Everyone loves her. Somehow, with all the mistakes, we did that one thing right."

He hadn't meant he didn't want Lucie, just that the whole miserable mess began that night.

"Sarah, I don't regret our night together. But if you hadn't…" Her scowl stopped him again and he accepted his part. "If we hadn't made love, then you wouldn't have had to marry."

He already knew what she thought about that night. Worst mistake of her life, she'd told him. He clenched his jaw.

"If I hadn't been with child, I would have followed you all the way to California, instead of listening to my mother. Why did I listen?"

"'Cause you thought me dead."

She bowed her head. "Yes."

"How did Samuel find out you were expecting?"

"He came upon me at our spot, down by the creek. I was crying and, well, he asked me if it was because I missed you. That was before we had word." She lifted her gaze and glared. "Before I had word, anyway. I had just done some counting and realized what was amiss. I asked him what to do."

"What'd he say?"

"To write you a letter. So I did. I still have it. News of your death came the next day. We had a funeral, buried an empty box. Lord, I've never felt like that before. I thought nothing in this world could hurt so much."

Before he could move to comfort her, those gray wolf-eyes flashed at him.

"Turns out I was wrong. Lucie was five when I met Ben Harris after church. Funny that finding out you were alive hurt more than thinking you dead."

Thomas clasped her arm and steered her to a rocking chair in the shade of the hotel's front porch, then sat in the one closest to hers.

"Samuel was with me. They shook hands, and Samuel asked about the gold fields. He so regretted not going."

"He didn't miss much."

"How he envied you both when you and Hyatt left. When he talked about California, he got a faroff look in his eyes. The farm, the baby and me, well, we all tied him down. He was too responsible to go. Deep down he wanted to follow his brothers."

"Follow? He was the elder. The farm was his. Dad left me no illusions on that account. I told you, I had to make my own way."

"And so you have."

He couldn't tell if she was congratulating or mocking him. He gritted his teeth. "I've made a fine living."

"With no one to share it with."

They glared at each other.

Finally he said. "You going to finish your story?"

"I think not."

"Fine, let's get a room." He stood and waited.

She remained seated, refusing to look at him.

"You coming?"

"Not if you are renting *a* room."

He dragged his hat off his head, resisting the urge to throw it down like a gauntlet. "You'll have your own room, Sarah."

She rose, regal as a queen. "Very well, then."

Sarah waited while he registered and secured two rooms on opposite sides of the hall and then arranged livery for the horses. He walked her upstairs and handed off the key. Behind them a porter lumbered up the stairs.

"I want to wait for that newspaper story to run. In the meantime, I'll see about finding an outfit heading east." He hesitated, wanting to be rid of her and not understanding why he lingered here in the hall. "See if your room is all right."

She turned the lock and stepped inside. He followed her but she stopped him with a hand, glancing toward the porter.

"In here," she said to the boy. "Those are mine. Thank you." She pressed a coin into his hand.

Thomas stood in the hall, gripping his hat. The porter unlocked his door and hauled Thomas's gear within.

"Dinner?" asked Thomas.

"I think I'll take mine in my room."

He scowled. It was because he'd cut off her story about Samuel that she shunned him. "I'll pick you up at seven."

"I don't think so."

How was it possible for one woman to put him in such a constant state of irritation?

She stood with her hand on the crystal knob now, ready to slam the door that he'd paid for in his face.

The porter cleared his throat. Thomas scowled. "Skedaddle."

The porter glowered and descended the stairs.

"Honestly," said Sarah, following the boy's departure. "You know how I hate public scenes."

"Do I? Do I know the first thing about you?"

Her grimace fell away, replaced by a crestfallen expression.

He turned to go. With the first three steps he meant to leave her. For reasons he didn't understand, he found himself returning to the narrow doorway, looming over Sarah.

"And I don't want to hear any more about Samuel."

"But he gobbled up any news of you."

He leaned forward, and she flattened against the door to avoid touching him. Her current position gave him a fine view of the round curve of her breasts. He lifted his gaze to meet hers. She regarded him with caution and he knew she understood the height of his passion.

Easily, he gripped her arm and pulled her back into the room, kicking the door with the heel of his boot. In an instant, he dragged her up against him. The warmth of her body electrified him, like a bolt from the sky.

He thrust his hands into the soft, rich hair at her temples, forcing her gaze to his.

"Every time you say his name I see him with you. I see you in his bed." He pressed his cheek to hers, bringing his lips beside her ear. "I go mad when I think of you together."

She trembled in his arms like a captured bird. He knew he could throw her on the bed and fall upon her like a wolf. But could he erase Samuel from her heart?

One hand moved to cup the back of her head as the other trailed along the tender flesh at her throat. He pulled back to watch her ragged breathing. His fingers drew along the pale column of her neck, over her shoulder and down the lush slope beyond.

At last, he held her breast in his hand. Through the layers of her dress, her nipple hardened beneath his palm. He pressed and she groaned. Her eyelids fluttered closed, and her head dropped back in surrender, giving him access to her throat. He leaned in to kiss her, madness filling him as he devoured her. Her scent intoxicated him, and he dragged her against him, against the raw desire she raised in him.

She tensed in his arms and he stilled. Her face was now etched with dread and her head was cocked, as if listening. He listened, too, and noted voices in the hall.

"The door," she whispered.

He saw it was ajar, creaking open wider and wider. She trembled in his arms now, but not from his advances.

"What?"

An elderly couple appeared in the doorway. Sarah leapt away from Thomas as if scorched.

The woman's mouth gaped and then clamped shut in an expression of harsh censure. Her escort lifted his bushy eyebrows.

"Oh, excuse us." The man grasped his lady's arm and led them forward.

The woman's words rang clearly in the hall. "Excuse us? Excuse them. They're the ones engaging in shameful acts with the door hanging open. Revolting, simply revolting."

Sarah's neck and cheeks now flamed. Thomas moved to the door, preparing to close it, but she was there in an instant.

"Out," she ordered.

"What?"

"You heard me. You ruined my reputation once. I'll not have it again. I'll not be called a whore behind my back."

He couldn't keep his hands from clenching into fists. "Who called you that?"

"And my daughter. Do you know what all those dear little sons and daughters of our friends called her?"

He grasped her shoulders, to tell her he didn't know. How could he have known? "Sarah, please."

"Please what?"

Forgive me. I never intended to hurt you.

She gripped the knob until her knuckles turned white. "You have to leave."

He nodded, accepting her rejection as his due. He stepped into the hallway and the door was closed firmly behind him.

He stood on the faded carpet runner for a long time, his lips still tingling from her passionate kisses. After all the sorrow he had caused her, why would she let him kiss her at all? Because she doesn't know what happened—not all of it, anyway. If she did, she would have shunned him already.

If he told her, could she find it in her heart to forgive him?

To know the answer to that, he'd have to tell her about Hyatt. He imagined the fire of passion in her eyes turning to revulsion. Thomas's shoulders slumped and he walked away.

Chapter Eight

Thomas sent a note inviting her to dinner that evening and she sent her regrets. She paced to the window, pressing her palm to the warm glass as uncertainty built within her. This game of avoidance could not go on indefinitely.

Tomorrow the *Daily Bee* would release the story. Then she and Thomas would journey east toward the terrible plains where the Sioux had taken her Lucie. She gazed through the window of the hotel room Thomas had provided. She did not look outward but inward, back to her last meeting with Thomas. He had seemed so stricken when she had ordered him out. He'd looked as if he'd lost his last friend.

Perhaps he had. First his parents, then Hyatt and now Samuel. Thomas had no one, while she had Lucie.

Sarah had never wondered if he had missed her. All these years she had thought of herself as the girl he willingly left behind. But the look in his eyes belied that notion. He had never forgotten.

Why hadn't Thomas written her? He wouldn't say. What could have happened that made him think she could change her mind about them? She recalled Hyatt's eager face and the fuzz that covered his cheeks. He didn't yet have his first beard but had so wanted to be a man. Her heart ached with grief. What had happened to poor Hyatt?

Samuel had known—and kept it from her all these long years. Why had he not told her the truth?

Sarah considered possibilities until she came to the most terrible. Samuel had lied to keep her for himself. If he had given her the truth, that Thomas lived, would she have married?

She pressed her hands to her eyes as the hoarse cries came again.

Samuel knew her too well. At the first word of Thomas's survival, she would have gathered Lucie and walked a thousand miles to find him.

"Samuel, you tricked me."

She recalled the day she had met Ben Harris. Samuel had been engaged in conversation with him outside the church. Sarah recognized her old schoolmate and smiled her greeting.

Samuel tried to send her off. She remembered clearly now. He told her he would meet her at the wagon, but she ignored him, anxious to hear of Ben's trip to California.

When he had mentioned Thomas, her heart had hurt so badly she thought it had ruptured. She pressed a hand over her breast now at the echo of the grief that had swept through her.

"Alive?" she had breathed.

Ben had grinned and nodded. The sun's rays had burned her face, her eyes. The world went brilliant white. She heard Samuel calling her name as he seemed to spin before her in dizzying circles. Then she fell away into darkness.

She had never fainted before in her life, not even when she had found Lucie gone.

Lucie.

She sank to her knees beside the bed, resting her forehead upon her folded hands.

"Please, God, let me find her alive. Bring her back to me. Let Thomas forgive me and help me forgive him."

And she realized that she asked God for what she had not

asked of Thomas. They must reconcile if her prayers were to be answered.

Why had he allowed her to think him dead? What terrible secret made him fear to return to her? She could think of nothing that could break the bond between them, save his leaving her. But now she longed to hear his side of events.

She would begin by telling him the truth and hope to win his trust. But how would she manage that when she could not even be in the same room with him without wanting to kiss him?

Sarah smoothed the wrinkles from the bedspread and then sat upon the coverlet, clutching the bedpost. It was her fault that Thomas thought he could kiss her like that, because she had once crawled into his room like a wanton woman and given herself to the man she loved. She'd never had a drop of resistance where Thomas was concerned, and it seemed that that had not changed over time.

Cold panic washed down her spine. She knew full well that she could not find her daughter without his help. She needed Thomas if she was to have any chance of success. She must make him understand that their entanglements threatened their mission. The scandal of their last joining had hurt her, but more importantly it had hurt Lucie. Her daughter had done nothing to deserve the scorn that had fallen upon her innocent head. Another scandal would certainly hurt her chances of gaining sympathy for her cause so she would explain to Thomas what must be—for Lucie's sake. It was the woman's role to suppress such improper impulses. Her job—and she had failed again.

She must speak to Thomas and make him understand.

Sarah rose, drawing strength from her need to help Lucie. She must speak to Thomas about Samuel. If he could not forgive her for marrying, at least she could make him understand the circumstances. And she must set down the limits to their relationship. Until they found Lucie, she would keep her energies focused on her child.

The courage to step across the hall came easily. The nerve to knock on his door took more time to summon, but she did it. Her second knock was more forceful and still garnered no reply.

At last she conceded that he was out, and so she waited with her door cracked to hear his approach. Not until after her usual time to retire did she recognize the sound of a heavy tread and then the metal scrape of a key against a lock. Rousing herself from her doze, she opened the door and drew a breath to call him. She hesitated.

He stooped and examined the keyhole and then the key before trying again to couple the two, missing badly.

She stiffened with suspicion. One deep breath confirmed her initial assessment. He smelled of stale beer and cigar smoke.

Drunk.

Just as Samuel had been more and more often in the final years. Seeing Thomas fall prey to the same demon forced a wretched cry from her lips.

He turned to peer back at her, still stooped as he gave her a lopsided grin.

"There's my girl."

"You're drunk."

He straightened. "Guilty."

"We're leaving tomorrow. You promised."

"Did I? Well, you should know I can't be trusted to keep a promise any better than you."

That arrow struck straight to her heart, but he paused only to draw breath before continuing.

"But anything to keep my best gal happy."

He hadn't called her that since the Sunday before his leaving. The fact that he did so now, without any inkling of the burning sadness the endearment raised in her, shocked her near speechless.

"Don't you call me that."

He just grinned.

"Go to bed, Thomas."

"All righty." He turned and then seemed to remember something because he faced her again. He wobbled and tipped into the wall hard enough that she feared he would break through the plaster. "Whoops."

"Honestly." She snatched the key from his hand and inserted it with more vigor than necessary into the hole.

A click and twist brought the door open. She stepped back to wave him in and he staggered forward, reaching the bed and falling facedown. The frame groaned from the frontal assault but did not buckle. His legs dangled to the floor. He looked like a boy about to get a good paddling. Likely he deserved it more than most.

She stood in the doorway, hands thrust on hips, staring daggers at him. He was beyond her scorn, so she sighed and let the anger clarify to heartache.

"Just like Samuel," she whispered.

Tom lay motionless.

"Is that the only way you men know how to solve your troubles?" she asked, but received no reply.

"That or punching things," she muttered. Lifting her voice again, she called to him. "I should leave you there."

A door opened and a woman peered out. Sarah stood frozen at her regard. The woman lifted an eyebrow before retreating and Sarah could breathe once more. She crept across the carpeted hall and retrieved the lantern from her room. Silent as a thief she returned, pausing only to remove Thomas's key from the door. Such carelessness invited robbers, and he carried all their funds. Perhaps she would speak to him about that. If he was going to act with such foolish disregard, then she would carry them.

Samuel had given her charge of all the money, or what little had been left after bankruptcy. A terrible possibility struck her like a blow. The money!

She shook his shoulder until he groaned and then responded.

"Celeste, leave off, I'm resting."

Sarah straightened, shock starching her spine. He'd called her by another woman's name. This indignity kept her at bay a moment as she tried to stanch her outrage. Finally, her fears drove her back and she shook his shoulders until he bounced on the mattress.

"Wake up, Thomas. It's Sarah."

He rolled. "Sarah?"

His bloodshot eyes stared up in wonderment as if she were some apparition come to seek him out.

"Thomas, where were you? Were you gambling?"

"I leave the window unlocked every night just hoping."

"What? Thomas, the money. Do you still have it?"

He nodded. "I've got money now. More than we'll ever need, if only you'd come back to me."

Thomas struggled to an upright position with the aid of a firm grip on the foot rail.

"Oh, I forgot," he slumped as the look of hope drained out of him like sand from a bag. "You belong to him now." He lifted his watery gaze to her again. "Oh, Sarah. How I miss you."

"Tom, I'm here. Do you have the money to find Lucie?"

"Lucie?" He swayed.

"Where is it?"

He made a grab for his boot and missed, then toppled back, this time lying sideways across the bed.

Sarah closed the chamber door, sealing them in. Unease crept upon her. She was again in a compromising position. If anyone saw her leaving, she could hardly explain why she was here alone at night in his bedchamber. But she was not here for bed sport. Her intentions were equally wrong.

She knew she had no right to search him but that she would do it just the same. Her hand slid into his front pockets, finding a drawstring purse. She ripped at the strings and counted the coins. The total reached less than fourteen dollars. She hurled the coins upon the coverlet.

"Oh, Tom. Damn you for failing me twice."

She felt the familiar burning in her eyes, but forced back the tears as she gathered his coins and placed his purse on the bed-side table before turning to go. His symphonic snore stopped her. Biting back her disappointment, she lifted one foot and tugged at his boot. With some effort she released him from the leather. The second boot took more elbow grease. When his foot cleared the rim, a billfold flopped onto the floor.

Her gaze pinned it like a cat targeting an escaping mouse. In a moment she snatched it up. It was stuffed with bills. Hundreds of dollars fanned out before her. Relief washed away her fear.

She righted the boots, tucking the toes beneath the bed, and then laid the billfold beside the purse. Why did she always believe the worst of this man when all he had ever done was love her and believe his older brother when Samuel told him she had been untrue?

She should have followed her heart instead of listening to the whining drone of her mother's relentless insistence that she marry, she and Lucie would have been free when word came that Thomas lived. It hadn't been his brother's lies that had separated them all these years, but her weakness.

"I'm sorry, Thomas."

He lay insensible, groaning as she lifted his legs onto the bed. Remembering that Samuel often drank to the point of illness, she feared to leave him. Thinking of Samuel this way stirred her misery. She remembered when the drinking had changed from moments of celebration to a daily affair. She now realized that his altered habits had coincided with his betrayal of his younger brother. When she had discovered that Thomas lived, Samuel's drinking grew worse again.

Samuel had been there when she'd heard the news from Harris. When she woke from her faint, Samuel knelt beside her. She didn't see him at first, didn't see anything past the joy.

"He's alive," she whispered.

He gave her a harsh shake.

"He's forsaken you. And you are *my* wife."

She hunched, recalling the pain of the instant when she understood that her lover lived and that he had abandoned her. He was as lost to her as if he were dead, for he walked the earth and she could not go to him.

Her gaze met her husband's, and she knew all her efforts to love Samuel were in vain. In that terrible moment she knew he saw the truth—that if Thomas had come for her, she would have left him.

So she had wept, while he had grown sullen. Now she knew that Samuel had known all along that Thomas was alive and never told her. He had kept his secrets locked in his heart, imprisoning her.

Sarah stared down at Thomas, who was lost in the oblivion of strong drink. Her best beau. Gently, she rocked him onto his side and bolstered him with a pillow. She paused to check her work and he rolled upon his back again. Again, she set him on his side. This time she was forced to hold him in place. This would not do.

If the drink made him so insensible as to render him unconscious, surely he endangered himself.

She crept across the floor and locked them in his room. Then she returned to his side.

"Tom?"

He made no reply but continued his light snore. She swept a lock of hair from his forehead and stooped to drop a kiss upon his brow.

She placed the key beside his things and rounded the bed. To unfasten her shoes, she sat beside him, working the stubborn buttons through the leather eyelets without benefit of a hook. She removed nothing else before snuffing the lamp.

Then, for the second time in her life, she lay in his bed.

Chapter Nine

A shove from the women sent Lucie stumbling into the large lodge, where she fell to her knees before the gathering of men. Lucie trembled, certain that they meant to burn her at the stake. Eagle Dancer presented her to a chief called Fast Bear.

Her mother had kept her from much of the talk of Indians, but on the trail, when the sun had set and the wolves howled, the men and women spoke of little else. From within the thin walls of canvas she had listened to every grim description of evil deeds. Now they rose in her mind to haunt her.

A warrior named Yellow Tomahawk produced a pipe and she was largely forgotten as they smoked and talked. The men shared venison stew as her stomach grumbled a loud complaint. More terrible than the fear and the hunger was her unabated thirst. She could no longer swallow.

At last many of the men departed and two women entered. The older one grabbed a braid of Lucie's hair as the younger tugged at her clothing, making exclamations of wonder. Eagle Dancer laid out the things he had bartered for. She gradually understood that she was obtained with the blankets, while the horse was traded for the items before her.

She recognized her mother's blue Ohio star quilt, two cast-iron skillets and a copper kettle. There was also a butcher knife and the Wagner's Reader from their wagon. Lucie had not had a lesson in the three and a half months of her captivity. Her gaze wandered to the quilt as heartache hollowed her insides. How she missed sleeping snug and safe beneath that quilt. But it would not protect her now. Nothing would.

Chases Storms lifted the book and laid it open upon her lap. "Talk words."

She did, reading to them in her own language as the chief, now wrapped in her mother's quilt, watched with a solemn expression. The younger woman clapped her hands.

Fast Bear held out a twig and spoke to Chases Storms, who offered her the stick. She held it without understanding until he swept a place clear in the sand.

"Make stick words."

She wrote. Lucie Marie West, 1864.

The two men exchanged a smile. They then handed her a letter and told her to read it. She unfolded the page, and she began in English.

The men waited until she reached the signature of Lt. John Gaffney, 5th Cavalry.

"What does it say?" asked Eagle Dancer.

Lucie searched her limited vocabulary. "It say blue pony boy missing his goods." She could not think of the word for money or pay and thought they had none. "He ask for..." She used her hands in a game of charades to count imaginary money.

Eagle Dancer nodded. Fast Bear scowled fiercely, scooped up the book and departed without another word.

Lucie did not know why she felt like a traitor. The communication was valueless. She had revealed nothing of importance. As she followed Eagle Dancer out of the lodge, she could not shake the feeling she had made some mistake. He told her to wait beside a strange teepee. In a few moments he brought a woman.

Lucie's heart leapt into frantic beating, for one look at the light brown hair and hazel eyes told her she met a captive. Lucie was so overcome with joy, she hugged the young woman. They sat together as Lucie shot questions at her like gunfire.

The men moved off, sitting together to gamble. Eagle Dancer glanced toward Lucie on occasion.

"What is your name?" asked Lucie.

"I'm Alice French from Decatur, Illinois. And you?"

"Lucie West. I'm from Illinois, too. Kaskaskia."

They hugged again, like long-lost family. Alice pulled back first.

"How long have you been here?" she asked.

"A few months. The Sioux attacked our wagons and killed the men. I think my mother got away. At least I did not see her killed or captured, nor did I see her scalp lock with the others."

Alice's head dropped and her words simmered with rage. "They killed my parents and little brother, when they took me. We were homesteaders in Kansas."

"How long ago?"

"Seven years."

Lucie gasped. So long?

"Now Fast Bear means to marry me." Her venomous expression vanished and her eyes twinkled. "I'd sooner die than lie with a heathen beast. I may be leaving soon." She produced a pencil and the Wagner's reader. "Write your name here and if I reach the fort I will give it to them as proof you are alive."

The creeping unease grew stronger, at seeing the book Fast Bear had held as he'd stormed out of the lodge. After a moment's hesitation, she snatched up the pencil as her heart fluttered with hope for the first time since her arrival. In a moment she wrote her name. Alice wrote hers beneath it.

"I've told them a lie." Alice shifted her gaze toward the men. "If they believe me, they may bring me to the fort."

"What lie?"

"They brought me a letter to read. I told them it said there was a large reward for me. That any Indian who brought me safely to the fort would receive five boxes of ammunition and three rifles. Fast Bear wants more arms. I think he will take me himself."

Lucie's jaw dropped. Words failed her as she realized what she had done.

"Alice, did the letter say that a soldier was missing with the payroll?"

Alice smiled. "Yes, how did you know?"

The answer to her own question dawned upon her a moment later. She clutched fistfuls of her own hair and howled.

"No! You did not read it. You did not."

Lucie rested a hand upon Alice's arm to calm her. "I didn't know. I'm so sorry."

Alice pulled tufts of hair from her head as she wept. "I won't marry him. I'll run."

"No, you must not. Help will find us. My mother is searching."

Her eyes pinned her. "How do you know?"

"I just do."

Alice threw up her hands. "You don't even know if she's alive. They are not coming." Her shoulders hunched and a bleak expression masked her features as she stared at the ground. "Seven years—do you understand me? Seven, and you are the first white I have spoken to, except for a boy who does not remember his language or his people. The rest are half-breed savages. You are the first and you betray me." She threw herself facedown in the dirt and wept.

A shadow fell across Alice's back. Lucie turned to see Fast Bear standing over his slave. He hauled her to her feet and dragged her off as Alice sobbed and struggled.

Lucie's mouth remained open as she watched Fast Bear slap Alice and then pull her out of sight.

"You will catch a fly in that mouth," said Eagle Dancer.

Lucie scowled at him. She wished to accuse him of trickery, but he was her only friend. Well, not friend, but protector. He gave her food and did not allow the children to throw sticks at her.

She feared to anger him, but needed to know what fate awaited her. "Why you buy me—Alice?"

He shook his head.

"Why?" Ice filled her stomach as he smiled down at her sitting at his feet like his pet hound.

He squatted and lifted one of her braids. "I want you."

Lucie drew back. "I am too young."

How she hoped he would believe it. She knew two girls of fourteen already married. She did not fancy being one of them, especially if her husband was to be this man.

"I will wait."

Lucie faced the same fate as Alice, unless her mother came. She prayed again to be rescued as she considered escape.

Three days later Eagle Dancer came to the lodge of his mother, where Lucie now lived, and told them that soldiers were coming. The village had to move.

Lucie was put to work lifting and carrying under the direction of Yellow Bird. This woman, at least, never raised a stick of firewood to thump her across the shoulders, but she was as watchful as a hawk.

In a mere matter of hours, thousands of teepees were struck. Babies were bundled into leather bags and hung like sacks of grain from saddle pommels. Yellow Bird tied two tent poles to her horse, leaving them to drag behind the black and white pinto. Here she stacked the buffalo hide used as shelter along with all her household belongings. She ordered Lucie up onto the horse and loaded her down with bags and bundles.

The caravan set out. At midday they forded a river, the men riding across on horseback, unencumbered by anything but weapons, while the women threw themselves into the water like cattle and swam across.

Lucie squeezed her legs about her mount, praying she would not tumble into the water, as she could not swim. Behind them came the sound of war, shouts and gunfire.

She glanced behind her, longing for a glimpse of army blue. Yellow Bird shouted.

"Do not look back. Your place is here now."

The fury in the woman's voice frightened Lucie into compliance.

The woman riding beside Yellow Bird shouted at Lucie as well. "If we see them, I will kill you first. Do not think to escape so easily. Pray they do not come for you, for they will find you dead."

The afternoon wore on. Dust blanketed Lucie's skin as the column of Sioux moved north. When once she prayed for delivery by the army, now she feared their victory.

Yellow Bird explained that the Sioux killed their captives before surrendering them. Should the army win this battle, Lucie would die.

The sound of a galloping horse brought her about. Fast Bear charged toward her, pulling up on the rein too late. His horse bumped hers, unseating her. She landed hard and the items she carried spilled about her on the ground. Fast Bear tugged again on his rein and his horse reared up. Lucie fell back, narrowly escaping the flailing hooves.

"Where is she?" shouted Fast Bear.

Lucie cowered. "Who?"

"My slave!"

Alice, he meant Alice. Lucie looked about her in confusion and tried to form a coherent sentence. "I do not see this one."

Fast Bear howled and wheeled his horse away, tearing off at a gallop.

Had Alice heard that the soldiers were just behind them and fled?

Such an act was foolish desperation. Now Fast Bear pursued his slave. If he caught her, Lucie knew Alice's only escape would be through death. Alice had told her she chose death before the dishonor of marriage. Lucie drew herself to her knees and closed her eyes praying for Alice's safety.

The kick to her shoulder sent her sprawling to her face. Yellow Bird was on her, swooping like her namesake as she dragged Lucie to her feet.

"Pick it up, toad."

Chapter Ten

The bright sunshine streamed through unfamiliar curtains, reaching Thomas's throbbing eyes. His temples pounded with the results of last night's efforts. Had it been Sarah's birthday, he wondered. No, the warm air told him it was not October.

He recalled the hotel and Sarah in the same instant. He rolled onto his back and groaned at the sensation of his head splitting like wood beneath a dull axe. His hand fell to his side and touched something soft and warm.

That brought him sitting up despite the pain. Had he been so drunk he'd brought home a whore?

Sarah mustn't find out.

He tried to remember last night as he blinked down at the female curled at his side. Auburn hair spilled across the pillow. He gasped.

Sarah lay beside him, his Sarah, in yesterday's rumpled dress. He longed to peek under the coverlet and see if she wore silk stockings. Images of the New York garters filled his mind as his gaze galloped the distance from her hidden heel to her soft cheek.

She blinked and rolled onto her side to face him.

"How's your head?"

"Painful."

She sat up and swung her legs off the bed. Thomas struggled to rise to his elbow to catch a glimpse of her ankle but the hem of her skirt fell like a veil. He dropped back onto the pillow as Sarah reached the water jug and poured a glass. Returning, she offered it to him. He drained the contents in three thirsty gulps, then wiped his mouth with the back of his hand.

"Why are you here, Sarah?"

She sighed and turned to the window, lifting the lace edge to stare out onto the street.

"I've never seen you so drunk. I was worried."

Shame washed over him as he realized she'd witnessed him at his lowest moment. Could he show her nothing but weakness and mistakes?

"Thank you for looking out for me," he said.

She nodded her acceptance and then cleared her throat. Her thumb rubbed nervously over the top of her opposite hand, and Thomas braced for whatever Sarah was preparing to say.

"I have to apologize," she said.

Confusion wrinkled his brow. Whatever he'd expected, it wasn't that.

"You? For what?"

She spoke quickly now, as if in a rush to get it all out. "Last night, when I found you, I thought—that is, I found your empty billfold."

Thomas automatically lunged for his boot, only to find it missing. Fear gushed through him.

"No, no. It's all there." Sarah pointed to the side table. "I found the one in your coat while removing it. I assumed you had lost our traveling money at gaming. I'm sorry, Thomas, for having misjudged you."

Had she? He'd been so drunk that any thug could have rolled him for his money. Damned irresponsible. He silently vowed to do better.

He could not fail her this time.

"Do you drink often?" she asked, failing in her attempt to make the question sound casual.

His first thought was that he only drank when he mourned her loss. But he would not give her that information.

"Some," he said.

She raised her chin, her expression changing to disapproval with the simple narrowing of her lovely gray eyes.

"I thought I knew you better."

He dragged himself up, forced by the pressure of his bladder.

"You don't know me at all."

Some of the starch went out of her spine. "Perhaps not."

"You hungry?" he asked.

She nodded.

"I'll meet you downstairs in thirty minutes, then."

He could see by the tightening of her lips she didn't like being dismissed. She said nothing as she sat to don her shoes.

"Have you a buttonhook?" she asked.

When he shook his head, she sighed and stood, carrying her shoes.

He had dreamed of having her in his bed so often he'd lost count, and now he was tossing her out. Her scorn and the sickness of the drink combined to deter him from pursuing his impulses. It seemed the timing was always off with them—except that one night. That evening, the timing had been perfect.

He thought of Sarah, young and lithe, her body working in rhythm with his, and could not stifle the sigh of longing.

He grasped her free hand, conscious that he reeked of stale beer.

"Don't judge me by last night, Sarah. I'm asking to make a fresh start with you."

She glanced down. "Is that even possible after so much?"

"I'm willing to try and mend some fences."

She studied him. He resisted the urge to squirm.

"We have to talk about Samuel."

The denial sprung to his lips, but he bit it back.

"Why?"

She drew a long breath as if gathering her strength. "Because he asked me on his deathbed to find you. I didn't think I had the strength. When they took Lucie, I found I did."

"Because you had no one else to turn to."

"True."

"What did he say, exactly?" Thomas found himself leaning in, yearning for his brother's words. His eyes burned with unshed tears as he waited.

Sarah hesitated. "He asked me to tell you he loved you and that he was sorry. He asked for your forgiveness."

"Why?" But he knew. He understood that Samuel had known the truth of Lucie's paternity and had lied to keep him away. Had he also lied about his father's contempt and his mother's reproach? How much of Thomas's beliefs were built on sand?

Damn Samuel for interfering and damn himself for believing him without speaking to Sarah. The list of wrongs stretched from here to Illinois. He lifted his gaze to meet Sarah's.

"He told me we were going to Oregon, but I think he wanted to see you. He had been sick a long time and the journey weakened him. Then he got cholera. He tried to write you, but was too far gone. He made me promise to tell you he was sorry."

She turned away to look at the rays of light streaming through the lace curtain.

"Why did he leave the farm?"

Her head sank to her chest. "He didn't leave it, Thomas. He lost it to debt."

"What? Samuel was the best farmer in Illinois."

"He changed. Even went to doctors about his troubles, but they didn't help him."

"You're saying he got too sick to run the farm and had to move on?"

She hesitated.

The tension built in his chest as possibilities popped up like weeds in a garden. "He wasn't right in the head—is that it?"

"No, not that. He just grew sad, quiet and..."

Thomas gripped her arm. "And?"

Her eyes swam with tears when she lifted her face.

"He drank, Thomas. He drank all the time."

His hands slipped away from her as Sarah's words collided with the picture of his strong older brother. The man he'd envied all his life, the man who had everything.

His denial came quickly. "No."

"Yes." Her pronouncement was final and her expression brooked no argument.

Still he shook his head, refusing to believe that Samuel could have won Sarah—through lies, that was true, but still, he had married her—only to lose her to drink.

He stared at her in astonishment. Acceptance filled him slowly.

"He gambled, too, and made a public spectacle on more than one occasion." She glanced away as her words tumbled out. "Hard to hold your head up sometimes. It was difficult on all of us, but especially on Lucie."

"Why?" whispered Thomas.

"Samuel?"

He nodded.

"For a long time I thought it was because I wasn't a proper wife to him. I never loved him enough, you see." Sarah's gaze flicked to his and then back to her hands. She clasped and unclasped them as if kneading dough.

Thomas sat frozen on the bed. Shock did not even begin to cover his state of mind. Samuel had drunk and gambled himself into poverty, dragging them along with him. The urge to deny her words rose again, but he pushed it back. The miserable set of Sarah's shoulders assured him this was the truth.

But not all of the truth.

Samuel probably could not live with his lie. It must have eaten

him up inside like a cancer. Thomas imagined lying to keep
Sarah at his brother's expense. The jolt of pain that shot through
his insides assured him that Samuel had suffered. Thomas swallowed the lump rising in his throat. All these years he had cursed
them and all these years they had been cursed.

Their marriage had been childless and unhappy. This tragedy
had spared no one.

"He couldn't live with himself," said Thomas.

Sarah nodded. "All this time, I thought it was me. But at the
end he asked for my forgiveness. I gave it without really knowing what he had done."

"Now that you know, do you still forgive him?"

Sarah's head sank. He'd never seen her look so downtrodden.
Tentatively, Thomas laid a hand upon her shoulder. She covered
it with her palm and met his gaze.

"I do."

Thomas pressed his lips together, wondering if he were man
enough to do the same.

"I'm sorry to have to tell you about our troubles, Thomas. I've
never spoken to a soul about them. But you needed to know how
he suffered from his lie. I do believe it killed him. I thought that
once you knew, it might make it easier."

"What?"

"Forgiving him. You must, Thomas. Or it will eat you up
inside, too."

Thomas glanced back at the prairie behind them. The world
seemed divided by the two ruts of the wagon wheels stretching as
far as one could see in both directions. Late September brought the
possibility of early snows, but they had hurried along, traveling with
a military convoy of ammunition, food and whiskey for the army
in Dakota Territory. The presence of a small cannon, prominently
displayed, brought some comfort to him. With more than a hundred mounted fighting men, their column seemed impressive, but
Thomas knew the Sioux warriors could number in the thousands.

They met several Sioux along the trail. Men and women begged for handouts. Major Swenson seemed of the belief that these Indians were merely scouts and that if they found a train poorly protected, they could quickly rally their warriors to massacre.

The fort could not be far off now. Thomas searched the never-changing eastern horizon for some sign of civilization. Deer Creek Fort lay behind them and at day's end they would reach Fort Laramie.

He wondered if the eastern newspapers had acted as he had hoped. Before leaving Sacramento, Thomas had sent a copy of the *Daily Bee* with Mr. McClatchy's wonderful scathing article by Wells Fargo to the eastern newspapers in Philadelphia, Boston, New York and Washington, D.C. Mr. McClatchy had once worked for the *New York Times* and had given him a letter of introduction addressed to the owner, outlining his purpose and requesting their assistance in pressuring the military to act on behalf of white captives.

With luck the letters and the McClatchy article had already hit their mark and, like a rock thrown into still waters, they would soon cause ripples across the plains.

Sarah's horse tripped and stumbled. She quickly recovered the slack reins and glanced Thomas's way.

"I think I nodded off again."

The monotony of this section of the journey lulled everyone. But out there, beyond that sea of grass, their enemies prowled like wolves and Lucie waited in bondage. She might be only miles from their train.

"Nearly there now," he assured Sarah.

She smiled. "I don't think I'll ever be able to walk normally again."

"We've come a long way."

She nodded.

They had traveled far in miles, but not at all in their troubles. Since Sarah's revelation regarding Samuel, they had not spoken of the past, unless it was of Lucie. Sarah seemed different when surrounded by others. Her eyes flicked constantly to the men in the unit and she spoke polite nonsense much of the time. When he tried to broach the subject of their history, she said that she would not air dirty laundry in public.

Thomas glanced about the vacant prairie. "In public," he muttered.

What had happened to the bold, carefree spirit he had fallen in love with? The answer came to him like a crushing weight upon his chest. He had killed her, by leaving her alone and pregnant to face the scorn of everyone she ever knew. Dread of disdain now marked her.

He resigned himself to keeping the topics of discussion to the weather and traveling conditions. In this way they managed an uneasy truce. The tension still stretched between them like a telegraph line, but he preferred that to reliving his past and she seemed to prefer it to jeopardizing the respectability accorded a grieving widow.

Sarah showed a narrow chink in her armor when she spoke of Lucie. She told him all she could of his girl, but Samuel's ghost seemed to follow them with each step. Thomas did not know what to do. He did not think Sarah would ever forgive him and knew he would never forgive himself for leaving her.

"Tom?"

Something about Sarah's tone put him on instant alert. He glanced about, seeing no visible threat, then lifted an eyebrow at Sarah.

"I have something—well, I think you should have it."

Something of Samuel's. Oh God, not his wedding ring. He swallowed back his apprehension.

"What?"

She reached into her saddlebag as the horses walked along and drew out a folded sheet of green paper. He recognized it as the cover of a photograph. She hesitated a moment, gripping it, and then extended her hand toward him. He accepted the offering. When Sarah took an instant too long releasing the gift, he knew what lay inside.

He opened the cover and stared down at Lucie's face.

Pale ringlets cascaded over her slim shoulders—strawberry blond to match his own, according to Sarah. He needed no convincing to see the pale eyes that echoed her father's and the same slim nose. Goosebumps lifted on his arms to see his features recast as a young girl. His hand quaked, sending tremors vibrating upward to his heart. The resemblance was so strong it stopped his breath a moment. He studied Lucie for signs of her mother and gradually saw Sarah's freckles, her bright smile and stubborn chin. Here was the blending of their souls made flesh.

Their daughter.

How difficult it must have been for Sarah to stare at a face so similar to his each waking day.

Thomas lifted his gaze to meet Sarah's. His words came out strangled and thin. "She's beautiful."

Tears ran down Sarah's cheeks and she nodded.

"Thank you," he said.

"She's so much like you and not just in appearance. A real hard worker, but fun loving. She can be an imp, playing tricks on folks, just as you once did."

Sarah looked away, wiping her face.

No one had described him as fun loving in years, and he hadn't played a practical joke since…he thought back and he stiffened as he realized that the day Hyatt had died, he had changed in more ways than he even recognized.

He stared down at the photo of the girl and knew he would give his last breath to bring her back to her mother.

A shout came from the front of the column of soldiers. Thomas glanced up to see the front guard topping a small knoll.

"They've sighted the fort," said Thomas. He took a final look at his daughter and then tucked her image safely into his breast pocket. Sarah didn't have to give him this picture, but he was so grateful.

Before the hour passed, they entered the high earthen walls of Fort Laramie. Their arrival raised several curious eyebrows among the soldiers drilling in the street. It was well past the season for travelers and their appearance from the west was out of the ordinary.

Thomas noted three women gathered in the shade of one of the walkways, leaning so close together that their heads nearly touched. Beside him, Sarah drew back her shoulders, straightening in the saddle. He recalled her opinion of the officers' wives. When the bedraggled survivors had limped into this sanctuary, instead of organizing a rescue party and a speedy search for captives, the officers had continued on with their evening ball. One glance told him that Sarah still seethed.

Before his foot touched the dirt, one of the women was picking her way across the road, carefully avoiding the scattered manure.

She paused before Sarah. "Mrs. West, how unexpected to see you again."

"Mrs. Douglas." Sarah dismounted and turned her back on the woman as she flipped up the near stirrup and loosened the cinch.

Mrs. Douglas cast a look back to the two women who lurked in the shadows. They both motioned her forward. She drew a breath.

"How goes your search?"

Sarah's face reddened and she dropped her chin as she turned to face the woman. Thomas recognized the signs of attack, but the Douglas woman merely stood there, smiling stupidly with her hands clasped before her.

Thomas extended his hand. "I'm Thomas West, ma'am."

She briefly clasped his fingers, seeming grateful. "Oh, how lovely to meet you. Pauline Douglas. My husband is second in command. Did you say West?"

"Yes, ma'am." He smiled, watching her try to figure out their relationship, but offering nothing further.

Her gaze went to Sarah, who stood with lips pressed together and arms folded. She turned back to Thomas.

He tipped back his hat. "Perhaps you can direct us to the head man's office?"

"Are you assisting Mrs. West in her search?"

"That's right."

"How kind." She motioned to a corporal. "Mr. Abby, do take our guests to Major Brennan." She grinned at Thomas. "Welcome to Fort Laramie, Mr. West." Her smile faltered as she turned to his traveling companion. "And welcome back, Sarah."

Thomas cast Sarah a stern look, causing her to hesitate before saying whatever it was she had intended.

At last she said only, "Thank you."

Abby motioned. "This way."

They were escorted across the road to the offices of the commander.

Major Brennan stood as they entered but looked none too pleased to see them. He was a thin man whose bushy brown mustache seemed to emphasize his weak chin. Thomas stared into watery blue eyes beneath a broad shiny forehead and thinning hair.

"Major, I'm Thomas West." He extended his hand and the man hesitated before accepting his open palm. "And this is Sarah West."

He waited in vain for Brennan to offer them a seat.

"We've met," he said. His expression turned sour as he nodded at Sarah and then focused his attention back on Thomas. "Your name is also West?"

"I'm, well—"

"My late husband's brother," Sarah said.

Brennan glanced at Sarah before glaring at Thomas. "I've been expecting you. You're the man who likes to kick the hind end of a badger and see what happens."

Sarah's gaze flashed from Thomas to Major Brennan. He saw she was working herself up for a frontal assault and lifted a hand in a foolish attempt to ward her off.

Thomas kept his tone civil. "I haven't seen any badgers here-abouts, nor Sioux, either, though I am hopeful for your assistance in a personal matter."

"Lucie West. Yes. I am aware of your mission. The whole damn country is aware, thanks to you." He threw a copy of the *Daily Bee* upon his desk. "My brother sent me this. These—" he withdrew a stack of letters "—come from Washington."

"Then you are mindful that I am willing to offer a reward for her safe return," said Thomas.

Brennan's eyes flicked from Thomas to Sarah and back again. He seemed about to speak when Sarah interceded.

"Why haven't you sent a search party?"

The major leaned forward, resting his weight upon his knuckles. "Well now, Mrs. West, you and I had this conversation about four months ago. I told you then, I didn't have the resources or the authorization to go tracking hostile Sioux."

Thomas admired the way she straightened her spine, rising up like a mother bear to defend her cub.

"Have matters remained unchanged in that regard?" she asked.

"Somewhat. I still have no resources, but, thanks to your inter-ference, I now have new orders to kill all hostile Indians on sight."

Thomas wondered who decided which Indians were hostile, but Sarah sighed in relief.

"Wonderful," she said.

"You might not think so when you hear the rest. We caught up with a band two weeks ago and killed two dozen before they escaped. They had a white woman captive with a little boy."

"You recovered them?" asked Thomas.

"We recovered their butchered bodies."

Sarah gasped and Thomas's hand went to her elbow to steady her.

Thomas didn't like the man's bluntness. The officer obviously wanted to frighten Sarah and succeeded. She swayed as Thomas tightened his grip upon her.

"Major," he said, glaring at the man.

"The Sioux don't give up captives, Mr. West, unless it's for ransom. Perhaps you didn't know that when you started this…campaign." He thumped his fist down on the folded newspaper. "If you had, you might have reconsidered, because if we get close to the band holding Miss West, the Sioux will slit her throat and leave her body in the dust of their fleeing ponies."

Thomas guided Sarah to the chair in front of the man's desk and then leaned across the cluttered surface.

"Major, your insensitivity in this matter is outrageous."

"And so are your efforts to undermine my authority here. I've been instructed to inform you as to the actions being taken. The government will get those savages onto reservations or kill them all. This is a war, sir, and Miss West is a prisoner of it."

"Do you have any contact with the Sioux?" asked Thomas.

"There are some friendlies who trade here. I suggest you make a ransom offer to them. If your gal is alive, they might take you up on it. Course, what they want most is ammunition and weapons."

"Then I'll supply them," said Thomas.

"You'll not. Trading arms with Indians is now illegal."

"Do they favor money?" asked Sarah.

"They do and I'll tell you why. They'll take your gold and use it to buy guns at one of the trading posts that isn't so particular about law or morality. Then they'll use those weapons, which you provided, to murder as many whites as they can get a bead on. You'll be helping them kill your own kind and take more captives. I just wanted you to know the cost of your daughter's return in Christian lives."

Sarah's shoulders slumped. It was the first sign of weakness Thomas had seen. Her defeated posture only strengthened Thomas's resolve.

"Are you refusing to assist us?"

"Oh no, Mr. West." Sarcasm dripped from his words. "I have orders to see Mrs. West is happy enough that she doesn't give any more interviews to the newspapers. I'm to give you all necessary assistance as long as it does not conflict with my orders or jeopardize the safety of this fort."

"I see. Then we'll talk again, say, tomorrow?"

The major nodded and walked them to the door. "Until then."

Thomas guided Sarah through the door and out of earshot.

"Isn't he the little drop of sunshine?" muttered Thomas.

Sarah turned to him. "Have we made a mistake?"

"What mistake?"

"I don't want to be the cause of another family's misery. I don't want to give the Indians guns to kill other settlers."

"Now you listen here. We are doing what it takes, anything it takes to get Lucie back. If that means giving them money or horses or the damned shirts off our backs, we'll do it."

She clutched his coat. "But what if the army attacks the band she is with? You heard him. They'll kill her."

"Then we'll work quick and get her free before the worst of it comes. The Sioux will go down, but they'll go down fighting. Soon this whole damned territory will be a battlefield and I mean to find my daughter and get us clear before then."

Chapter Eleven

They met with Major Brennan the following day after lunch.

"I'll direct you to the next Ogallala Sioux that comes in. You can send him back with a letter making your offer."

"They can read?" asked Sarah.

"Your gal can. Maybe you could insist she write the reply as proof she lives. You might get lucky and have some word from her."

A knock sounded on the door. Brennan barked his permission and in marched a young soldier with pink cheeks and a neck covered with razor burn.

"Well?" asked the major.

The soldier looked from Thomas to Sarah and hesitated. Finally, he cleared his throat and addressed his commanding officer.

"We found something four miles west of Little Butte."

Brennan lifted his eyebrows and gave his underling an impatient look. The young man stepped around the desk and presented a small book bound in brown leather. Then he bent and whispered in the major's ear as if they were old school chums.

Sarah's hawk-like gaze narrowed in suspicion. Brennan flipped open the book jacket and scanned the page, still listening to his underling.

The corporal straightened.

"Any others?" asked his superior.

The soldier shook his head.

"All right. Dismissed, Corporal."

The soldier scurried from them as fast as he could manage without running.

The major drew a deep breath and Thomas knew the news was bad. He pressed his feet into the floor, bracing.

"We found a body."

Sarah inched closer to Thomas.

"It's a young woman. She's been scalped."

Sarah's denial came before the man could draw his next breath.

"That could be anyone."

"She carried this book." He laid it open before him. "Inside were two names—Alice French and Lucie West." The major pointed. "That your gal's signature?"

Sarah shook her head. "It's not her."

"Mrs. West, look at it."

She lowered her gaze and then lifted her hand to stifle the cry.

"I need someone to identify the body."

Sarah rose woodenly to her feet, her eyes staring at the book. She reached out and drew her fingers over her daughter's name.

"Lucie."

Thomas rested a hand on her shoulder. "I'll go."

She fell into his arms, her luminescent gaze radiating her gratefulness. Then she stilled and stared at him in horror. "You've never seen her."

"I have her photo and your descriptions."

The major rose. "This way."

Sarah stood trembling in the center of the room as Thomas squeezed her arm and then stepped away.

"Wait here," he said.

For the first time, she did not insist he take her along, but only nodded and he understood that she used all her strength just to remain standing.

"I'll hurry back."

Thomas stepped into the cool September sunshine and gathered his resolve. The last time, when Hyatt had died, he had not been able to see the carnage. He recalled the terrible odor of blood and scattered flour mixed with burning canvas and wood. And the cries for God's mercy. Hyatt calling his name as Thomas staggered blindly forward. The shrieks had died as the wagon crumbled to earth. A terrible silence had followed.

"Mr. West? Mr. West."

Thomas lifted his head to find Brennan grasping his arm.

"Are you all right, man?"

"Yes." But it was a lie. He had never been right since that day.

"You've seen this before." It wasn't a question. "Well, then, best get it over with."

Thomas nodded, following Brennan as they headed for the wagon just inside the front gate. Thomas forced one foot before the next as his hand slid into his breast pocket to finger the portrait of Lucie, bright and smiling.

Had they come all this way only to find her dead?

He whispered a prayer that she was not in that wagon as he halted beside the major. Before him lay a dusty blue wool blanket buzzing with flies. The outline of a body was clear beneath. A sergeant, standing watch, lowered the yellow scarf he wore over his nose against the stench of death.

"She's been out there several days, sir. Buzzards got after her. Savages took her scalp and fingers."

Major Brennan lowered the brim of his hat and nodded. "All right then, let's have a look."

The sergeant threw back the blanket. The scent of death enveloped Thomas. The gall rose in his throat as he stared at the bloated corpse swollen beyond recognition. The girl gazed up from empty sockets devoid of eyes. Her head was a raw red wound where the skin had been hastily removed. At the fringes, light brown hair was all that was left of the fertile field that had once grown there.

Thomas had time only to bend at the waist before retching. When he straightened, the corpse lay covered beneath the thin blue wool and the flies, airborne now, buzzed in a cloud about the men. The major offered his handkerchief.

"I'm sorry for your loss."

Thomas wiped his mouth and pocketed the soiled cloth.

"Brown," he said.

"Beg pardon?"

"Brown. Her hair. Lucie's is red. I need a lock."

The man flipped up a corner of the blanket and used his knife to slice away a hank of hair. He extended the grisly trophy to Thomas.

He fingered the soft lock.

The relief that swept though him was so strong it buckled his knees. He rocked against the wagon a moment, gripping the strand. He had to tell Sarah.

"Are you certain?" asked Brennan.

"Yes."

Brennan nodded. "Alice French, then. Sergeant, muster a burial detail."

Thomas ran across the yard. He would not keep Sarah in agony one moment longer than necessary.

He dashed up the step and into the office without knocking to find her collapsed on the floor.

Thomas gathered her in his arms.

"Sarah, Sarah. Wake up now. It's all right. It's not Lucie. It's not her."

Her eyes blinked open and she clutched at him.

"Are you sure, Thomas?"

He held up the lock of hair and she grasped it like a lifeline, drawing it to her cheek and weeping. In the next instant she threw her arms about his neck as the tears turned to sobs.

"Thank God," she said, choking with emotion. "Oh, thank God."

Her tears continued as Thomas rocked her in his lap like a

child. At last, she quieted and then looked up, meeting his gaze. The expression of relief on her tear-stained face changed into something resembling horror. Her pale cheeks and pinched lips made his breathing catch.

"What is it?" he asked.

"I was so glad it's not Lucie, I didn't think…I didn't… I'm jubilant at another girl's death. Oh, Thomas, how she suffered, just like Lucie. And she has a mother, too. How could I be so heartless as to rejoice at her passing?"

"Sarah, you didn't kill her."

"I feel as if I had."

"That's nonsense. You would never hurt a soul."

Their eyes met and locked as they both knew it as a lie. She had hurt him, deeply.

"Perhaps this is punishment for my sins."

"You aren't a sinner. You and I, we're just unlucky."

She tucked her head into the crook of his neck, nestling against him. He closed his eyes and breathed the scent of chamomile blossoms, savoring this moment of tenderness.

"Unlucky. Yes. But lucky this day. What was her name?"

"Alice."

"God rest her soul."

He hugged Sarah, wishing he had the nerve to kiss her, grateful that she allowed him to comfort her just this once. Gradually, she lifted her head to show him red eyes and hair sticking out in all directions.

"Do you know what that book means?" asked Thomas. "We have the first real proof that she's alive."

She gasped. It was true. Sarah had never doubted it, but now they had evidence to show the world, clues to use in their search.

Sarah drew back, suddenly filled with urgency. "She's still out there among them. Oh, Thomas, they might do the same to her. We have to hurry. Something terrible will happen if we don't rescue her."

He let her go. "All right, little mother. We'll find her."

He brushed her thick hair back into place. The gentleness of his touch nearly made her weep again. How she missed his tenderness. He gazed down with an expression she had not seen since before he left. How she longed for those days.

She smiled up at him, realizing that her terror was gone, drained away by the confidence in his cornflower blue eyes. He eased back and she clutched at him, reluctant to let go. Then remembering herself and her surroundings, she allowed him to assist her up. The weakness had gone from her limbs. Hope now held back the dread.

"Do you really think there's a chance, Thomas?"

"We'll get her back."

He did not hesitate an instant. His certainty buoyed her, tipping the scales toward faith.

"I'm so grateful to you. I know you were well settled in California."

"This is more important. Maybe I survived that attack so I could save my little girl."

He took her hand and she did not pull back, accepting the comfort he offered. They left the office hand in hand, stepping out into the bright afternoon sun. She followed the direction of his gaze to the wagon by the main gate and could not repress a shudder.

Thomas dragged off his hat and mumbled a quick prayer, breaking the contact between them. They stood momentarily lost.

"We'll get the word out through as many Indians as possible," Thomas finally said. "The Sioux wander far and wide. No telling where they've taken her or who would have seen her."

Sarah gazed through the gate, past the river, to the endless prairie that stretched out to meet the sky. How would they ever find one little girl in that ocean of grass?

Chapter Twelve

The army did not chase their tribe far and soon Lucie found herself walking southward once more in another caravan, on foot rather than on horseback. Her arms ached from all the goods Yellow Bird forced her to carry, but at least she had rope to bind the load together.

After her last mishap, she planned to be more careful about dropping things. Her clumsiness had caused Eagle Dancer's brick-colored pipe, carved to resemble his favorite horse, to break in two pieces. She hunched her bruised shoulders in memory of the beating Yellow Bird had given her.

Fast Bear drew alongside her. She gazed downward. A slave did not stare directly; she had learned that lesson early in her time here. Something dangled in her face. She glanced up at the bloody scalp before her. It took a moment to note the waves of light brown hair.

"Your friend," he said and she understood.

Alice's escape had failed. Lucie staggered and fell to her knees as Fast Bear dragged Alice's hair over her head. Lucie cried out in horror slapping at the locks that snarled and snagged.

"Stop." She recognized the voice and the authoritative tone. The scalp was drawn away.

"It is a joke," said Fast Bear to Eagle Dancer, his voice losing its bravado and turning conciliatory.

"Joke with your own slave. Oh, yes, you no longer have one."

"I honored her by making her a wife and she ran. It was my right to kill her."

"It was. But you have no rights to this one."

Fast Bear put his heels to his pony and lifted the scalp, giving a bone-chilling cry as he charged away.

Eagle Dancer dismounted. "I am sorry, Sunshine."

Lucie swiped at her tears. All her prayers went unanswered. Alice had failed. She had told Lucie she would rather die than be taken by a savage and that was what had happened.

Eagle Dancer drew her to her feet and gazed down at her with a look of tenderness. "She was your friend."

Lucie sniffed and nodded.

"Did you know she would run?"

Her eyes widened. Of course she had known, but she could not tell. Her cheeks heated. She was such a terrible liar, he had his answer before she could deny it.

"No."

He sighed. "You should have told me. She would still be alive now."

Another arrow pierced Lucie's heart. Alice had been so unhappy and had been here much longer.

Eagle Dancer's grip grew uncomfortably tight on her upper arms. She lifted her gaze to his.

"Do not run, Sunshine."

She shook her head. "I won't."

He stared intently at her a moment longer and then released her. Lucie gathered her burden, clutching it tight to her aching chest.

She cried without sound so as not to draw attention as they marched along. She had felt jealous when Alice had run. Now she felt sick at heart.

Later that day she saw Fast Bear upon a rise, wagging the dreadful trophy and laughing at her.

"You run, too," he jeered. "Then I take your fire hair."

She stared straight ahead, refusing to look at him or his bloody prize.

On the morning of the second day she discovered another captive, dressed as a warrior and riding beside an old brave. At first, his dark brown hair made her believe he was a half-breed. Many women bore children to whites who later tired of their company and sent them home. But this boy, perhaps two years older than Lucie, had blue eyes.

She called to him, but he made no reply. Finally, she tried in Sioux and he looked her way, slowing his horse to allow her to catch up.

"You are a captive?" Lucie asked.

"No more. I am adopted son of Ten Horses." He motioned to his companion.

"But you are white," she said in English.

"I do not remember those words," he answered in Sioux. "Or my coming here. I was a child. Now I am a warrior."

"But you are white," she repeated in Sioux.

He made a face and kicked his pony to a trot.

That evening she asked Yellow Bird about the young brave.

"His people sickened on their travels toward the sun. Ten Horses found him with his dying father. The man wrote stick words on paper and then offered Ten Horses all his oxen and horses to take the boy east to the fort."

Lucie waited, breathless for the end to the tale.

Yellow Bird laughed. "Instead he takes the boy and all he wishes from the wagons of the dead. He makes the boy his son. He is called Sky Fox for the color of his eyes.

"They are ghost eyes, like yours. I say it is not wise to bring the enemy into one's home."

The woman glanced at Eagle Dancer, but he ignored her, keeping his focus on the new piece of stone he carved for a pipe.

The next day, Lucie struggled with the larger load Yellow Bird had laid upon her. As the day progressed she fell farther and far-

ther behind, until she saw not one familiar face. Late in the afternoon, when the women set up their camps, Lucie continued
on, but as dusk approached, the first twinges of panic arrived.

Lost.

Fearful of punishment she hurried along, bent by her load,
but she recognized no one in the group as she moved from one
campfire to the next. At nightfall she asked for help, but none
knew Yellow Bird.

The camp numbered in the thousands. She walked until her
legs ached. No one took her in or offered her even a gourd of
water to drink.

Fear of retribution urged her onward until exhaustion finally
caused her legs to tremble like a spent horse. She could not go
on and so she sank to the earth beneath a willow tree.

It was there that Eagle Dancer came upon her. She never
thought she would be grateful to see him, but found she was. He
offered her water from his skin. When she tried and failed to rise,
he lifted her in his arms as her father used to do and carried her
to his warhorse. Then he handed her the bundle of belongings.
He did not chastise or berate her, but simply lifted the reins and
led his horse along.

Lucie knew it was very improper for her to ride while he
walked. She glanced about to see if anyone witnessed this
breach. Men must keep their hands free to defend their families.
They did not carry burdens. That was the work of dogs, horses
and women.

The only time she ever saw a man carry anything other than
his weapons had been the time Running Wolf carried firewood
for his wife just before she bore him a son. But Lucie was not
so burdened as that.

They walked along and Lucie wrapped her fingers around the
ropes, determined to hold on. The rocking lulled her tired body,
but her mind raced.

What would Yellow Bird say?

Her empty stomach clenched as she recognized the cast-iron

pot, stolen from her mother's wagon sitting beside a fire. Yellow Bird stepped into the light.

"So she did not run away. Too bad."

She pressed her hands to her hips. "She could not keep up. You should beat her for her lazy ways."

Eagle Dancer ignored his mother as he took the bundle from Lucie and set it aside.

Yellow Bird gasped. He proceeded to clasp Lucie gently about the waist, drawing her into his arms. He held her like a groom preparing to jump over the threshold.

Yellow Bird's voice rose in outrage. "What is this? You carry her things. You carry her? Is she your slave or are you hers?"

Eagle Dancer set Lucie on her feet and reached for the bundle. Yellow Bird stepped between him and his objective.

"My son does not carry a woman's things," she snapped.

Eagle Dancer drew a deep breath and straightened to face his mother. "Your son has not eaten this day. Does his mother have his meal ready?"

She turned to the cooking pot. "It is ready. I have not been hiding from my work all day. I know *my* place."

Eagle Dancer cast Lucie a glance and she thought she saw the shadow of a smile. On that chance, she smiled back and then hurried to unpack the sleeping skins she carried.

When she finished, Yellow Bird sent her to gather wood. By the time she returned, she nearly wilted from hunger. Her stomach had long since given up growling and her body now sent little shards of red light exploding before her eyes.

She dropped the stack of branches and sank to the earth beside the fire. There she found two small chunks of antelope left in the pot.

Yellow Bird smiled viciously, waiting for Lucie to issue some complaint about her portion. Knowing better than to speak, Lucie held her tongue and ate, then used her fingers to scrape the burned leavings from the pot. Her stomach, alive with this meager offering, now growled and rolled mercilessly.

As Lucie worked to glean another mouthful of dinner, Yellow Bird disappeared to see to her personal needs, leaving Lucie alone with Eagle Dancer.

"Did you try to run, Sunshine?" he asked.

Her eyes widened with surprise.

"I was lost."

He lifted his bowl from beneath the cover of a deerskin hide and offered her a full portion of cold supper. She snatched the bowl and ate like a dog, gulping her meal.

"I know my mother is unkind. Understand that my father died of the spotting sickness. She blames your people for this. Now she has only me."

Lucie finished her meal and placed the bowl with Yellow Bird's inside the cooking pot.

"Thank you," she said.

"Have you had your break with the moon?"

Lucie frowned, trying to comprehend his question.

"I do not understand."

His hopeful expression changed to resignation and he nodded. When his mother returned he drew her aside to speak to her privately. Lucie strained to hear their conversation, knowing she was the subject of heated discussion.

It was just before sunset when Brennan called them to his office. Thomas held the door for Sarah and then stepped inside to find Major Brennan. The room seemed crowded with Indians.

Before Brennan's desk stood two men. Behind them, three Indian women sat on a narrow bench, as motionless as statues.

Thomas glanced at the men. The first was a Sioux warrior, judging from the leggings and moccasins visible beneath the red Hudson Bay blanket draped over his shoulders. His pock-scarred face and hunched posture made him look small and weak, until you looked at the fire in his black eyes. Thomas watched the Indian with suspicion.

Beside him stood another Indian, but this one was dressed in an army jacket, brown trousers and worn black boots. He held his broad hat in his hands before him.

Brennan rose to shake Thomas's hand, ignoring Sarah completely.

"Mr. West, this is Black Tail." He motioned to the Indian huddled beneath the blanket. "He's Ogallala Sioux and friendly. He is agreeable to carrying ransom offers back to his people."

"Who are they?" asked Sarah, indicating the three women sitting beneath the window behind them.

"His wives."

Sarah gasped.

"They take as many as they can feed," said the major.

Thomas stared at the smiling Indian, who looked away an instant after their gazes met. Anger burned low in his belly as he realized that some young buck might right now be taking his little girl for a wife.

"I have the letter you requested," said Sarah.

She handed this to the major.

Brennan accepted the envelope without comment. He used it to indicate the other Indian.

"This is my interpreter, John Standing Forest. He has explained what we require."

Sarah did not even glance at the other man, keeping her attention on Brennan. "Tell Black Tail to deliver this letter only to Lucie."

Brennan nodded and the interpreter spoke to Black Tail. The man's hand emerged from beneath his blanket to take the letter.

Brennan spoke to his interpreter. "Tell him that if he brings Lucie West back safely, we'll give him horses and cooking pots, but until he returns, his wives stay here."

The translator explained the major's words and waited while Black Tail spoke.

"He wants to take one of his wives to cook for him. It is a long way north."

Brennan shook his head.

The Indian spoke again and the interpreter translated.

"He agrees to leave two as hostages to guarantee his return."

Thomas spoke in level tones, staring at the warrior. "The women stay here."

Black Tail apparently did not need a translator for this. He raised his voice, slapping the letter upon the desk.

Brennan lifted a hand calling for quiet and turned to the interpreter.

"He says he will not leave his favorite wife behind."

"Tell him he leaves them all or they are free to go, but they are not welcome to trade here again."

When he heard the translation, Black Tail's expression showed his unhappiness more clearly than words. He snatched up the letter and marched away without speaking to his women.

The major looked at the three and then to his interpreter. "Take them away."

Alone with only Sarah and the major, Thomas voiced his concerns.

"How do you know he is friendly?"

"Likely he is not. For all I know he's of the same band that struck the train of emigrants last week. They attack us one day and lay down their weapons to trade here the next. If it was up to me, I wouldn't let a solitary one of them inside these walls."

"Do you think he'll deliver the letter?" asked Sarah.

The longing in her voice nearly broke Thomas's heart. She had nothing on which to pin her hopes but the fickle enemy letter carrier and his desire to retrieve his wives.

"He might," said Brennan. "Either way, we won't hear anything for weeks. Best to settle in to wait."

"Thank you for your efforts, Major." Thomas replaced his hat and held the door for Sarah.

Outside, she marched along the planking with ill-disguised rage.

"Weeks he said, as if I care. If only he brings her back to me."

Thomas increased his stride length and grasped Sarah's arm, bringing her to a halt.

"It will take time for this tree to bear fruit."

Her rigid stance dissolved and her shoulders rounded. Her desolated countenance echoed her desperation. "I know you are right."

He eased the pressure on her elbow and guided her toward her room. They walked in silence, save the strike of their heels on the walkway.

Sarah slowed her pace, now dreading to be trapped alone in her little room. Her heart ached and she longed to seek comfort in Thomas's arms. Tension crept into her as she considered asking him in.

He drew to a halt beside her door, and she found herself holding her breath in indecision. She wanted him to hold her, but feared him being seen entering or leaving her quarters. Sarah glanced first to the right and then the left, searching the shadows for witnesses.

Thomas opened her door and stepped aside.

"Sarah?" Thomas's expression showed his confusion at her hesitation.

She crossed the threshold and faced him.

"Do you want to stay, Thomas?" As soon as the words left her mouth, she knew she had made yet another mistake.

She had never been able to quell the longing he stirred in her soul, but she was not ready to face the consequences of another night together. She had only wanted him to hold her.

But Thomas was already inside the room and judging from the intensity of his stare, she knew he had other intensions entirely.

She qualified her invitation. "You could rest beside the bed."

His advance halted abruptly and his brow sank low over his eyes. "The first time you slept in my bed was magic. The second, I was downstairs sleeping in my parlor and the third I was too damned drunk to recognize the opportunity. I'm not drunk now, Sarah."

She stood frozen with her indecision.

He laid a hand on her arm. "If I stay, I won't be sleeping on the floor."

The room was dark. She looked up but could not see his face. His shadowy outline hovered near. The repercussions of her last act of impulsiveness rose up before her like a specter, sending cold terror washing down her spine.

He leaned forward to kiss her and she turned away, giving him her cheek. He stiffened and drew back, gripping her shoulders. She did not look at him, but stood mute.

His hands slipped away. "I best go."

She did not try to stop him, though he waited for a long moment for her to do so. When she did not, he spun about, departing with long urgent strides.

Sarah closed and bolted the door and then sank to the bed in the darkness. Could she do nothing right where Thomas was concerned?

Sarah sat for some time. At last, bone weary and sick at heart, she rose and lit a candle to ready herself for sleep. But sleep was a long time in coming.

Her restless mind yielded violent nightmares. She stood gripping a lock of Alice French's brown hair as savages chased Lucie across a stormy prairie, capturing her and dragging her to their leader. Then she realized their chief was Samuel and it was he who held Lucie hostage. The thin, tinny notes of First Call brought her upright.

How could she have such a dream? Samuel never hurt Lucie.

Then she remembered his lie. The evil untruth scrawled across a page as he claimed Lucie as his own. That letter had driven Thomas away while holding them hostage all these years.

After Ben Harris had come and gone, she'd brooded for a time. Then she went to Samuel and told him what she wanted. He wept. The raw pain of his sobs still echoed in her ears. So she had stayed. She had not known of the letter then, only that he had rescued her and Lucie, had given them a home. She felt like an ungrateful cur for wanting to leave him. When he was drunk he would tell her to go, that he didn't deserve her and then he would weep, clinging to her legs as he knelt before her. By then he was ill and she could not bear to leave him.

Enough!

She swung her feet over the edge of the bed and came upright, clutching her head in her hands.

Sarah washed and dressed, pausing after braiding her hair. She stared at her reflection in the tiny mirror.

Major Brennan had warned it would be weeks before their courier returned, if he ever returned.

What was there for her to do to fill the minutes and hours and days? She glanced with desperation about the empty room. For the first time in her adult life she had nothing to do. No laundry to wash or meals to make. No chickens or pigs to feed, no house and family to tend. She found the respite unsettling. All her life, there never seemed to be enough time to finish what had to be done. Now she had no work, no purpose. Without the farm, Samuel and Lucie, she ceased to be of use. Fear crept over her heart like ice on a pond.

If she never found Lucie, what would be her purpose?

Your purpose is to find her and bring her home.

But Sarah had no home—no farm and few possessions. What would Lucie come home to?

Sarah dug in her packs and found her bag of scraps. She drew out her needle, thread and scissors. Next she turned to her clothing bag and pulled out a faded denim shirt that Samuel had once worn. She paused, remembering the fabric covering her husband's strong back as he plowed the fields. The elbows went first and then the collar. She lifted the garment to her nose and sniffed but found no trace of him.

She lifted the scissors and began to cut. Her old oatmeal-colored skirt would suit for the background fabric. She fingered the tattered hem. The garment still bore many useful yards.

She drew a heavy sigh. Lucie would remember Samuel's

shirt and her old skirt as well as she. Sarah would give her daughter a piece of her parents she could keep. It would help her recall her father, or the man she believed to be her father. Samuel raised her up with love, but Lucie had heard the rumors. Children could be cruel and they had no qualms about repeating the words of their folks.

Sarah reached into the bag again and Lucie was here with her as well, in the pale green scraps from her Sunday dress, altered and then outgrown, and again in the white of her nightgown and rich purple of her favorite pinafore. Sarah held the fabric to her cheek for a moment, but before the tears could fall she lifted the scissors again.

Snip, snip. The pieces went into a pile, darks on the left, lights on the right. When Lucie came home, this quilt of memories would be waiting.

Chapter Thirteen

The first time Lucie bled she managed to keep it from Yellow Bird. The following month her luck ran out when her nemesis found a bit of stained petticoat Lucie had used as a rag. The folded cloth had shifted as she carried an armful of wood and then fallen from the makeshift sling she'd fashioned.

Quick as a swooping hawk Yellow Bird dove, talons gripping the bloody rag.

"You have broken your link with the moon." Her voice accused as if this was a dreadful sin.

The wood slipped from Lucie's arms as she cowered before the woman's wrath. Yellow Bird grasped a branch, thick as Lucie's arm, and lifted it high against the blue sky. Lucie covered her head with her arms as the shower of blows rained down upon her.

When Lucie lay motionless in the dust, no longer rolling or scrambling to escape, the beating ceased.

"Get up, you wicked white slug."

Lucie managed to curl her knees to her chest but could not rise. How long she lay aching and bruised before the teepee she did not know. She had broken her link with the moon and with time. It rolled on without her, minutes or hours—she knew not.

She woke to the ringing shriek of Yellow Bird. In the last month Lucie's understanding of their language had improved. Like a fog burning off the mountain meadow, the words had become clearer to her.

"Do not touch her. She is dirty!"

Hands pressed to her forehead and arms lifted her. She floated in the warm anchor.

"Papa?" She tried to open her eyes but the swelling kept her blind. She inhaled the scent of sweetgrass and leather. Not her father. She stiffened.

"She is just a child."

She knew the voice of Eagle Dancer.

"No longer. Now a maiden."

Lucie heard him gasp. Had Yellow Bird shown him the evidence of her deceit?

"From here forward, only I discipline this one."

"But you do not discipline her. That is why she is so spoiled."

Lucie forced an eye open past the unnatural swelling and looked up into his strong hawkish face to see his bronze skin and a narrow mouth. She smiled and watched the corners of his eyes lift.

Yellow Bird squawked from behind them.

"You will need cleansing. She will draw away your power. This girl contaminates you."

Eagle Dancer ignored his mother as he walked away. He took Lucie to an unfamiliar teepee and left her there.

"This is a place for women. I will send someone to tend you."

"My thanks."

He knelt beside her, then stroked her cheek with his thumb.

"You are a woman now," he said.

Her breathing caught and she found her mouth too dry to swallow. With the beating, she had forgotten. This was why she did not tell Yellow Bird. Eagle Dancer planned to take her when she became a woman. By his judgment she now was.

"Eagle Dancer, I still feel like a girl."

His gaze traveled slowly over her, making her feel as if his hands already touched her. The hairs lifted on the back of her neck and she sank further into the sleeping skin.

"We will talk soon. Rest."

He turned and left her. Lucie curled into a ball and closed her eyes. Everything ached now. After some time the tent flap lifted again. Lucie peeked through swollen eyes to see Eagle Dancer's only sister, Shadow.

"My brother sent me to tend you."

Judging from her expression, she was not pleased with the added responsibility. She lowered her pack and Lucie saw the round face of her infant daughter, Minnow, tied into a carrying bundle.

"My mother tells me you have broken your link with the moon and did not tell her so. This was foolish. Do you wish to risk my brother's life?"

"His life?" Lucie stared in astonishment.

"You deserved that beating."

There was so much she didn't understand here. Lucie tried to sit up but found her arms too bruised to hold her. "I have done nothing to hurt Eagle Dancer."

"You are unclean. Everything you touch during these days and nights is dirty. A warrior must not accept anything from your hand until you regain your link with the moon."

Lucie thought this stuff and nonsense, but she nodded gravely as if they presented her with one of God's own commandments. She added this new rule to the list with "women eat last" and "women don't touch a warrior's weapons."

"Thank you for explaining this."

"While you still bleed, you stay in this place."

"What will happen to Eagle Dancer?"

Shadow scowled. "He must undergo a cleaning ceremony and fasting. Everything you touched must be destroyed."

Lucie did sit up now. The quilt her mother made, the lovely quilt she watched her stitch as a child, stolen by Eagle Dancer and used by his mother to carry belongings. Lucie always slept with one hand on the precious reminder of her life before. Had Yellow Bird noticed?

Now she understood Yellow Bird's wild fury. The wood Lucie carried, the hides in which she slept, all would be destroyed. No wonder the woman tried to kill her.

"You are a very foolish girl." Shadow considered Lucie a moment and then sighed. "Take off your garments."

Lucie hesitated. "Will you burn them?"

"I will wash them."

She left Lucie huddling in a tanned elk skin. Alone and naked, Lucie assessed the damage inflicted by Yellow Bird's club. Her thighs bloomed in blue and purple welts. Her arms had received fewer blows, judging from the bruises. She stretched her back and groaned.

Alone, bruised and bleeding, Lucie rolled onto her side and cried. Her tears had dried upon her face before Shadow returned at midday carrying several bundles. Lucie smelled food and righted herself.

Shadow stared at Lucie's legs and pointed. Lucie flushed at the sight of blood smeared upon her thighs.

"You must use the water and skins to clean yourself regularly. Discard the bad water over there."

Shadow showed her how to wash away the blood and sit upon a soft tanned bit of hide.

"While you are here you will pray."

Shadow washed her hands in clean water scented with sage and then offered Lucie a bowl of stew.

"My brother says you are to have all the meat you can eat. I told him that he spoils you, but he does not listen. So here is your meat."

Lucie ate the contents quickly before Shadow changed her mind. Over the next four days, Lucie rested, slept and ate. Her strength returned. Her vision cleared and the ringing in her ears abated.

The fresh food and absence of work seemed all her body needed to heal. Now that she was not bone weary, her mind returned to the restless search for ways to escape the Sioux and her upcoming marriage. She thought often of Alice French's escape.

A chill lifted the hairs on her neck. Perhaps she was only a coward, but unlike Alice, she thought marriage to an Indian preferable to death.

The Indians had little modesty. She saw men couple with their wives across the fire sheathed only in a buffalo robe. It seemed they did not care who watched. The grunting and cries made the act seem painful. But she also heard laughter and that confused her.

On the fifth day, her bleeding ceased and panic bubbled up in her like milk left to boil. Her time in this sanctuary was at an end.

She stretched her legs and groaned. The bruises, now yellow and blue, ached only when she moved. She stood and hobbled about the tent. Soon Shadow would come and see no fresh blood on her pad.

Lucie had an idea. She took a stick from the fire pit and sharpened it to a point. Where could she cut that Shadow would not see? Lucie studied her hand and the spidery blue veins at her wrist, the bottoms of her feet and the inside of her thigh. Still naked, her body shielded only by the hide she wore as a cape, any wound might draw notice.

She pressed the stick against her thigh and found the flesh pliant, seeming to refuse the pressure of her attack. At last she decided on the wrist. Instead of a gentle pressing, she gripped the stick with fingers slippery with sweat and plunged the stick into her flesh.

Her grip slackened and fell away. The stick quivered, still embedded like an arrow. Spots danced before Lucie's eyes as she reached for the shaft and pulled. Blooded poured from the puncture and down over her knobby knees.

The scream brought Lucie's head up to see Shadow standing inside the tent with both hands pressed to her mouth.

The pot of food she carried rocked wildly at her feet.

"You stupid, stupid girl," she shouted.

In an instant she reached Lucie and encircled her wrist in a vicious grip. She turned her head to the tent flap and called for help.

Lucie swayed. The effort of breathing seemed too much for her. She closed her eyes. A stinging slap struck her cheek.

Shadow hissed at her. "You stay awake."

Lucie nodded and rocked back, kept from falling by Shadow's strong grip. Faces appeared about her. They swam like reflections in a pond and then, like fireflies, blinked out.

Next she came aware, she lay back in Yellow Bird's teepee. She glanced about to see Yellow Bird scowl and Eagle Dancer smile.

"You wicked girl," uttered Yellow Bird. "Because of you I had to burn a sleeping robe and the cloth blanket."

Lucie glanced about and discovered her mother's blue Ohio star quilt was gone. Until that moment she had not known how much she would miss it. Tears welled in her eyes.

"Stop that and tell me why you stabbed yourself."

Lucie glanced at her wrist, noting the leather wrapped securely about her arm. If she told the truth she might anger her only ally. But what reason could she give?

"I tried to puncture the leather to make a cape," she offered. "My hand slipped."

Eagle Dancer lifted his brow and stared at his mother.

Yellow Bird shook her head. "She lies."

Eagle Dancer's expression grew grim. Then he stood and left the teepee, leaving Lucie at Yellow Bird's mercy.

Her captor rounded on her the instant the tent flap fell. This time she did not lift a stick of wood, but her hand. She slapped Lucie across the face so hard her teeth sliced into the soft flesh of her cheek. Blood filled her mouth and she spat upon the ground.

"You will not have him," said Yellow Bird, clouting her with a fist.

Lucie's ear rang from the blow. She fell to all fours still spouting blood from the gash at her cheek. She choked as blood burned through her nose.

"Get out."

The kick landed on Lucie's backside as she scrambled for the door dressed only in the deer hide cloak. She fell out onto the ground and the flap closed behind her. Lucie crawled behind the teepee, huddling there.

That is where Eagle Dancer found her hours later. Again he carried her, but this time to the river. He washed away the blood and left her there, returning later with her torn blue dress and shift.

Lucie's cheeks burned in shame, but she did not hesitate, throwing off the cloak and sweeping into her shift as quickly as she could manage. He helped her into the dress, managing the buttons when she could not.

"Do not make me go back there," Lucie said.

Eagle Dancer's gaze swept over her face. "No."

Her shoulders dipped in relief.

He lifted her chin with one strong finger and winced at the sight. Lucie could only imagine her appearance. She could see clearly out of her left eye, but the swelling nearly blocked the view from her right.

He swept a hand over her hair in a vain attempt to control the tangled mess. No one had seen to her hair since her arrival here.

"Why do you even want me?" she asked.

He wrapped a coiling strand of hair about his finger. "When

I saw you on the wagon, I wanted you. Your hair shines like afternoon sunshine."

Her hair again. If not for the unusual color, she might be safe with her mother. Another possibility struck. She might also be dead.

"Follow," he said.

He walked along at a slow pace, allowing her to keep up without running. At last he stopped before an unfamiliar teepee. The flap was lifted open, giving a glimpse of the fire within, so he entered without permission. Lucie ducked inside and recognized Shadow nursing her baby. Shadow's placid brow wrinkled as she caught sight of Lucie. The two men in the lodge nodded at Eagle Dancer as he took a seat.

Lucie squatted inside the door.

"Our mother beat her again," said Eagle Dancer without preamble.

The man closest to Shadow lowered the feathers he split into fletching and regarded Lucie.

"She will kill her one day."

"I think so, too. That is why I ask that she stay here until she can make a lodge."

Make a lodge? Lucie wondered at this as Shadow threw up her free hand.

"She does not know how to make a lodge."

The men stared at her in silence.

"I have a babe and a husband to care for. I do not have time to teach her."

"She will help you with Minnow," said her husband, Blue Elk.

Shadow eyed Lucie as her grip tightened protectively on her baby. The men continued to stare at Shadow. At last she heaved a great suffering sigh. When she spoke, her words were tight with resentment.

"I will teach her. But you, Brother, must bring the hides."

Eagle Dancer smiled. "And she will sleep here."

Shadow opened her mouth to protest but her husband answered.

"We will be happy to help our brother."

Shadow huffed and turned her back on the man. Lucie recognized the expression of censure from Yellow Bird. The men exchanged commiserating looks.

From that afternoon forward, Lucie stayed in the teepee of Shadow and Blue Elk. Another warrior, called Black Tail, arrived the following day and stayed as the guest of Blue Elk. The warrior stared at Lucie when the others were busy. His feral gaze made Lucie as jumpy as a frog in a heron's nest.

Black Tail told stories at night of how he tricked the whites at Fort Laramie into thinking he was friendly. They traded with him, not knowing that he had taken three scalps in the last raid. Lucie's dislike for the man grew.

She struggled to stifle her disgust at his bloody tales, succeeding in holding her tongue. Where she came from, trickery and lies were a sign of low character, not opportunities to boast. She would have been mortified to tell anyone she was capable of such treachery.

Black Tail was the only dark spot in her new situation. Although Shadow was not pleased to have Lucie, she did not hit her or shout. The food was better here and Lucie had less work. Eagle Dancer did not sleep with them but visited after dinner. He brought two buffalo hides and Lucie set to the arduous work of tanning them under Shadow's direction.

The task of stretching the enormous skin upon the upright frame exhausted Lucie. Shadow seemed impatient with her progress. Lucie lifted the tanning knife and began dragging it over the underside of the buffalo, scrapping away the bits of fat and sinew still connected to the hide. Flies buzzed about the bloody skin, and she batted them away.

"Why does Eagle Dancer need a new lodge?" asked Lucie.

Shadow stopped and stared, dumbstruck. At last she closed her mouth and spoke. "All women make the home for the husbands." She waved a hand at the lodge behind them. "I made this for Blue Elk two summers past."

Understanding dawned. She wasn't making a lodge, she was making the home she would share with Eagle Dancer as his wife. Lucie sank to the earth, kneeling before the great hide, the knife still in her clutched hand. Minnow howled from inside the tee-pee. Shadow scurried off, leaving Lucie blinking stupidly at her knees.

Eagle Dancer considered her a woman and as soon as she finished this work they would be wed. Fear rose in her throat like ice water jumping the banks of a river. Her head snapped up and she glanced this way and that, searching for some way to escape. Her attention fell back to the knife and her bandaged wrist.

She stilled.

This was the only way left. She stared at the blackened blade and shuddered. She gripped the handle.

She recalled the girls she had met on the trail. They had walked along for hours discussing Indian attacks and capture. Rebecca Woodland had vowed to die before she allowed an In-dian to ravage her person. Lucie wondered if the silly girl really had the courage to die. She glanced at the buffalo skin and won-dered if she had the courage to live.

Then Black Tail came upon her. He walked close behind her and dropped a letter into her lap, then came to rest beneath a cot-tonwood tree that supported one side of the hide she scraped.

Lucie knit her brow as she stared down at the writing, recog-nizing her name and the writing simultaneously.

Her mother lived!

A cry escaped her.

"Quiet, stupid girl," Black Tail whispered.

Her fingers shook as she lifted the letter and pressed it over her heart. Her mother's writing, here in this wilderness.

She did not cry out again as she tore open the envelope and drew out the folded page.

Dearest Lucie,
This man has agreed to bring you to us. Go with him and
do as he asks. He is a friend. I miss you with all my heart.
Do not give up hope. We will be reunited soon.
With all my love,
Your mother, Sarah West

Lucie lifted her gaze to Black Tail. Could this man who
bragged of killing whites be her savior?

Chapter Fourteen

Busy hands kept Sarah from insanity during the following five weeks. In all this time, they had received no word from the Sioux warriors who took up the challenge of recovering her daughter. October's warm afternoons vanished with November's frost. Soon the winds would howl. Through the long stretch of days, Sarah worked steadily on Lucie's quilt. She had chosen the pattern called basket of flowers, set on point, recalling that her daughter once admired a neighbor's quilt of that design. Sarah bent over her task, plying her needle to create small, neat stitches.

If only she could so easily mend the pieces of her torn relationship with Thomas. He had been cool and distant since she had stupidly invited him into her room. She had apologized, of course, but could tell by the distance yawning between them that she had hurt him deeply once again.

She lifted the quilt top, determined to finish her task, and tied the last knot connecting the final block in the sashing. With a snip of her scissors, the thread severed.

She thumped the fabric upon her lap. Lucie must come home before the snow. The sound of scattered gunfire brought her back to the moment. This shooting did not sound like the orderly rounds fired at rifle practice. Shouts from the ramparts confirmed her suspicion and she set aside her work. One glance to the catwalks showed the soldiers running hither and thither.

Thomas jogged across the yard.

"What is it?" she asked, gripping his arms more tightly than she intended.

"Small band of Sioux picked a fight with one of our patrols. They're too far from the walls to hit."

Across the yard, Captain Douglas climbed the ladder to the catwalk and, apparently coming to the same conclusion as Thomas, ordered a ceasefire. Far off, beyond the thick walls, came the pop of distant gunfire.

"There are only ten warriors. Seems like suicide to engage a full patrol," said Thomas.

Thomas drew her back to the shade of the porch. She resumed her seat but felt taut as a bowline.

Her gaze stayed fixed on the captain as he shouted and waved like a madman. Major Brennan arrived, taking his place beside his second officer. She had never seen the commander on the wall before. Unease made her skin prickle like a pincushion.

The bugler was summoned, and he lifted his silver trumpet toward the west, issuing his call.

Sarah spotted Corporal Abby hurrying across the yard.

"Corporal?" she called.

For a moment she thought he would not stop, but he did, jogging to her porch rail.

"What is that signal?"

"Retreat, Ma'am. Brennan is calling Captain Coffland back to the fort." He tipped his hat and scurried away.

Sarah turned to Thomas, who was already on his feet.

"Wait here."

He stepped away and she lunged for him, clasping his hand in hers. It was the first time they'd touched in many days. The simple entwining of fingers sent a jolt of awareness through her. Why did this happen only with him?

"Be careful," she whispered.

He gave her hand a squeeze. "Always."

She resumed her seat in the hard chair as he climbed the wall, and she waited for him to glance back. He didn't. After he disappeared into one of the guard towers, she realized she held the top for Lucie's memory quilt crumpled in her fists.

Sarah laid the wrinkled cloth upon her knee and tried to press away the evidence of her desperation. Giving up, she laid the project aside in favor of gripping the arms of the chair until her knuckles whitened.

Up on the walls, the soldiers leaned toward the west as the skirmish played out before them. Gradually the sounds of gunfire faded. The afternoon sun cut a band of golden light across the men above her, but it no longer reached the yard. All went deadly quiet.

Sarah slapped her palms upon the smooth maple arms of her chair. "What is happening?"

Thomas returned some time later.

His slow pace told her two things. They were not in danger and something terrible had happened.

She waited in mute dread for his words.

"Coffland disobeyed orders. He followed the Sioux over the knolls to the west, along the river and out of sight."

The dread coiled her innards into knots. "Will they send a search party?"

Thomas shook his head. "Not until morning."

"That will be too late."

"Captain Douglas made that point. Major Brennan thinks it's already too late and will not send good men after a captain who disobeys orders. Gunfire's stopped and there's no telling how many Sioux are waiting over that knoll."

"Are we in danger?"

"Since the minute we set foot in this god-awful territory. The Sioux are fearless enough to attack a fort with two cannons, but not foolish enough. The major is right to keep his men here."

"They will have to go out eventually."

"But not a half hour before sunset."

"They're all dead, aren't they?"

"I hope so."

Chilling memories filled her mind—the sickening thud of an axe striking flesh, the cry of wounded men. She trembled. Thomas's jaw clenched as he dealt with the demons in his memory.

Sarah wanted to ask him to put his arm around her. She craved his strength and the comfort of his scent.

She had betrayed him by marrying his brother. Thomas did not owe her any comfort. She gathered the rumpled quilt top and her needle.

She began stitching the border. Thomas leaned on the porch rail, staring out over the wall, keeping his own counsel until she could no longer see to stitch. On her lap lay one completed side of the border.

Thomas turned to her. "'Bout had enough?"

She stretched her cramped fingers and drew her aching shoulders together. Her body had grown as stiff as the wood beneath her.

"Yes."

Above them on the parapets, soldiers stared westward, as hope of the return of their comrades died with the day.

Sarah broke the heavy silence.

"Do you think she's still alive?"

Thomas returned his attention to her. "Indians often take young ones to replace ones who died of disease or in battle. She survived the attack and sent a message to us in that book. If she doesn't do anything foolish, like try to run, she'll be waiting for rescue."

"What if she runs?"

Thomas answered only in the grave and steady contact of his gaze. Foreboding froze her blood.

"She's a bright girl. But she might grow desperate." Sarah stood, lookinig out across the empty yard. "I'm so frightened for her."

Thomas came up beside her, close enough for her to sense his uncertainty. He hung back, seeming to want something. She regarded him in the fading light. Could it be he needed her comfort as much as she craved his?

The thought startled her. With awkward slowness she reached out, touching his arm. He jumped and she felt stupid for having made the gesture, but she hesitated a moment longer and in that time he grasped her hand.

His sure grip held the confidence she lacked, and she gave him a tentative smile.

"Gonna be a long night," he said.

She wondered if he asked indirectly for her company. She nodded her agreement.

"You hungry?" he asked.

She shook her head. "I can't stomach seeing the worried looks on the men's faces in there." She nodded toward the mess.

"I'll bring you something. We can eat right here on the porch."

"All right."

He hesitated and then drew back his hand. With it went the calm she did not even realize he had brought her. She watched him go and found herself tidying up her sewing basket and moving her things aside, making room for him. Then she brought the small table outside. The evening star appeared in the sky and others followed. If not for the horror awaiting them outside the wall, she would say it was a beautiful evening.

Thomas returned in short order carrying steaks and pinto beans. They ate the meal in silence. When she laid aside her fork, Thomas took up the conversation.

"Are we ever going to feel comfortable together again?"

She started at his words. They expressed her own feelings so closely, she could only stare in stunned silence. At last she found her tongue.

"I don't know."

"Well, I don't like it."

Neither did she. Sarah missed confiding in him and laughing together.

"We should be able to hold a civil conversation. I'm the girl's father."

"She doesn't know that."

He shot to his feet, outrage in his voice. "What?"

She remained seated and laced her fingers in her lap to keep from drawing her hands into fists. The truce, it seemed, had ended.

"I thought you said there was talk."

"Yes. Lucie was born only a few days after Samuel married me. That was two weeks after the news came of your death. Everyone knew you and I were sweethearts and Lucie looks so like you. Most folks guessed the truth."

"So everyone in town knows but my daughter."

Sarah straightened and met his outraged glare.

"She never asked and I never told her."

"Why the hell not?"

"What would you suggest? That I tell her that her mother acted like a wanton woman or that her real father promised to come back to me but never did? That the only reason I married the man she called Daddy was to keep the shame from her innocent head?" Her voice rose. "Do you think I married for myself? I didn't want to live. If not for our child, I would have tied a rock around my neck and jumped into the river!"

She'd imagined it many times—even gathered the rope.

Astonishment echoed hollow in his voice. "You would not."

She stared, daring him to deny her words again.

"Sarah, you couldn't."

"But I nearly did. It hurt that much. First the news of your death, and then the news that you lived. That was worse. Because I'd trapped myself and Samuel. Our life together was never the same after that."

"Did you love him?"

Sarah stared at the dark outline of Thomas, leaning against the upright beam.

"Yes."

His sharp intake of breath sounded as though she'd punched him in the gut.

"I loved him second best all his life and he knew it."

Thomas fell back against the beam hard enough for Sarah to feel the vibration in the soles of her feet.

"You stood between us every day of our marriage and now that Samuel is gone, he stands between you and me." Sarah rose to her feet. "I'm tired, Thomas. I'm going to bed." She turned, but his words called her back.

"Samuel would want us to work together to find Lucie."

Sarah nodded. Yes. That was right. He loved Lucie. If Samuel's memory drew them apart, Lucie joined them like lock and key.

Chapter Fifteen

The knock upon Sarah's door in the early hour preceding dawn brought her awake. She scrambled to her feet and dragged Lucie's quilt top over her shoulders. When she opened the door, she found Thomas dressed to ride. At the hitching post behind him, his buckskin stood saddled and ready.

She had lived through this once already. For a moment she only blinked stupidly. At last she found her wits enough to form a question.

"Are you leaving me again?"

His eyes grew round at this. "No."

Relief flooded her like sweet spring rain. It was short lived, however, for he continued.

"I'm only going with the men to scout beyond the western knolls." He held out an open hand, as if begging for her understanding. "Then I'll be back."

The last time he told her he'd be back he'd been gone fourteen years and would still be gone if she had not gone to fetch him. The fear of Indian attacks and all the other deadly possibilities that lay just beyond these clay walls rose up in her mind.

"Don't go." She repeated words from long ago.

"If we find any warriors alive, Brennan can trade them for Lucie."

She gripped the latch, trying to draw strength from the cold iron beneath her clutching fingers.

"May I come?" she whispered.

He glanced away, shuffling his feet as if anxious to be rid of her.

"It's only the soldiers."

"And you."

He nodded, then dragged off his hat. "Sarah, this isn't fair. It isn't like the last time. I'm only going—"

"As far as Captain Coffland?"

"You have to trust me."

It was no different from the last time, because she still trusted him. Damn his honest face and sincere eyes. He meant to come back. But just like that day, she understood that things do not always go as we mean them to go. All manner of tragedies loomed, hungry as wolves, ready to rip them apart once more.

What would she do if he didn't come back?

"You must promise me that this is the last time."

He didn't pretend not to understand her.

"All right."

"You don't leave me again until we find her."

His eyes narrowed, and she wished she could call back the words. Why had she said until—until we find her? Because she knew she had no right to hold him longer than that. His face flushed in a way she instantly recalled. Was his anger caused by her mention of their parting, or by her insistence on weighing him down with promises? She longed to know.

Instead of asking she said, "Lucie needs us both. What hope do I have of rescuing her alone?"

"Sarah." His voice sounded condescending, as if he found it aggravating to have to explain this to her. "I'll only be gone a few hours this time."

She lifted her fists, still clutching her quilt top. She meant to strike him in the chest, just above his heart. Instead, she pressed the balled fists into the sockets of her eyes.

"I can't face this alone. I'd rather die out there with you than face this alone."

He drew her in and she let him, swaying like a sunflower in the breeze. He held her tight against the reassuring strength of his body. She wrapped her arms about his neck and pressed her face into the warm comfort of his neck, breathing in the scent of him. His hand stroked her uncombed hair.

"Do be careful," she whispered.

He drew back a few inches, and she lifted her chin to gaze up into his compelling face and sparkling eyes.

She understood he would kiss her then and she tingled with anticipation. She felt the aching pressure in her breasts as they met the hard planes of his chest. He cupped her chin and tilted her head. The first contact was the softest brushing of lips. It was a delicate flame touched to dry tinder. In that instant she ignited, the yearning within escaping in a soft moan.

His reaction was instant. He deepened the kiss as he pressed her close. She wrapped them in the quilt as the years fell away and she held her Thomas once more. He was back, loving her and letting her love him. Sarah's fingers danced through the thick waves of his hair, sending his hat cascading off his head. The quilt top slipped from her shoulders as his hand slid down her spine to stop at the hollow of her lower back, the calloused palms rough through the light cotton of her nightgown. With the slightest contraction of his arm, he pulled her flush against him, pressing tight as lovers in the dawn.

He tensed and she hesitated. The distant strain of a trumpet broke the link between them.

She stepped back, her fears consuming her once more, making her unable to release the lapel of his coat.

"Let me go, Sarah," he whispered.

Her fingers uncurled, and her arms fell lifeless to her sides.

"I'll be back," he said, his eyes begging her to believe him.

She didn't, but she managed a nod. She knew he intended to return and the rest was in God's hands.

He stooped to retrieve his hat and also lifted her makeshift shawl.

"Needs a heavy batting," he said, passing her the quilt top.

Then he recovered the reins of his horse. In one clean motion he swept into the saddle and turned his mount toward the gate.

She waited for him to look back, lifting a hand in farewell. He never turned. As he crossed behind the stables her raised hand collapsed earthward, and she sank into the chair on the porch. From far across the compound came the thunder of many horses surging together as the men left the safety of the walls.

How long she sat, crumpled like a heap of dirty laundry, she did not know. When she became aware, the blacksmith's hammer rang out in a steady rhythm and sunlight filled the yard. She stumbled into her room, draped in her daughter's quilt top like a madwoman.

How near she felt to madness. It was there, just beyond that wall. The turn of fate, the taking of her last loves, and there would be nothing here for her in this world.

Then nothing would stop her from jumping into that river, nothing and no one. Inky black despair threatened to fill her like poison. She shook it off, rising upon unsteady legs.

He would come back this time.

Why hadn't she made love to Thomas when she had had the chance? Sarah moved to the window, staring out at the yard. Somehow her decisions concerning Thomas forever led to regret. She could not seem to do things right. Always her mind and her heart divided. But no longer. Her love for him was stronger than her fear. When he returned, she would remedy her mistake…if he returned.

Just over the rise in the valley, between an outcropping of rock and the river, they found Captain Coffland and his men strewn upon the ground like wheat before the scythe. The scouts quickly determined they were alone with the dead. All of the party was accounted for.

The Sioux had taken no prisoners, thank God, but the fallen soldiers had been stripped naked. Slash marks across the face, extremities, and torso showed the bodies had been mutilated after death. The corpses little resembled the elite fighting force that had followed their misguided captain over the hill in pursuit of a few hostiles.

"Ambush," said Sergeant Farrow, glancing about at the landscape instead of at the bloody ground. "Them Sioux led him right to the slaughter."

Thomas looked at the gash across the torso of the nearest man, a skinny fellow with more beard than brawn. His ribs lay exposed and his punctured intestine lay bloated and stinking.

"Send back for the wagons," said Farrow. "Marshal, you muster a burial detail. Looks like we'll have a proper cemetery by nightfall."

Farrow found Coffland's body and stared down at the scalpless head.

"Stupid bastard," he said and then spit on the ground beside the corpse.

"Why did they cut them up?" asked Private Taylor.

Farrow snorted. "Savages believe that how you die is how you go to heaven. They're forcing our men to enter the afterlife all cut up and stinking. Heathens, with no notion of Christ the Savior. Damned for it, too, each bloody one of them."

Thomas thought the entire plains damned by the war that had just begun. He left the work of loading the stiff bodies to the soldiers and went with the scouts to learn the direction the band of raiders had taken. Two hours into the mission, he realized he had picked the most dangerous job possible and the one that kept him away the longest.

"I should show more sense," he muttered.

He'd spent so much of his life acting for himself, without regard for others. But now he had responsibilities.

As they journeyed along the trail left by the Sioux, his unease grew. Too late to turn back, he decided, and too dangerous to travel alone. He buckled down and vowed to start thinking of Lucie and Sarah before himself.

For the first time in his life, his death would now matter to someone else. Sarah needed him. The thought warmed his insides as he recalled her kiss. For a moment there, he almost believed she still loved him. She'd asked him not to do this again, then added "until we find her," as if she didn't give a damn what he did after that. Took the wind clean out of his sails. Did she think he could just walk away?

Damned if he would.

The scouts found the place where the band had broken in two, and halted.

"They'll just do that again in a few miles," said Farrow. "I see no reason to risk our scalps. Besides, the best way to track them is through the arrows they left behind."

Soon they were galloping toward the fort.

The audacity of the attack struck the soldiers hard. To kill a patrol just beyond the fort, well, the act was atrocious and damned brave. Thomas thought back to yesterday and the Indian he'd watched through a spyglass from the fort wall. The brave rode a dark horse decorated with white spots and a yellow thunderbolt on the flank. Thomas thought the man must be crazy to stick his finger in the eye of the U.S. Cavalry. A crazy Indian on a pock-marked horse.

As they came within sight of the fort walls, Thomas noted an unfamiliar sight upon the parapets. There stood a woman in a dark blue dress.

Sarah.

How the devil had she managed to get up there when Brennan absolutely forbade her presence on the catwalk?

There was no telling what that woman was capable of.

His heart swelled with pride to see her solitary vigil. As he approached, he pushed back the unfamiliar stab of guilt at making her wait and worry.

For the first time in years, he had someone to come home to.

Someone whose kisses scorched him like a firebrand.

His stomach tightened as he forced down the desire that pounded through him with every beat of his heart. Damn, he wanted to kiss her again—wanted to do more than kiss her.

The suffering they had both endured had changed them. It could never be forgotten. Perhaps that was how it should be. The question was, how to move past it?

He glanced to where she waited cast against the blue sky and lifted his hand. She returned his salute and then disappeared as his party neared the gate.

She carried something in her hand as she swept across the yard. Of course, by now she knew there were no survivors. The burial detail was working just outside the gates.

He hoped she had not stood upon the wall as the evidence of the Sioux savagery paraded beneath her feet.

Had she seen the bodies?

He swung down as she approached and felt suddenly awkward. Would she greet him with another kiss or a tirade for going with the scouts? He walloped the dust from his sleeves and vest with his hat. Then he stood, waiting.

She hesitated, three steps back, as if held by some invisible line in the sand.

"I'm glad to see you unharmed," she said, her voice sounding strained. "Brennan wants to see you."

No kiss then. He tried to hide his disappointment. "How'd you get up on that wall?"

She smiled. "I ascended the ladder."

He lifted a brow and she smiled.

"I told the major he would have to physically restrain me and then, upon your return, he would have you to deal with. I never expected him to concede." She glanced over her shoulder. "Something has happened."

"What do you mean?"

"I'm not certain. But after the mail arrived, he called me to him and told me to bring you at your earliest convenience."

"Odd."

She extended several newspapers. "And these came."

He unfolded the first paper and she pointed to the headline reading Army Fails To Rescue White Captive. Beneath this was, Lucie West Still Missing, Army Makes No Attempt At Recovery.

"I see why Brennan wants to parley," he said. "Have you read it?"

"All of them." She took the reins from his hand and led his mount toward the stables as he scanned the article. He gave a whistle.

"They sure do make the army look bad."

"As well they should," she said. "Not only did they allow the trains of settlers to travel without the most meager of escorts, they also gave no word of earlier attacks to which they were privy. Had we known of the unrest, we would most certainly have traveled in greater numbers. In my mind, they are as much the cause of this as the Sioux."

Sarah handed off his horse to a private and waited while Thomas read the next article.

"Read this one," she pointed. "They are calling for the president to take some decisive action against these murderers."

"It is their land," said Thomas.

Sarah cast him an incredulous look. "And they can have it. I only meant to travel through."

Thomas decided discretion was the better part of valor and said no more on that subject. At last he folded the paper.

"Let's go see the major."

"He did not ask for me."

Thomas draped an arm around her and steered her across the yard. It was not the kiss he longed for, but it would have to do.

"Any woman who can force her way to the catwalk should find no challenge in gaining entrance to a little meeting."

She grinned at him and he thought it the prettiest smile in the world.

His arm slipped about her waist as they walked side-by-side past the dust-covered men returning from burying their dead.

Out in the courtyard, Sarah's step faltered. She shrugged off his embrace. He turned to see Mrs. Douglas noting their passage. Thomas sighed and tipped his hat to the woman, who inclined her head.

Thomas turned to important matters. "Did you see them?"

She gave a jerking nod and said nothing.

"Twice in my lifetime I've seen a massacre. I pray to God that this is the last," she said.

"Amen," he said.

"You were right before, Thomas, when you said that this is their land and they will fight our coming. It is only the beginning."

Thomas waited with Sarah in Major Brennan's office while the corporal sought out the commander. He appeared a few minutes later and glared at the papers Thomas held in his hand.

"You've seen them, then." The man looked like he was trying to swallow sour milk. "I've received new orders in today's mail granting permission to enter the Black Hills in pursuit of Miss West."

"Thank God," said Sarah.

"I wouldn't give thanks just yet. I'm also authorized to exterminate any hostile Sioux I meet and seek out and kill any man, woman or child giving succor to these raiders."

"But you will ransom Lucie," said Thomas.

The major shook his head. "I am to demand her release. If they refuse, I am to take her by force."

"But you said the Sioux kill their captives rather than release them."

"I am aware of that. Unfortunately for your daughter, the lamebrains who wrote my orders are not."

Chapter Sixteen

Black Tail told Lucie to meet him by the river at daybreak. It seemed foolish to leave at dawn when she would be so quickly missed. The night before her escape, she lay awake trying to decide what to do.

If she were caught, it would be her scalp hanging from a warrior's saddle. She did not know Black Tail or if he could be trusted. He might well lead her into a trap.

Her mother told her to go with this Black Tail, but her belly ached and that usually meant something was wrong.

But if she stayed, she would lose her one chance at escape. Eagle Dancer planned to wed her when she finished their lodge. She feared all that a marriage to this warrior entailed. He was so big and so old, nearly twenty, she thought.

By dawn she decided to put her faith in this stranger who boasted of trickery.

She rose before the bird songs and crept past the sleeping forms of Shadow and Blue Elk. From habit she grabbed two buffalo bladders to fill with water and took nothing else.

The family dog rose and stretched as she stepped out of the teepee. He trotted along with her as was his custom. How far would he follow?

At the river, she waited. The sky turned gray and birds flitted from branch to branch. There was no sign of Black Tail. When the sun rose, she felt in her bones that she had been betrayed.

Terror stiffened her limbs. Women came to the river to gather water. Any moment, she would be missed. She must go back and convince them she had not run. She threw off her dress and waded into the river. She dunked her hair and scrubbed her body in the icy water.

Lucie wrung out her hair and braided it tightly before donning her dirty shift and dress. The river mud squished cold between her toes as she filled the bladders with water.

Returning the way she came, she found each step a test of her will. Fear made her tremble, shaking water from the tops of the containers.

The dog appeared as she climbed the bank and trotted before her as she returned to the teepee. She hesitated as she noticed Eagle Dancer sitting with Black Tail before the lodge of Blue Elk. She nodded as if nothing was amiss and she continued, hanging the water on a peg inside the lodge. Shadow and Yellow Bird sat beside the fire.

"So, you came back," said Black Tail.

Lucie stood before the men, ordering herself to hold still and keep her hands relaxed at her sides.

"I thought you might, after I did not come." He tossed her mother's letter before him. Lucie glanced down, able to control all but her breathing which came in short frantic pants.

"What is this?" she asked, turning to Eagle Dancer.

His scowl deepened, but now seemed knit with confusion.

"Black Tail says you agreed to run away with him," said Eagle Dancer.

Lucie drew an indignant breath. "He lies. He begged me to run away with him but I said I am yours."

Black Tail's jaw dropped. He rose to point an accusing finger. "She lies. I showed her the letter and she agreed to come with me."

Eagle Dancer stood between the two. "One is lying." He turned to Lucie. "Why were you gone so long?"

"I dropped the bladders in the river. I had to take off my dress and swim out to retrieve them."

He studied her damp skin and wet hair. "Did he tell you to meet him this morning?"

Lucie wondered what Black Tail had said. She nodded. "But I did not go to the trees. I filled my skins at the river and came home to you."

Black Tail swore. "You cannot believe a slave over me."

Eagle Dancer studied his guest. "You spend much time at the fort these days. You have a new gun. How did you get it?"

Black Tail's face reddened. "I rode with Crazy Horse. We killed many blue coats."

"But you also went to the fort and got this letter. You are their messenger."

"They think I am friendly. But I kill the blue pony boys. I am a great liar, they believe anything I say," he boasted.

"You lie very well," agreed Eagle Dancer. His voice made his words seem more insult than compliment.

Black Tail bristled. "We will take this to your chief and see if he believes an enemy slave girl over a warrior with many coups."

Yellow Bird stood in the open doorway, a malicious smile curling her lips.

"I believe Black Tail. The girl betrayed you. First she cuts her wrist and now she runs. She will do anything to escape you."

Her son flushed scarlet. He turned to Black Tail. "I think you tried to steal her and when I followed you to the river, you made up this tale."

"What would I want with a white girl with legs like a walking stick?"

Yellow Bird stepped from her daughter's lodge and between the two men before they exchanged blows. "The council should know of this letter. You must bring it to them." She grabbed Lucie in a punishing grip. "I will watch your slave in your absence."

A shudder of pure panic washed down Lucie's spine. She wanted to beg Eagle Dancer not to leave her with his mother. She called out but all the men strode on together without pause. Lucie's heart sank as they disappeared behind a lodge. In the next instant she was hurled to the ground.

"Evil temptress. Now you lure another. Can they not see you are an ugly little turd? It is that hair of yours."

In a moment Yellow Bird clasped a fistful of Lucie's hair and pulled. With the other hand she lifted her skinning knife.

The knife descended.

Lucie screamed and kicked as the woman fell on top of her, but was unable to dislodge her weight. Certain that Yellow Bird meant to scalp her, Lucie fought for her life. In a matter of moments, it was over. Yellow Bird had her pinned to the ground, trapping both Lucie's arms beneath her knees.

Yellow Bird clasped one wet braid and yanked, forcing Lucie's head up. The blade sliced the braid in two, releasing Lucie from the painful grip. The second braid followed the first. Lucie's hair had once reached her hips. Yellow Bird had severed her tresses at her shoulder.

A circle of women now watched the spectacle as Yellow Bird beat Lucie across the face with her severed braids.

"You belong to my son. If you run, we will find you and kill you."

"I didn't run," Lucie cried.

"I will beat the truth from you."

Pretty Sparrow, the wife of the chief, stepped forward.

"She will not serve your son dead."

Yellow Bird raised her hand to beat Lucie again and Pretty Sparrow grasped her wrist.

"Let her up."

Yellow Bird released Lucie but not her scowl. "She must learn she belongs to the Sioux."

"So mark her. Then all tribes will know she is our captive."

The old woman's face brightened and she turned her beetle-black eyes on Lucie. "Yes. Thank you for your wisdom."

Pretty Sparrow inclined her head and departed, leaving Lucie at Yellow Bird's mercy. Her tormentor dragged her to Shadow's teepee.

The conversation was too fast for Lucie to follow. But she had heard Pretty Sparrow's words clearly. She'd said to mark her and Lucie's belly quaked as terrible possibilities rose up in her thoughts. A branding iron. It was how cattle were marked. Or they might notch her ear like a sow.

Her fright abated somewhat when she saw Shadow grinding charcoal into a fine dust. Charcoal would not hurt, nor would it be permanent.

Lucie watched as Shadow mixed in fat until she had a blue-gray paste that sucked at the pestle like thick mud.

Lucie released the tension in her shoulders. Perhaps they would only draw some mark upon her clothing. Then she saw the bone awl gripped in Yellow Bird's hand and panic seized her like a giant fist.

"Lie down," ordered Yellow Bird.

Lucie eyed the weapon with widening eyes.

"What will you do?"

"You do not question me!" Yellow Bird's voice rose to a screech like a hawk's. "Lie down!"

Lucie decided she had better run. Perhaps she could reach Eagle Dancer and he would help her. She shot to her feet, but Shadow grasped her ankle and Lucie fell hard on the dirt.

In an instant Yellow Bird lay upon her chest, pressing the air from her lungs. Shadow grasped her jaw, holding her steady.

"If you fight, the marks will be ugly," said Shadow. "Lie still and we will be quick."

Tears leaked from Lucie's eyes as Yellow Bird punctured the tender flesh of Lucie's chin. Again and again the awl pierced, until blood ran down Lucie's jaw and into her hair. She could not breathe. Her vision blurred. She wanted to faint, but the needle pricks came again and again, like the sting of a bee.

Finally, Yellow Bird wiped away the blood. Lucie breathed a sigh, thinking the ordeal at an end until her captor lifted the pot of ink and rubbed it on Lucie's chin.

Tattooed.

That was the mark. She had seen them on some of the women here, ugly blue stains upon their chins, ankles and arms.

Next Yellow Bird stripped Lucie's dress to the waist and turned her attention to Lucie's upper arm. The ordeal began again.

When Yellow Bird finally sat back, Lucie's chin and both arms were smeared with blue-black paste and blood.

Lucie's head spun as she tried to leave the teepee. She hoped to wash in the river to draw away the charcoal.

But the women made her sit, with her chin throbbing, until the blood dried. Only then was she permitted to go.

She ran to the riverbank. There she scrubbed the tattoos with sand until blood poured down her neck and stained the front of her dress. Her shorn hair fell before her, covering her horrible face.

It was there that Eagle Dancer found her, sobbing and scrubbing her chin. He dried her face and pressed a bit of wet buckskin to her chin.

"This is a mark you cannot rub out," he said. "This means you belong to the Sweetwater People. If you run again, any tribe that finds you will know that you are mine."

"I did not run."

His eyes reflected doubt.

He fingered the ends of her cropped mane and sighed. He swept her hair through his fingers, sending it away from her face. Perhaps he would not want her now that she was so ugly.

"The blue pony boys ride to our south."

Lucie held back the flash of hope that sparked at this news.

"We move to the sacred hills. Once there, we will marry."

Lucie clutched the bloody leather to her face. What would her mother say when she found her tattooed and married to an Indian? Shame burned through her. For the first time since her capture, Lucie wanted to die. She understood the desperation of Alice French and the humiliation that drove her to recklessness. Lucie squeezed her eyes shut to keep from crying out loud.

"What is this? I tell you that you will be my wife and you weep? I raise you from a miserable captive to a place of honor."

Lucie swallowed back her grief. He spoke the truth; she had never felt more miserable. "My chin hurts. I am thankful to Eagle Dancer for the honor he gives this one."

He nodded, his solemn eyes still studying her as if unsure he believed her.

"Your chin will heal if you stop rubbing it."

"I am ugly now." Her head hung down, causing her short hair to fall all about her face.

"Look at me, Sunshine," he whispered.

She did.

"Your hair will grow and you will bear these marks with pride. It means you are Sweetwater."

Lucie could not keep her chin from quivering.

He stroked her hair. At last the pain and sorrow grew too great and Lucie launched into his arms like a little girl seeking comfort.

He rocked her by the riverbank, whispering tender words to her. "Many women chose to have these marks to add to their beauty. You do not need them, for you already please my eye."

When she quieted, he led her back to camp. Shadow had already removed the hide from the frame of sticks and was tying two poles to the back of her horse.

Lucie helped her strike the camp. Within the hour the line of horses wove its way north. Lucie's chin throbbed with each footstep. That night they had no fires, but rested on the open prairie with the men encircling them.

Three days they traveled in a column. On the morning of the fourth day the men rode off to the west and the women continued their northward march. They hurried now, with many backward glances.

Before midday, Lucie heard gunfire above the ceaseless wind. Yellow Bird had already promised to plunge a knife into her heart if she saw the cavalry. Still, Lucie's heart bore hope. She imagined the soldiers rescuing her and taking her home.

The image shattered as she lowered her head in shame. How could she ever go home?

She had submitted to Yellow Bird and Shadow and anyone else who told her what to do. That was how she had stayed alive. She had not seen the great shame in it.

But now they had marked her face. Before her capture, people had told her she was a pretty child. Her wavy red-gold hair, blue eyes and pale complexion had always gained attention. Her mother said that a woman was more than a pretty face. Lucie had believed her. But she wondered whether a woman was also more than an ugly face. What if no one could stand to look at her now?

What if her mother could not bear the reminder of captivity branded upon her daughter's face?

Lucie rubbed her chin, picking at the scabs in hopes that the blood would drain away the coloring. Yellow Bird shouted at her and she ceased.

The men returned before sunset. Eagle Dancer rushed into their camp and pulled Lucie to her feet. She staggered at the unusually rough treatment.

"What have I done?" she cried.

He threw her onto his horse, bounded up behind her and kicked his heels into his pony's sides. The horse leapt away through the waving grass.

"Where are you going?" shouted Yellow Bird. Her voice, already distant as the wind, rushed past Lucie's ears.

Some small ember of hope whispered that he was returning

her to her people. The voice of doom laughed at this notion, croaking that he meant to kill her for her betrayal.

Lucie clutched at the horse's mane as they galloped over the open prairie.

Chapter Seventeen

$\mathcal{S}$arah paced the wooden planking before her quarters while Thomas leaned against a beam as if bracing up the roof. He nursed a tin cup of coffee that had long ago gone cold, but it gave him an excuse to linger in the cool evening air.

The bugle sounded call to quarters.

Sarah stopped before him. "We can't wait any longer, Thomas. Sooner or later a cavalry unit will find her and then the Sioux will…"

Thomas winced as an image of Alice French flashed in his mind.

"You proposing to head into Sioux territory without the cavalry?"

"I am." She came to rest beside him, perched on the railing like a bird on a wire.

He hated to be the one to point out the impossibility of her plan and wipe that hopeful smile from her face. He used a coaxing tone, trying reason on the most unreasonable woman he had ever met.

"Sarah, I'm near desperate, too, but not so much as to run off half-cocked and leave my girl without both parents."

"Who is allowed to come and go amongst the Indians?"

"Besides other Indians, you mean?"

Sarah pressed her lips together momentarily and then lifted a hand to emphasize her answer. "Traders. They still venture out."

"And more than one has lost his life of late. Most dangerous line of work there is." Still he was considering the idea. He could pay to tag along with a man known to the tribes and conduct his own search. Sarah was onto something here. He nodded.

"We could do it," she said.

This startled him from his musings. "We? What do you mean we? You can't go."

"I most certainly can."

"There are no women traders."

He lowered his chin, bracing as Sarah rose to her feet, her eyes narrowing to slits.

"Trappers have wives. Why not traders?"

"Squaws, you mean. You don't fit that description."

Sarah folded her arms across her bosom. "Let me guess. You figure to ride out and leave me with the promise to come back again, right?"

He shifted uncomfortably but did not break eye contact. That was precisely what he planned to do. It was the only thing that made sense. He recalled, belatedly, that he had sworn to Sarah not to leave her again. But this was different. He wouldn't put her in such danger.

Her gaze flashed fire and he knew she'd sunk her teeth into old grudges once again.

He tossed the coffee into the road, taking his anger out in an overzealous throw. "This isn't like before."

"You are right there, because this time I'll follow you."

Hyatt had threatened the same thing. Stupidly, Thomas had conceded and led Hyatt straight into a massacre. He glared at Sarah, drawing his line in the sand.

"You will not! You'll stay here where it's safe. I won't risk Lucie losing us both."

"This was my idea."

"No, I say."

"I'd rather die out there than lose you again!"

His breath caught. He couldn't believe his ears. If he didn't know better, he'd think she had just told him that she loved him. Well, shouted it, actually.

"Sarah?" It was out of his mouth before he could stop it, like a whispered prayer. He clamped his lips together, determined not to beg for her love. But he would have if he thought it would do the least bit of good.

It wouldn't.

Something about this woman stripped away his dignity, leaving him with nothing but his childish fantasies that the perfect love they'd shattered could somehow be restored to them.

She said nothing, so he squared his shoulders, praying for a miracle—praying she could still love him. He stared down at her face. Her cheeks glowed crimson with emotion. Her eyes seemed to echo his desire. He struggled within himself not to reach out to her, his fear of appearing ridiculous now growing stronger than his hope.

She rested her hand upon his forearm. "Take me with you."

It wasn't wise. Lucie could lose them both and with them all chance of rescue. "But if I don't come back, you'll still be here."

Her expression hardened as the fury flashed like lightning in her eyes. "For what? To bury you? To collect her body after the cavalry attacks their village? It will take both of us to find Lucie. Don't you run off and die on me, Thomas."

He winced. He'd never met such a blunt woman.

The true reason for her concern settled on him. She didn't want to lose him, but her worry did not stem from love. She felt that without his help, her quest would fail. Her insistence on coming along grew out of suspicion that without her vigilance, he'd up and die on her.

"You're staying," he growled.

She pushed him, and he dropped the tin cup. It bounced, then rolled noisily to a stop.

"Traveling with the traders was *my* idea," she said. "Why don't you stay here and wait while I go out and find my daughter."

"Our daughter."

She didn't dispute that, at least.

"You asked for my help."

"Then don't abandon me by the roadside like some broken wagon wheel."

Anger pulsed through his veins. He knew he was right in this, but she would twist it around and bring up past mistakes to make him feel like the blackest of villains.

He gripped her shoulders.

"You are a damn stubborn woman. For once in your life, do what I tell you."

She stared up at him, eyes blazing. "I did what you asked once, Thomas. This time I'll follow you."

"Won't listen to reason or do as you're told, just like Hyatt."

Comparing her to Hyatt seemed to shock Sarah speechless for her mouth dropped open for a moment. "Thomas, I'm not Hyatt."

"Aren't you? He followed, too. But not this time. I have enough blood on my hands."

Their gazes locked and she reached up to cup his face.

Thomas closed his eyes to savor her touch, recognizing his mistake too late. All the worry liquefied into molten desire at her touch. God how he wanted this—wanted her. His gaze flicked from her slightly parted full lips to meet her startled expression. She felt it, too.

Was she preparing to flee like the antelope or strike like the panther? To push him away as she had done each time he persued her.

She neither fought nor fled. Instead, she licked her lips, causing an avalanche of desire to break loose within him. His fingers tightened on her shoulders.

"Sweetheart," he murmured.

Her fingers delved into his hair as he tipped her mouth to accept his kiss. His lips and tongue assaulted her, and she returned the firebrand with her own.

He groaned as the need to press himself to her overwhelmed him. Could it be fourteen years since he had held her naked in his arms? The desire had only grown fiercer with time. Why was it that of all the women he had known, only this frustrating female made him tremble like a green boy? Why couldn't he get her taste from his mouth or her memory from his mind? His blood coursed past his ears like a waterfall, deafening him.

He dipped his tongue into the shell of her ear. Her gasp sent a sweet shot of desire to his core.

She clung like ivy. He glanced about to find them hidden in the shadows of the porch. Behind him, the door to her room beckoned. Would she come to her senses if he moved them?

Fear gripped him. If he lifted her into his arms and carried her to her bed, would she accept him or recall only that he had failed her?

She moaned and rubbed against him in open invitation, bringing her hips into aching contact with his erection.

"Consequences be damned," he muttered, scooping her into his arms, charging through the door and kicking it closed behind them. He kissed her, in an effort to distract Sarah from their new location. He laid her on the bed and slid down upon her. But she pressed at his shoulders, giving him the rejection he feared.

How could he live even one more night without feeling his Sarah naked and wanting beneath him?

The memories returned of her daring innocent self all those years ago. He had taken what she offered and then blamed her as his seductress. All this time he had not accepted his part. Now he recalled her hesitation and how he had plied her with warm kisses and reassurances, just as he did now. He felt sick with regret.

No. Not this time. He would not lure her again, even if he was panting mad for her.

He drew back. She rose to sit beside him, but instead of re-

treat, she reached for the buttons on his shirt. His eyes rounded
in shock. In a moment she peeled the garment from his shoulders.

"Sarah, are you certain?"

She hesitated, her fingers trembling. She stared up at him with
large, luminous eyes. "Don't you want me, Thomas?"

He grasped her hand.

"I want you." He squeezed her hand. "Still."

She rose before him like a shadow in the darkness. He stared
but could make out no more than her outline in the night. The
last time he had her in the darkness, seeing her only with his
body and his hands. How he wished he could see her now. He
clenched his jaw and groped for the box at the bedside table and
struck a match. It flared white for an instant.

Sarah hesitated, frozen in the light. Thomas touched the
match to the wick of the single candle by her bed.

"Thomas?" Her voice quavered, driving him mad.

"I want to see you, Sarah. Please."

She drew a breath as if for courage and nodded, then released the eyelets of her dress. With agile fingers she peeled
away the sleeves and released the fastening at the waist. The
dress pooled about her ankles. Once free, she caught the collar
on the nail beside her bed, and then turned to face him, wearing
only her camisole and petticoats. He stared in appreciation.

Sarah had never needed a corset to narrow her waist.

Next, she lifted a leg to the foot rail, gripping a buttonhook
as he discarded his shirt, boots and socks.

She tucked her shoes neatly beneath the bed and straightened,
laying her open palm upon the smooth surface of his chest. "I've
always regretted not seeing you the first time, as well."

He smiled, wondered if his body would please her eye. Doubt
nipped like a terrier at his heels. He straightened his shoulders
against the uncertainty. The price of seeing all of her was to allow
her to see him. Tonight, he would gaze into her eyes when he
entered her. That thought made him shiver with anticipation.

Her hand slid down the center of his chest and over the ridges of his stomach. He gasped as her fingers paused at the button fastening his trousers. With a tug and push, she had him undone. He gripped the dark wool as doubt accosted him.

"Sarah, I don't want to make another mistake."

"I know what I want." Her lovely brow lifted. "Do you?"

Oh, certainly he did. Nothing had ever aroused him as much as the desire flashing in her eyes. He rose to his feet and reached for the cords that held her petticoats, unfastening one skirt after another. They fell about her like petals from a white rose.

He paused with his fingers perched on the lip of her bloomers, his knuckle brushing the sensitive skin of her soft belly.

She gasped and trembled at his touch. He drew back the cord, releasing the bow and knot. She stepped from them gracefully and then drew off her camisole, removing the final barrier.

He stared in wonder at the picture she made in the soft golden candlelight, her body pale and her nipples rosy and taut. His fingers itched to touch her, but he seemed frozen with wonder as she reached to release her auburn hair from its long braid.

He noticed then that the thatch of hair at the juncture of her legs was lighter than the hair upon her head, nearly the same fiery color as his own wild red head once had been. Looking up, he saw her chest rising in quick rhythm as he inched closer.

Thomas stroked the long column of her throat, his hand stilling at the plane of her shoulder as his eyes continued their descent. Her breasts looked larger than he remembered and the flat belly he had once stroked now showed a sensual curve.

He smiled, lifting his gaze to meet hers.

"I'm a girl no longer," she said. Her voice carried with it a note of apology that nearly broke his heart.

"Thank God for it."

Her eyes rounded for a moment as if she could not credit his words. Perhaps she believed the truth shining in his eyes, for gradually the startled expression vanished as a smile curled her lips.

"I'd see you as well."

He frowned. Now he would have to face her scrutiny. The uncertainty returned. A man's body was not as beautiful as a woman's.

What changes would she see?

"Coward," she whispered.

Unable to resist the challenge in her eyes, he drew down his pants and long johns, tossing them on the chair.

Standing still for her was the hardest thing he'd ever done. No, the second hardest. Leaving her behind had been worse. It was why he never turned back to wave on parting. He knew if he did, he'd never have the strength to go.

He stanched the urge to devour her as she lifted her index finger to his chest, dragging it over his shoulder and sweeping down his back as she walked in a slow circle about him. He twitched at the contact, like a fish upon a hook, knowing he had no chance of release from this torment save the one she could grant him.

At last she stood before him again.

"I wish I had seen you then."

"I was a skinny boy." *Without the sense to know the treasure I sought stood right before me,* he thought.

"No longer." She granted him a smile and laid a hand on the broad muscle of his chest.

His breath caught as she stroked him.

He reached then and dragged her against him, savoring the sweet pressing of warm flesh as their bodies came together.

Her moan of pleasure brought an answering growl from deep in his throat. He lifted her chin to give her a gentle kiss, promising himself that he would not rush as he had when they were so young. This time he would savor her sweetness and draw out their pleasure.

His intentions dissolved the instant her tongue flicked out and stroked his. His grip tightened about her and he dragged her to the bed where they fell side by side, their legs sliding and gripping, bringing him to contact with the hot, wet core of her.

"Too fast," he breathed.

But Sarah's greedy fingers gripped him, guiding him as she lifted her hips in invitation.

No man could resist such a bold entreaty. He thrust home, sliding deep within her sweet flesh. He gasped as she rolled upon him as if he were her mount.

Rocking her hips, she sank even farther upon him, taking him to the hilt. Her tight, slick body squeezed, urging him onward.

She fell forward, flattening herself to his chest and then rubbing against him like a cat, her taut nipples dragging against him in exquisite torture.

He reached, stroking the soft outer flesh of her breasts, and then flicked his thumbs over her nipples. She moaned and tossed back her head, sending her wild hair brushing his thighs. He sat up beneath her, swinging his legs off the bed while Sarah stayed locked to him. She rocked against him, renewing her rhythm. He needed to stop her or she'd have him undone. She slid against him and, as she hovered near, he captured one of her nipples in his mouth. She stilled, crying out as she gripped his head, pressing him to her sweet flesh. She gasped as if relishing the sensation of his tongue on delicate flesh. He moved to her other nipple as his fingers stroked the wet tip of the first.

She arched, sending her body still closer to him. Then something snapped in her and his Sarah turned wildcat, bucking and straining against him. Her strong legs gripped as he moved to kiss her throat.

Her cry told him she had found her release. A moment later her body quaked about him, gripping and squeezing his erect flesh. The sensation was like nothing he had ever experienced. To feel her satisfaction rippling past his turgid flesh was the most erotic experience of his life. The knowledge of what caused this exquisite torture, coupled with Sarah's body open upon his, was more than he could stand. He flipped her to her back and pressed himself deep, taking her in wild thrusts. The gripping escalation robbed him of thought as he strove to his summit. It came with explosive force, sending him toppling upon her as if shot in the back.

After a time he became aware of himself once more. He almost smothered her beneath him, yet she stroked his back. He turned his head and kissed the palm of her hand.

"I thought nothing could match our first time," she whispered.

He nodded his agreement. "We're magic together, you and me."

He eased off of her and she nestled against his side, throwing a long leg over his hips. The curling smoke of desire roused a sleeping ember, but he was too exhausted to fan the fire. He guided them to lie in the conventional direction on her narrow bed, with one goose down pillow shared beneath both their heads.

"I want to do that again," she whispered, her fingers stroking the shell of his ear.

He chuckled, capturing her hand.

"Soon," he promised and dragged the blanket over their cooling flesh. His body twitched as sleep came to steal him away from his Sarah. He turned his head and pressed his lips to her temple. It was there that sleep captured him.

Sarah drew lazy circles upon his chest. She inhaled the familiar scent of him and breathed in the fragrance of her body upon his fingers. How could it be that with all the pain and sorrow that had passed between them, they should meld so perfectly, as if they had been separated by only one day?

She leaned close and whispered into his ear.

"Thomas, damn your stubborn hide, I still love you."

Drawing back, she saw that her words gleaned no reaction. That was best. For now she would keep her own counsel on this matter. She did not know if he could forgive her for her marriage and worried about the secrets he kept.

Why would he not confide in her?

Still, with all their troubles, they had a connection even time could not destroy. Their lovemaking proved that. But was it enough to keep them together?

In her dreams, it was always his hands, stroking, possessing. Only this man filled her with desperate longing and made her blood race as if she were still that young girl with all her dreams intact.

Could they regain that joy? Perhaps it only comes once in a lifetime—a transient passion, not meant to last. But passion was not all that connected them. There was Lucie.

When they found her, he would see this connection made flesh and he would not leave this time. They could be a family. Until this moment she had only dreamed such things might be possible. Now her heart clung to that hope.

Sarah turned to Thomas and pushed a lock of hair from his forehead. Her dreamy state gradually ebbed as the sweat cooled upon her body.

Reality returned as she watched him sleep. He meant to leave her already, to run off into the waving grass and leave her to watch and wait. She felt in her heart that if she let him go, he would not come back.

As for tonight, she would take the joy that had always been denied her. Tonight, she would sleep in Thomas's arms.

She closed her eyes and did not rouse until she heard the bugler blow first call. Thomas slipped from the bed. She dozed again and when she opened her bleary eyes, he stood pouring water into the bowl and washing with one of the soft flannel cloths she kept on the nails above the basin. She watched the efficient stroke of the rag with sleepy eyes, wishing that the washstand had a mirror so she could see the front of him, as well. When he finished, he retrieved his razor.

She smiled and closed her eyes, listening to the scraping of the blade across his chin. Samuel's lie had stolen these moments of quiet intimacy from her.

She dozed, dreaming of swimming in a deep pool. She dove and the weeds at the bottom tickled the sensitive skin of her thighs and belly.

The sensations grew more arousing until she realized it was Thomas stroking her body from neck to knee. His feathery touch drew her from slumber and into a state of high excitement. His clever fingers moved between her legs to the folds that protected her secret places as he leaned to take her nipple into his mouth. Quaking sensations built within her belly, radiating outward. She breathed his name as she anchored her fingers into the hair on his head.

He chuckled against her, his breath fanning her breast. How dare he laugh when he tortured her so?

No more time for thought—the bud bloomed, sending her arching back to the mattress, as the sweet contractions rippled outward. Her body went from taut to exhausted collapse in one blissful moment.

She lay helpless in his arms as he stroked her. When she opened her eyes, she found him staring.

"I've never seen a sweeter sight." He nudged her thighs apart with a knee.

She welcomed him into the lea of her legs.

"Last night, I meant to watch you when you found your pleasure, but I couldn't control myself. Today, I've had my wish."

"Then you'll be granting me the same pleasure." It wasn't a question, so much as a demand.

His breath stopped for a moment as he stared down at her. "You want to watch me reach my—"

She nodded, grasping his shoulders.

He propped himself up upon his hands as she guided him home. She stared in wonder as he moved, his attention never leaving her. His pace quickened and a crease formed between his brows. His expression grew tight as if he felt some great pain. She stroked his cheek but resisted kissing him, unable to draw her gaze from the riveting picture of him thrusting into her as the muscles of his chest and shoulders bulged.

He stared at her in wonder as his body pulsed within her. She squeezed and he moaned as he collapsed beside her. She stroked his fiery hair as if comforting a child, words of love perched upon her lips. She didn't speak them.

The knock upon the door came as an unwelcome intrusion. Thomas groaned.

"Mrs. West?" A pause. "It's Corporal Abby. I found the trader, like you asked."

Thomas rose upon his elbows and glared at her.

Chapter Eighteen

Sarah scowled back at Thomas as he drew away, breaking the connection between them.

Abby continued talking in a raised voice outside the door, as if she'd answered. "I told him you wanted to see him right away. He's waiting at the mess."

"Go away," bellowed Thomas.

There was a long pause. "Mr. West, sir? I'm sorry to disturb you."

"Then get away from the bloody door."

Another pause. "Yes, sir."

Thomas swung from the bed and snatched his long johns from the chair, thrusting his legs into them. Then he jerked into his dungarees and boots.

Her outraged voice followed him. "How could you do that!"

"How could I...? You—you went behind my back."

"And you just let the entire camp know I'm sleeping with you."

It was true. "Sarah, I'm sorry."

She swung her legs to the floor and reached for her camisole, sliding into it like a fish into water. As she drew on her bloomers and petticoats, he stared at the delicate pink ribbon threaded through lace to dangle at the cleft between her breasts.

"Thomas, I have no wish to quarrel," she said. "We'll go see the trader together."

Thomas reached for his shirt. He knew he was in for a fight, but it was a fight to keep Sarah in a place where the Indians couldn't burn her wagon around her.

"No, Sarah."

She did not disagree, as he expected, but rather took a step forward, bringing a palm to rest on the naked flesh over his beating heart. Her lips parted as her gaze locked with his.

"Thomas, please." Her fingers stroked his fevered flesh, branding him with their heat and setting off a pounding ache farther south. When it occurred to him what she was about, his excitement vanished like a flash of powder in the pan.

He gripped her wrists. "Is that what this was?"

Her smile faded. "Is that what *what* was?"

He pointed at the bed. "This! You trying to get me to change my mind about taking you? Is that why you slept with me?"

She recoiled. "Let go of me."

He did and she stepped back, her face flushed and her brow descending dangerously over her lovely eyes.

His naive illusions crumbled to dust. He thought their night together had been the truest act of devotion. But in the glaring morning light, it seemed something tainted. "Damn it, woman, you planned this seduction."

The corners of her mouth turned down as she pinned him with an icy glare. When she spoke her voice did not rise in anger, but came in low and frigid tones. "I thought there were two of us in that bed."

He buttoned his shirt. "I didn't use you."

"Didn't you? Then I missed your honorable proposal."

He stood there panting with fury.

"You said you knew what you wanted."

"That was before you took what happened between us and turned it into something dirty." She gave him her back. "Get out, Thomas."

Just like a woman to blame a man for something that she had done, he thought. He grabbed his gun belt and hat and stormed from the room.

There he halted, breathing hard as he grappled with his disillusionment.

She had used him and then denied the whole thing.

Thomas paced up and down before her room, his boots pounding the planks. He gripped the brim of his hat.

"Damn it!"

He flung his hat and watched it spiral out into the road, skipping like a stone on water before coming to rest beside a pile of fresh manure.

Movement in his peripheral vision drew his attention, and he turned to see Mrs. Corbit pressed against her door, her whey-faced baby upon her hip.

His scowl sent her gaze to the planking.

He strapped on his gun and retrieved his hat, brushing off the evidence of his temper tantrum. Sighing deeply, he tugged the thing low over his angry eyes.

Sarah had cut him deep. He didn't know how it had happened. One minute he was kissing her, feeling himself deep inside her, and the next he was shouting.

Had he guessed correctly—that she was trying to coerce him into taking her along, just like the last time she had slipped into his bed? Had she really ever wanted him or had she just wanted a way out of her father's house?

Blackness coated his insides like tar as he stanched the urge to vomit right there in the street.

How had it started?

Sarah had licked her lips. That was all. One small gesture and he erupted like some ancient volcano. He should have known he had no power to resist her. No other woman had ever manipulated him this way.

Why couldn't he control his lust for her?

The little voice in his head spoke with certainty. *Because it isn't lust, you damn fool. It's love.*

He made it to the horse rail as a wave of dizziness swept through him. He pressed a hand to his mouth as beads of sweat erupted on his forehead.

No. He couldn't love her, not when she so obviously did not feel the same.

There was no controlling his feelings for this exasperating woman. That was why he'd never found a wife, why he kept her damned picture by his bedside and why he jumped back into her bed the minute she crooked her little finger.

Thomas leaned heavily upon the rail. She only wanted to come with him. But he feared losing her, as he had lost everyone else he loved. Was it so wrong to want to keep her safe?

He shivered in the November wind.

Had she ever cared for him?

His chin sank to his chest.

Not the way he loved her, not the way he wanted to love her. She used him. He knew it and it still didn't stop him from loving her.

After all he'd done to her, he should count himself damned lucky he had something she needed. As long as he did, Sarah would stay.

What would happen when he had nothing to offer?

He swallowed his dread. Losing her once had nearly killed him. He didn't think he could stand it a second time.

Sarah sat upon the rumpled bed sheets. Humiliation burned in her face and neck as she realized that Thomas thought no better of her than the town gossips she so despised. Had he not just accused her of sleeping with him in order to trick him into taking her along? It was true she wanted to go, was near desperate to go, but she had taken him to her bed because she loved him. Thomas's kiss made her forget all her fears of scorn and consequences.

Now in the harsh morning light the world looked very different. Her fears returned to plague her, accompanied by more regrets. She had only wanted to talk about Hyatt. When Thomas had said she was acting just like his little brother, he could have knocked her over with a feather. She never guessed that this was the reason he was so insistent that she remain behind.

And then another revelation—Hyatt had followed Thomas. She'd always been told that Thomas had lured him from the safety of the farm. Now she saw another piece of the puzzle fall into place.

She knew Thomas carried a back-bending measure of guilt. Now she understood why. For some reason, he felt responsible for poor Hyatt's death. What else could he have meant when he said he had enough blood on his hands?

Sarah reached for her dress.

Why couldn't he tell her about Hyatt?

Thomas did not trust her. That much was obvious. If he did, he would not have been so quick to accuse her. Without trust, he would not confide his secrets, and nothing she might say would sway him otherwise. Without trust, there was nothing between them.

She pressed her hands to her face, wishing to vanish like a wisp of smoke.

Corporal Abby had heard Thomas. Who had seen him storm from her room?

She scowled past her headboard, to the adjoining wall she shared with Captain and Mrs. Corbit. She tried to recall her angry words. What had her neighbors overheard? Experience had taught her that women relished such gossip. A groan escaped her as she fell back upon the bed. Her life was repeating itself in a terrible cycle of shame and humiliation. She drew the pillow up over her head.

Nothing in this world could force her to leave this room. She would stay here until she dried up and blew away.

She huddled in the covers, suddenly freezing. The fire had gone out and the room was cold enough to see her breath.

Where was her child right now?

She remembered finding one of Lucie's shoes and pictured her child barefoot on this cold autumn day. Sarah bolted upright. She rose, fastening the eyelets on her bodice.

The one thing strong enough to bring her to face the self-righteous stares of her tormentors was her love for her daughter.

Sarah emerged from her door a few moments later to find Mrs. Chastity Corbit holding her toddler over her shoulder.

The woman and her husband, the requisitions officer, had two rooms adjoining Sarah's northern wall. Had she seen Thomas's exit a short time ago?

"Morning, Sarah," said Chastity.

Sarah's cheeks heated as she nodded her hello.

"Baby's colicky. Been up most of the night."

"I'm sorry."

Chastity brushed a strand of hair from her forehead. "I hope we didn't wake you."

Sarah stiffened as another notion sprang up in her mind like a frog from a pond. Had this woman heard their lovemaking? Mortified, she could only blink. The answer she feared came a moment later.

"If you are looking for Mr. West, he's over at the mess hall."

Sarah turned to go.

"He seemed mighty hot under the collar."

Sarah slunk across the yard. It would be only a matter of time before this woman shared her tasty morsel with the other cats. How had she let this happen again?

Thomas was indeed in the mess hall, engaged in conversation with a stranger. The man wore a heavy buffalo-skin coat, buckskin leggings and high, fringed moccasins, like an Indian. His thick brown hair lay loose and tangled, except for two even plaits behind his prominent ears. A bit of feather fluttered from leather cording holding one of his braids. Dark eyes, a crooked nose and a greasy beard, streaked with gray, gave him an intimidating air. Sarah paused, hoping this wild man was not the trader she had come to meet. The barbarian noticed her first and stood.

"Mademoiselle. I am Pierre Roubideaux." The man's French accent cut heavily through his words.

This was indeed the name the soldier had relayed to her.

She gathered her resolve. "Sarah West."

Corporal Abby had failed to mention what a bear of a man Roubideaux was. Perhaps his bulk was mainly coat. She could only hope.

He offered his hand and she hesitated, glancing to Thomas for reassurance before stepping nearer. He neither encouraged nor dissuaded her by word or action, so she extended her hand, clasping the large rough surface of the trader's palm.

"A pleasure."

The man held her when she tried to draw back and lifted her hand for a kiss. The wet press of his lips nearly caused her to shudder, but she restrained herself as he released her hand.

She gave Thomas a quizzical look, trying to gauge whether his fury had passed. He met her gaze with cold regard. She preferred Thomas's disdain to the trader's familiarity, so she sat beside Thomas on the bench.

Mess was officially over and the men reported for work detail, leaving the room nearly empty.

"Thank you for seeing us," she said, as if Thomas had been expecting her to join them. "Has Mr. West explained why we wished to speak with you?"

"He said he's aiming to join up with me and see if he can find your little gal. That might work out."

"Did he mention that I wish to accompany you?"

The trader glanced at Thomas, who kept his expression inscrutable, but she saw the blood vessel at his temple pulse.

"Not a good idea. Indians have a tendency of stealing horses and women."

"I'm sure you could protect me."

The trader laughed. "You'd be betting on the wrong horse. If the Sioux wanted you, I'd trade you over before I'd fight 'em. I've a business to protect."

Sarah's uncertainty prickled. "Likely I'd stir little interest. I'm not a young woman."

"But you're a handsome one and that hair of yours is bound to increase your value."

She didn't like the way Roubideaux surveyed her now, as if measuring how much he could get for her. She inched closer to Thomas.

Behind him, the door opened and Mrs. Corbit entered, still lugging her whining child. Their eyes met as the woman hustled to the cook. Sarah heard her ask for bread soaked in milk before she sidled closer, ears cocked to eavesdrop. Sarah fisted her hands and laid them on the table.

Thomas spoke to the trader, forcing Sarah's attention back to the problem at hand. "I've told Sarah that she should remain here."

"Then she stays."

Thomas nodded.

She wished she could just get Thomas alone for a few minutes so she could find out about Hyatt.

Roubideaux flicked the crumbs from his beard and rose. "I'll introduce you to my wife in the morning, West."

"Wife?" Sarah glanced at Thomas, but he gave her no information so she turned back to Roubideaux. "Does she travel with you?"

"Every damn step."

She scowled at Thomas. Why hadn't he mentioned there was already a woman going along?

Sarah kept her voice conversational, leaving the resentment to burn below the surface. "She doesn't eat with you?"

"Watching the supplies. Besides, Indians ain't allowed in here."

Sarah failed miserably to cover her surprise. Behind the trader, Chastity's smile turned wicked.

Roubideaux laughed, showing rotting bottom teeth. "My gal is Yanktonai Sioux. She's niece to one of the chiefs, fellow named Five Blankets." He turned to Thomas. "Heard of him?"

Thomas shook his head.

"Well, being related to such a man helps me a heap more than being licensed by the government, I'll tell you that." Roubideaux touched the brim of his hat. "Goodbye, ma'am." His gaze met Thomas's. "I'll see you at the gates at first light, West. Pack your own food. Plan for a month."

He left them. Thomas finished his biscuits without a word to her.

She kept her voice low, so as to frustrate their uninvited guest. "Thomas, I need to speak with you."

"You aren't coming."

A glance at Mrs. Corbit showed her rapt attention was focused on Sarah. Their eyes met for an instant and then the woman glanced at her babe, who sucked on a soggy bit of toast.

Sarah leaned in. "Thomas, surely you don't plan to leave me. Not after you promised."

"Don't I?"

Her jaw dropped. She should have known. Hadn't he already proven how little promises meant to him? No, that wasn't fair. He had planned to return. That wasn't his fault.

Thomas rose. "I've plenty to do."

"Thomas, wait."

He didn't. Instead, he pulled his hat down over his eyes. "You can find me easy enough after you've had your breakfast."

Sarah sat a long while upon that bench. A private brought her biscuits with gravy, pinto beans and black coffee.

"Ma'am? You all right?"

She blinked at him. "Oh, yes, thanks."

Sarah stirred the beans until she had something resembling a tiny racetrack upon her plate. Again aware of her surroundings, she noted that Chastity had disappeared, scurrying off to spill her story, no doubt. Sarah slapped down her fork. Well, let her. Sarah had other troubles just now.

"Ma'am?"

She lifted her head from her hand and stared at the private whose bushy mustache did not disguise his youth.

"Major Brennan sent me looking for you, ma'am. He'd like a word."

Brennan had never summoned her. In fact, he usually actively avoided her. Her mind flashed back to the last time he'd called—the day they had found Alice French.

A barrage of possible troubles assailed her. The worst came first. Lucie was dead. He had word or had discovered her body.

"Did he ask to see Thomas?"

"Don't know, ma'am. Just know he sent me to find you."

Her words croaked out like a toad's. "What about?"

"He says to tell you that the Indian is back. The messenger."

She flew to her feet.

Thomas appeared at the door and hastened to her.

"Is the Indian alone?" she asked the private.

"Ma'am?"

"Is my daughter with him?"

Sarah couldn't help clutching her fingers about the private's nearest arm.

"Oh, no, ma'am."

Thomas grasped her elbow and they were off.

Chapter Nineteen

Eagle Dancer did not halt their wild ride until the village had disappeared behind the rolling hills. He sprang easily from his lathered horse and reached for Lucie.

She hesitated, staring down at this man who had been both protector and tormentor. Would he kill her now?

He motioned with his hands but did not speak, his face an inscrutable mask. That was when she realized that he was alone and she sat upon the horse. If she kicked, she might escape him. He would have a long walk back to the village and she would have a day's head start on horseback.

She glanced around. The view was the same in every direction. Only the sun showed the way to go. East or south to her people. To the south she would also find more Sioux, and the mark upon her chin now told all where she belonged.

When she glanced at him again, she found him holding the rein in his fist. She swung her leg over the horse's shoulders and reached for him. He gripped her waist and brought her gently to her feet in the high grass.

"When will you learn to trust this one?" he asked.

She rubbed her chin. "You do not trust me."

He scowled. "Trust must be earned."

Lucie said nothing. Eagle Dancer stared for another moment and then turned to his horse, removing the saddle and sheepskin blanket before leading his mount to the stream that cut between two hills. The horse sucked greedily, his black lips drawn back to show yellow teeth.

Lucie dropped to her knees beside the horse and placed her lips to the cool water. Eagle Dancer cupped his hand and drank as well, then he hobbled his horse.

Lucie sat on the bank, her knees drawn up in protection as she wondered if she would have an opportunity to steal his horse.

"Why have you brought me here?"

She had already thought of several possibilities. The speed with which he appeared and the swiftness of her abduction from the tribe spoke of danger. At first she thought he meant to kill her, but why travel so far? Then she thought he meant to ravish her, but that did not explain their flight. Perhaps he tired of waiting for her to finish their lodge. She was proving a poor student and Shadow often shouted at her. In her mind, the teepee's completion was to be postponed as long as possible. Like Penelope weaving a shroud, she actively sabotaged her work to avoid being forced to wed.

Eagle Dancer squatted beside her, comfortable on his haunches. He folded both arms upon his knees and studied her for a time.

He reached out a hand to stroke her head, combing back some of the hair that fell before her face.

"Do you think I mean to kill you?"

"Perhaps."

He snorted. "You are my slave. I could kill you in the village and no one would stop me."

"Why then?"

"I am afraid others will kill you."

She stared as a quicksilver shot of terror flashed down her spine.

"What have I done?"

"It is your people's work. But you are the nearest white and with so many dead, I fear they will hold you to blame, but I protect my most precious possession." He stroked her cheek.

Lucie remained still, thinking that he was her only protector and it would not do to anger him by drawing away. Still, she did not fancy being a possession.

"What has happened?"

"A wagon train passed some miles to the south." He indicated the direction with his arm. "Behind them, they leave boxes of bread."

His head sank to his chest and he rolled back to sit beside her.

She held her breath in anticipation. The haunted expression on his face told her he had witnessed something terrible.

"I was with them. The bread was divided into equal shares." He rose and went to his saddlebags, drawing out a parcel wrapped in hide. "I know you miss your mother and your people. So I saved my share to bring to you."

Lucie swallowed back her trepidation, resisting the warmth that filled her at this news. "Thank you."

His hands trembled as he opened the parcel. "The others did not wait. Many men ate their shares right there beside the wagon trail." His jaw tensed as he ground his teeth together. "They fell to their knees, clutching their bellies."

Lucie stared in horror at the bread.

Eagle Dancer threw back his head and gave a high-pitched cry that froze Lucie's blood. She clamped her hands over her ears to block out the wail.

She could not seem to keep her eyes from him as he drew back his arm and hurled the bread to the ground, then crushed it to powder with his feet.

He turned to her, panting with rage. "Poisoned."

Lucie rose to stand beside him. Sensing his agony, she reached out and rested a hand upon his forearm.

Tears filled his eyes as he stared at her. "Many good men

died on the ground, writhing like sick dogs. Your people did this."

"It was a cowardly act. I am shamed by it."

He blinked, sending tears down his cheeks. Then with the quickness of a pouncing lion, he captured Lucie and dragged her to him. His arms crushed her in a desperate embrace.

"I might have brought that death to you. I might have lost you."

She rested her cheek upon his warm chest and listened to the pounding of his heart.

"The survivors are crazed with pain and rage. They will make more war and take more lives in retribution. You are of the enemy, but still I cannot bear to see you harmed."

"I have not made war on your people. I only meant to travel through this land on the way to the western ocean. Take me back to the fort, where I will be safe."

He put her at arm's length and stared at her with a look of fury.

"I will not. Soon you will be my wife. You must stop thinking of escape and accept your place, now."

Lucie stared up at him and lied. "I never tried to leave you. Black Tail is a liar and would steal what is yours."

He gave her a look full of suspicion. She tried another avenue.

"You say I am not safe with your people. Where are we to go? Where can we live in peace? My people will kill you and yours will kill me."

Lucie thought her argument very wise until Eagle Dancer's face turned red and the blood vessels at his neck bulged. She watched them pulse and feared what he would do.

"We stay together."

"They'll blame me, kill me and you will lose me to death."

He did not deny it and that frightened Lucie even more. What she first saw as an opportunity to sway him into taking her to her people she now saw as a real possibility. She tottered on her feet as the seriousness of her situation settled heavily upon her narrow shoulders.

"In a few days, I will go back and see if it is safe for you."

"And leave me here alone on the prairie. The wolves will find me."

"I will hide you from them."

"What if it is not safe? What if the others follow you?"

"I will protect you."

Thomas noted that Sarah trembled as they walked together toward Major Brennan's office. They found him standing at the window inside his headquarters with two corporals flanking the Indian named Black Tail.

"West, he has come back empty-handed." Brennan nodded at Sarah. "I'm sorry, ma'am."

"Where is my daughter?" she asked the Sioux.

Brennan cleared his throat. "We are waiting for the translator. All we know is that he is alone."

Sarah's eyes narrowed as she studied the bare-chested warrior, who stared straight ahead. She fidgeted in the strained silence, waiting.

Brennan opened the door and shouted at the guard posted before his entrance.

"Where's the bloody man?"

"Coming, sir."

The soldier pointed, and Thomas saw the half-breed trapper hurrying across the yard, still buttoning his shirt.

Brennan stepped aside to let him enter.

"You remember John Standing Forest?" he asked.

Thomas shook the man's hand and Sarah nodded her greeting. The trapper lifted a hand to Black Tail and muttered something to which the man responded in kind.

"Ask him about Lucie West."

The men talked and Sarah tugged at a button on her blouse until she managed to pull it free. She picked the loose thread from the fabric and wound it about her finger until the tip turned scarlet. Then she slid off her bindings and tucked them, with the button, into her pocket.

At last Standing Forest turned to Brennan. "He says the girl is dead."

Sarah shot to her feet, staggered, and then, finding her balance, stalked forward, pointing an accusing finger at the Sioux.

"He's lying."

Brennan ignored her. "What happened?"

"He says she ran and was captured." He glanced at Sarah. "He gave details. They ain't pretty."

The warrior interrupted.

"He says he wants his wives back."

"Not without Lucie," said Thomas.

John Standing Forest spoke to the Sioux warrior. "He doesn't have her."

"Do you believe him?" Thomas asked the guide.

"Hard to say. I believe he wants his wives back, one in particular."

"The bargain was Lucie West for his wives. He failed and brings no proof that what he says is true." Thomas turned to Brennan. "His wives should stay here."

The trapper spoke to Black Tail, whose face turned red. The warrior began to shout at Standing Forest. The corporals unholstered their revolvers. Thomas dragged Sarah behind him as Black Tail regarded the business end of two 44-caliber Colts.

"He says the girl is dead and the bargain is broken."

"What proof does he have?" asked Thomas.

Standing Forest asked Black Tail. The man reached into the small pouch at his waist and withdrew a blood-stained rag.

Sarah cried out and snatched the tattered cotton from his hand, holding it before her like a prayer book as she dropped to her knees. She pressed the bloody bit to her cheek, weeping.

Brennan cast Thomas an impatient look. Rage flared in

Thomas's gut, but he moved to collect Sarah and guide her from the office.

He helped her cross the yard to her room and sat her on the bed, before wrapping an arm about her narrow, shaking shoulders.

"Th-this is her dress." She held up the cloth.

He stared down at the tattered blue swatch.

"I made it from one of my old calico skirts, so she'd have something new for the journey."

She cradled the fabric to her cheek and sobbed.

"Oh, Thomas, my heart is breaking."

He held her gently and rocked back and forth as her tears wet the front of his shirt.

At last her weeping grew less hysterical and he thought she might hear him.

"Why do you believe him?"

She lifted her head.

"What?"

"He could be lying."

"But the dress."

"Only proves he saw her."

"The blood?"

"Whose blood?"

Sarah bit her lower lip, holding it between her teeth as she stared up at him.

"You're just saying this to give me hope. Thomas, if she's gone there is nothing for me."

He hesitated and then spoke his heart. "I'm still here."

Her hopeless expression remained unchanged. "She is the tie that binds us. What do we have without her?"

"Each other."

Sarah shook her head. "I can't go on if they have killed my child."

He shook her shoulders and she gasped in surprise.

"You don't know she's gone. All you've got is the word of

an enemy who could very well have failed to collect her and is now willing to do whatever it takes to get his wives back."

"But she might be gone. Thomas, we might never know."

"Might? You gonna quit on 'might'?"

Her shoulders shook as the sobs took her again. Thomas rose.

"I'll find my girl or real proof before I'll lay down and quit."

He stood beside the bed, knowing if he stayed he would say something else he'd regret. He reached the door before she called him back.

"I thought Lucie might heal what has passed between us, that we might become a true family. But if she is gone—"

"Stop saying that. Did it ever occur to you that we have to work out our own troubles? It isn't up to our daughter to do it for us."

Sarah collapsed on the bed. "What if she's gone, Thomas?"

He crossed the room in angry strides. He didn't like this helpless woman before him. He wanted his Sarah back.

"What if she's not? What if she's out there on the prairie counting on her ma?"

Sarah sat up at this, but a moment later her shoulders slumped once more. "I don't think I have the strength to find her dead."

She frightened him now. What if this broke her? He tried to think of what might bring her back from despair. Comfort was his first impulse, but that hadn't done it. Another idea struck him. Sarah didn't need solace. She needed a poke with a stick. She needed to rekindle the stubborn force that had driven her to seek him out in the first place.

"Stay here, then, and wring your hands. I'll go north without you."

She rose to her feet.

He repressed a smile of satisfaction. "Trader leaves tomorrow. But you stay here. You can make me a quilt."

Sarah glanced at Lucie's quilt, now complete with batting and backing, missing only the finishing binding. Then she scowled at Thomas.

Good, she's fighting.

"You will not leave me this time."

She was back, furious and frustrating and oh, so beautiful. Her breathing came in sharp blasts through flared nostrils and her color was high. Damn, he wanted to kiss her.

"You could get yourself killed," he jeered, fanning the flames and then remembering it was a real danger.

"Better that than stay here and die by inches."

The poke in the eye had worked too well. His stomach clenched and he faced the possibility of leading her into disaster.

"I'll follow you."

He saw Hyatt before him, hands on hips, uttering the same threat. God help him but he faced the devil's choice once more—either he could lead her into danger or leave her here to follow alone.

Chapter Twenty

Thomas crossed the yard and paused to see the sentries questioning a boy who stood beside a painted horse with an Indian bridle. He was dressed in only a loincloth and buckskin shirt.

Pierre Roubideaux was there, as well.

Thomas approached, realizing the boy was younger than he'd first thought, perhaps only fifteen. His lanky arms and legs gave him height, but little muscle. His skin was burnt to the color of the tanned leather he wore and he spoke to the trader with a voice that occasionally cracked. Thomas stepped closer and saw the piercing blue eyes. The sun had lightened his brown hair nearly blonde at his crown.

"He says he was adopted by the Sioux after his capture. He don't recall how to speak English, though. He didn't so much escape as run away after he accidentally shot a tribe member while hunting. Hard luck that the boy he killed was the chief's youngest son. He figured he'd better skedaddle."

"Where has he come from?" asked Thomas.

"Up north somewhere, or so he says," replied Roubideaux.

"Got blue eyes," said one of the sentries. "He ain't no half-breed."

"Best take him to the commander," said his partner.

"Ask him if he's seen any white captives, women or girls," said Thomas.

Roubideaux spoke to the boy, while Thomas sweated out the reply.

The trader nodded to Thomas. "He's seen a few."

"One named Lucie West?"

The trader and boy spoke again before the trader turned back to Thomas.

"He didn't talk to them. Him being adopted into the tribe, he didn't want to remind them that he was white."

Thomas's heart pounded. The boy might have seen Lucie.

"Take him to Major Brennan," said the sentry.

The trader nodded and led the way.

Thomas headed to the mess hall and found most of the company eating their noon meal. He banged a tin cup on the table for attention. The men quieted.

"We got a white boy, just come in. He ran away from the Sioux. He might have seen Lucie. I need photos of your daughters and sweethearts. I want to see if he can pick Lucie out of a bunch."

Several of the men rose from their seats. Within a few minutes he had twelve images of white women. He headed for Brennan's office, but paused at Sarah's room.

He hesitated. If the boy had not seen Lucie or had witnessed her death, Sarah would be crushed. But Sarah had said from the start not to leave her out.

A thought struck him. What gave him the right to order her to stay at the fort? She wasn't his wife—never would be, if he kept acting like she was his property. He had the money, that was true, and that gave him some power. He also felt responsible for her safety. But how would he feel if the situation were reversed?

A chill swept through him as he understood her fury. He'd be damned if he would allow himself to be left behind. He would follow that trader to hell and back to find Lucie, and Sarah would do the same. She wouldn't stay in the fort no matter what he said. That left him with no choice.

He knocked.

She called him in and he found her just closing her saddle-bags.

"I got some news."

She stared at him in watchful silence.

"A boy just came in. He might have seen Lucie."

Sarah headed for the door. He grabbed her arm to halt her and explained his plan. Together, they marched to Brennan's offices for the second time that day.

The boy now sat before Brennan's desk. The major sighed heavily at their appearance.

"I thought you were leaving."

Pierre Roubideaux snorted. "Tomorrow."

"He doesn't know if he's seen your daughter. He never spoke to any other captive," explained Brennan.

Thomas put the stack of photos on the desk, his daughter's image there among the rest. He paused before withdrawing, afraid of what the boy would tell them. He might very well confirm Black Tail's story that Lucie had been murdered. Thomas clenched his fist and stepped back.

"Some of the men provided me with photos. Lucie's picture is there, as well. Please ask the boy to have a look at them."

Brennan nodded and the trader took over, speaking to the boy as he laid out the images upon the desk as if setting out a hand of poker. Thirteen photos of girls and young women. Thomas tried not to stare too hard at the one he had carried over the plains.

The boy leaned forward and studied the lot. Sarah moved closer to Thomas, her fist pressed to her mouth. The muscles of his shoulders tensed as the boy lifted a finger. It hovered a moment and then descended on the photo of Lucie West.

Sarah gave a cry of pure joy and threw herself into Thomas's arms. He squeezed her close, breathing a sigh of relief.

The trader and boy spoke and then he delivered the news.

"He says he saw this one about ten days ago. He says she tried to speak to him, but the other boys made fun of him, so he ran away."

"Is she well?" asked Sarah.

"She's under the protection of a warrior named Eagle Dancer. The boy says he plans to marry your gal."

"Marry? She's only a girl."

Roubideaux shrugged.

"Where is she?" asked Thomas.

The boy and trader spoke again.

"With the Yankton Sioux—the Sweetwater branch. He is of the Bitterroot tribe, also Yankton. Last saw her when they were traveling away from the soldiers. Been moving a lot 'cause of the troops engaging them. He reckons they'd be somewheres in the sacred Black Hills."

"The what?"

"What you call the Badlands," said Roubideaux.

"I can't send my troops that far north," said Brennan. "Plus that's still Indian territory. I've no jurisdiction."

Sarah's shoulders sank in relief. "Thank God."

"Well, someone must be up there, if this boy has seen soldiers," said Thomas.

"Sixth Iowa Volunteer Cavalry under General Sully," said Brennan. "Out of Fort Rice."

"Objective?" asked Thomas.

Brennan met his gaze and held it fast. "Engage hostiles."

Thomas's heart beat hard. They had to reach Lucie before Sully did. He turned to the trader. "Have you been to the Black Hills?"

"Know them well."

Sarah looked at the boy who now lifted one photo after another. Was he searching for a face familiar to his own heart?

Suddenly he seemed the loneliest child in the world. Surely his family had been murdered when he was captured. He was now at the mercy of Christian charity. Who would take care of him?

Her gaze never left him as she spoke. "What will happen to the boy?"

Brennan puffed up like a grouse as he mulled his answer. "We'll look for his family."

"That will take months and may yield no harvest. I'd like to offer to take charge of him while you conduct your search."

Brennan's condescending smile was cold. "Mrs. West, I understand your need to replace what is lost. But I think the boy would be better served if I fostered him with one of our married couples."

This comment rendered Sarah speechless. Had he said "replace"? To think she would grasp the first orphaned child she found as a substitute for her cherished girl was ludicrous. Wasn't it?

Indignation stiffened her spine and at last she found her tongue. "I am a mother and fully capable of taking charge of him."

"He's half-wild, speaks no English and needs a woman who can raise him up with good *Christian* morals."

Now he questioned her morals?

But she knew.

Brennan's gaze traveled meaningfully to Thomas and then back to her. Her face flushed as the insinuation vibrated in the air. News of Thomas's early morning retreat from her bedroom had reached the top man. Immorality was reason enough to turn her down and insult her.

How smug he looked.

Thomas crossed the invisible line of authority, cornering the commander behind his desk. "I ought to punch you in the nose."

"You do and I'll see you spend the winter in the stockade." Brennan clung to his authoritative tone, but his eyes told another story.

"Be worth it, though." Thomas grabbed the major by his lapel and cocked his fist. Brennan closed his eyes and braced.

"Corporal Abby!" Brennan called out at the same moment Sarah shouted, "Thomas!"

Thomas paused to glance at her and she shook her head vehemently.

He faltered, giving her a beseeching look, seeking her permission to strike in her defense. She withheld it. He sighed and turned his attention to Brennan, who had opened one eye to see what had caused the delay.

Corporal Abby crept forward, seeming none too eager to step between them.

"Apologize," growled Thomas.

"I could have you both cast out."

"But you'll apologize for the insult first."

Thomas released him and Brennan cleared his throat.

"Mrs. West, I meant no disrespect. But as commander, you must allow me to choose whom I see fit."

She inclined her head in acceptance and Thomas moved to her side.

Abby stepped before them, blocking their departure.

"Oh, let them go," snapped Brennan.

At the evening meal, Sarah sat with a clear view of Mrs. Douglas, Mrs. Corbit and Mrs. Fairfield trying to teach the boy how to hold a fork. They had cut his long hair so he more resembled a white boy than an Indian. He still retained his moccasins, though he wore a faded red cotton shirt and overly large wool trousers that billowed about him like an untrimmed sail. The trousers seemed to be causing a great deal of scratching in areas that made Mrs. Fairfield grasp his hand and shake her head.

"I'm sorry, Sarah," said Thomas.

She started. "What?"

"I'm sorry Brennan said those things. He's a damn fool."

She held his gaze, willing herself not to cry. "Maybe he's right. Perhaps I don't have the moral fiber to raise a child. That might be why God took my child from me."

Thomas's brow sank low over his eyes. "That's nonsense!"

"Is it? The whole camp knows we slept together. If I were a good Christian woman, I would not have let my lust sway me, again."

Her words did nothing to allay his scowl, but instead made his expression darken another degree.

"Is that all it was to you—lust?"

She dropped her gaze. She didn't know what it was, only that it was a mistake. "I'm a single woman and despite the fact that I know what is right, it seems I cannot keep from getting a reputation. Not then, not now." She gripped her coffee mug, letting the heat radiate through her palm. "I wasn't trying to trick you either night, Thomas. Truly, I never was."

She peeked up at him and found him staring, but not glowering.

"Then what did happen?"

She wanted to say she loved him and that she wanted to be with him. But she feared taking the risk. Here in the crowded room, she could not bear another humiliation.

"What do you think it was?" she asked.

"We have a spark between us. It's always there, even now." His eyes held the glow of desire. Sarah's cheeks heated under his gaze. "I thought time and distance had killed it, but it's stronger now. Sometimes it's so strong that it blazes like a grease fire and neither one of us is tough enough to clamp a lid on it."

She nodded at the truth of this.

He glanced at her uneaten dinner and half-empty cup. "You done?"

She nodded.

"Let's go, then."

The cool evening breeze hurried them along. The dark sky glistened with stars. Sarah huddled in her shawl as Thomas guided her across the yard to her room, where they sat on a bench, shrouded in shadows.

He sat only a foot away, but she could not see his expression in the darkness.

"Thomas? Remember when you said that we had to resolve our difficulties?"

"Yeah."

"How do we do that?"

She heard him draw a breath and sigh. "I guess we just sort things out between us."

"Then I want you to tell me about Hyatt."

She met only silence.

"Please, Thomas."

"Sarah, I'm going to tell you. But give me a little more time."

Time. Fourteen years had not been enough, but she would give him what he asked for.

"All right then." She turned the conversation to the trader. "I know you have funded this expedition and I am beyond grateful. But—"

"You aren't staying put."

"No."

He snorted. "Figured."

"I'm sorry."

She thought he nodded.

His voice sounded weary. "I'd be as mad as a hornet if you ordered me to stay put. I didn't think of that until now. Plus, I guess I have no right to tell you to stay or go, seein' as how I never made you an honorable proposal."

Her words were barely a whisper. "You did once."

The resignation rang hollow in his voice. It was as if he could see what would happen next but was unable to prevent it. "I only wanted to keep you safe."

"I know."

Chapter Twenty-One

Eagle Dancer kept Lucie away from his people for three nights. The day following the Antler Dropping Moon, his brother-in-law Blue Elk appeared.

"What news, brother?" asked Eagle Dancer, holding Blue Elk's horse's reins as the man slid to the ground.

"No captives have been killed."

Lucie barely had time to heave a sigh of relief before Blue Elk continued.

"Our braves have traveled far south to attack any whites they could find."

Eagle Dancer nodded at this while Lucie trembled, imagining the warriors swooping down on other families. She prayed no wagon trains had been trapped at the foothills of the Rockies by the snows.

The three of them journeyed back to their tribe, where Blue Elk found his harried wife tending their teething and feverish child. Her temper was short as she scowled at Lucie and then turned to her brother.

"I'm tired of waiting for this worthless one to do a day's work, Brother. I have seen bugs make better progress gnawing through wood."

Blue Elk exhaled loudly through his nose and addressed Eagle Dancer. "She gathered the women to complete your lodge. I told her that we need our food stores for the winter and not to feed other men's wives."

Minnow sat at her mother's feet, wailing and reaching. Shadow scooped up her daughter, brushing the tears from her cheeks and then turning to Eagle Dancer.

Lucie had always known this day would come, but she still hoped that she could avoid what was sure to follow.

"Your bride is ready, Brother."

Silence followed Shadow's pronouncement. White women did not marry Indians, even if the man was a warrior and well respected by his people, even if he was kind to her and held her in high regard. Her mother would not understand. No one would. She would be dirty, ruined. There was no greater shame for her. Her heart nearly stopped as she realized there was one greater.

What if she had his child?

"Where is the lodge?" asked Eagle Dancer, his voice eager.

Shadow pointed at a nearby teepee. It stood with taut sides and newly cut lodge poles. No soot darkened the freshly tanned hide at the peak of the structure and no paintings ringed the exterior.

A great grin split Eagle Dancer's face, making him look younger. He nodded his approval, crossed the path and circled the structure. Rounding the front, he ducked inside. Lucie waited, frozen to the earth beside his war pony, as the long tail swished rhythmically back and forth across her stomach.

Lucie pressed her hands to her face to stifle a cry. Shadow gave a mirthless laugh.

"Why are you whining like a dog in heat? Are you so anxious for my brother's lance?"

Lucie straightened, feeling her face burn in shame, but did not trust herself to speak. The lump in her throat seemed to choke her. How she longed for her mother.

"You go to him this night, little one. No more tricks. No

more delays. From now on you can eat his food, assuming you know how to cook it."

Lucie managed to nod as a hot tear splashed down her cheek.

"He is a good man with a big heart and a gentle hand. My mother is right—you do not deserve him." Shadow turned to scowl at Lucie. Her eyes narrowed as she spied the tears. "If you weep before him, I will see you pay."

"There is sand in my eye," Lucie lied.

"Then wash at the river. Quickly, before my brother sees this dishonor."

Lucie needed no urging to go. The river was one of the few places where she could escape Shadow and Yellow Bird. She worked her hair into two short braids that only brushed her shoulders, tying the ends with a long pliant strand of river grass. She did not have long to enjoy her privacy. Eagle Dancer arrived moments later, finding her on her hands and knees washing her face.

"Come now," he ordered.

His serious expression raised alarm bells in Lucie, who wondered whether Shadow had told him she wept.

In her time here, Lucie had witnessed three funerals and two wedding ceremonies. The weddings were short with their own version of vows. God, of course, was absent, as these people still lived in ignorance of His great glory.

Lucie rose and only then discovered that her knees were clacking together. She wobbled along beside her groom, feeling her stomach rolling the dried buffalo meat she'd had for breakfast. She felt she should gather flowers, at least, and was sorry she had no fine dress or veil. What would her mother say about this man who was to be her husband?

She cast a glance at him and noted that he stared straight ahead as they made their way to the village. His profile showed the hawkish nose and square chin. She did not find him handsome, but neither was he hard on the eye. His wide bare chest fascinated her, as did the muscles of his shoulders and back. He had shown her kindness, but not enough to let her go. Although he never mistreated her, he often left her with his mother.

Once she was a wife, would Yellow Bird continue to belittle and beat her? She did not wish to marry, but they left her no choice. And if she must wed, she hoped her status as Eagle Dancer's wife would afford her some peace.

She had much to learn, although gathering sticks and water, doing every foul task his mother could devise and watching Shadow's baby had prepared her somewhat to keep house like an Indian.

"I'm not a very good cook," she said.

He gazed down at her and smiled. "You will have much practice, for I will keep your cooking pot full."

Chapter Twenty-Two

Sarah arrived first at the stables. The Indian woman appeared as Sarah saddled Freckles. She glanced about for someone to introduce her and then in the hopes that the woman would glance her way, but neither happened, so she advanced cautiously.

She studied the stranger's face, deciding the woman was her junior by several years. Her black braided hair showed no gray and her smooth skin glowed with health. Her figure was hidden beneath a white Hudson Bay blanket. The bold yellow, green, red and black stripes crossed her narrow shoulders and back. The woman retrieved a mule from the stables and shed her blanket to tie a pack saddle in place. Sarah moved closer, waiting for the woman to notice her, but she continued her work, lifting load upon load onto the mule as Sarah hovered nearby.

"Are you Mr. Roubideaux's wife?" asked Sarah.

The woman turned, met Sarah's gaze with dark, serious eyes and nodded.

"I'm Sarah West. I'm riding along with you."

The woman said nothing to this.

Thomas had spoken to the trader about his change of heart, so she was expected this morning, though she wondered if Roubideaux had shared this news with his wife.

"Do you understand me?"

Another nod.

"What is your name?"

"I am called Water Blossom."

Sarah offered her hand. "A pleasure to meet you."

The woman stared at Sarah's hand and then reluctantly touched her fingers to Sarah's palm.

"You are searching for your girl."

"Yes, that's right."

The serious eyes gave nothing away as she nodded again. Then she pointed to the mule. "I have work."

"Of course. May I help you?"

Water Blossom's brows lifted at her offer. Then she looked over her shoulder, as if afraid to be caught committing some crime. Finally she shook her head. "I do."

"Very well." Sarah stepped back.

Water Blossom had two mules loaded and had readied both saddle horses before Roubideaux arrived.

Thomas appeared next, unshaven and bleary eyed. "Ready?"

In answer she turned Freckles to the mounting block. They headed out of the gate with the trader in the lead, followed by Thomas, Sarah and finally Water Blossom leading the mules. All that day, she saw no game, no cavalry and no Indians.

At dusk, Roubideaux called a halt and Water Blossom set the camp, moving silent as a shadow in the twilight. She again refused Sarah's offer to help, leaving Sarah nothing to do but feed and water Freckles, who seemed happy with that arrangement.

Sarah held her gelding's halter as he munched his grain and molasses from the sack. She wore her new coat and found it warm even against the chilly wind that numbed her ears and nose. The days never warmed up enough to suit Sarah now. Thomas staked the horses' leads and Sarah made her way to the fire. As she lifted her hands to feel the heat of the flame, she wondered if Lucie had the same luxury.

* * *

On the third afternoon of traveling, they reached the place that Roubideaux called his trading post. Sarah did not know what she expected, but certainly not a squatty little sod house and lopsided barn. The barn, at least, was made of wood and the corral looked sound. The mules' ears pricked up at seeing the resting place and the creatures happily trotted through a gap in the gate. Sarah left the men with the animals and helped Water Blossom carry bundles into the house.

The interior of the post was damp, barren and cold, but Water Blossom soon had a fire in the hearth and a thick stew in the pot.

After a long silence, Water Blossom spoke. "I think we find the Yankton Sioux tomorrow."

It was the first time Water Blossom had initiated a conversation and Sarah smiled what she hoped was encouragement.

"How do you know?"

Water Blossom pointed at the hearth. "They see smoke, I think."

"But I've seen no one."

"That does not mean that no one see you."

Sarah repressed a shudder. These were Water Blossom's people, but Sarah's enemies.

Water Blossom stirred the stew, keeping the contents from burning, and the conversation ended as abruptly as it had begun.

Sarah's smile faltered as she tried to rekindle it. "How long have you been married?"

"Roubideaux is not my first husband. My father accepted his offer of ten horses and told me that I mourned no more."

What did that mean, she wondered, but before she could ask, Water Blossom continued, lifting the spoon to emphasize her words.

"Before this I had a fine husband. He gave me a son." The spoon drooped until it plopped back into the pot.

The woman's chin trembled. Fingers of dread gripped Sarah's heart, for she knew already what Water Blossom would say.

The woman worked her jaw as if crushing the grief between her teeth. Sarah held her breath as Water Blossom cleared her throat.

"They grew ill with the rotting face disease."

Sarah's eyes widened at this. "With what?"

"Your people call this small pox. But the pox were not small. They cover my boy's body and inside his throat until he cannot breathe. I held him as he struggles for life and then draws breath no more." Water Blossom raised both empty hands as if offering her dead child to Sarah. "I am broken by this when I see a mark upon my husband's face."

Sarah breathed her denial as she imagined losing Lucie and then seeing the same plague upon Thomas.

Water Blossom stared hard at Sarah as if she had brought this plague to this woman's house. Sarah's face flushed in guilt. Perhaps she had. Certainly her people had, bringing it west along the wagon trail. She knew that small pox had wiped out entire villages and now felt thoroughly ashamed that she had once thought this a very good thing.

Water Blossom stirred the stew, but her mind was obviously with her first family. "This is a terrible disease. Our medicines do nothing. The rotting face takes my beautiful husband, as well. When my husband died I do not wish to live. I lay down and waited for spots. But spots, they do not come."

Water Blossom had no child to sustain her. Sarah turned to meet Water Blossom's steady gaze.

"We both lose a child, but you are the lucky woman."

Lucky? Sarah felt anything but that. "Why do you say so?"

"My child, gone away. Your child, maybe we get back."

Sarah gazed into the woman's dark eyes and knew she had an ally. "Thank you."

The silence again crept into the room, but this time it did not sit heavily between them. Sarah took a seat beside the hearth.

"My husband died of cholera on the trail."

Water Blossom met her gaze. "We have much the same. We lose men and now have new men."

"Oh, Thomas isn't my husband."

Water Blossom lifted an eyebrow. Sarah wondered if she was thinking of the two nights Sarah had slept beside this man she said was not hers.

"He will be soon, I think." Water Blossom nodded. "When you find your girl you will have everything a woman needs to be happy."

"I was married to his brother." It slipped out before Sarah could stop it. Why had she told Water Blossom this?

The spoon stopped. Dark eyes regarded her. "Then he have to marry you—yes?"

"Have to? No, why?"

"Husband's brother marries widow, take as second wife. West have first wife?"

Sarah's eyes widened in shock. The common ground they had discovered now shook badly beneath her feet.

"Is that what Indians do?" She could not quite get her mind around this. It was a terrible sin to have more than one wife.

"What else to do? Man dies and woman alone with babies, babies. Brother's duty to feed these all."

In an odd sort of way, that did make sense.

"It doesn't work like that with us."

"He leave you to raise brother's girl alone?" Water Blossom seemed scandalized by this.

"I chose his brother over him. He is still angry."

Water Blossom seemed to think about this before speaking. "He say this?"

Sarah shifted on the crate upon which she sat. "Well, not exactly. But he has not forgiven me."

"He has not or you have not?"

Sarah was struck by the truth in this. She did not know if Thomas had forgiven her. She'd never asked. But that was not all that stood between them.

"Also, he has a secret. Something that happened to his younger brother. He won't speak of it."

"Men guard their pain, women guard their hearts. Perhaps he will never tell. It should not keep you from loving him."

"I think it keeps him from loving me."

The spoon stopped its circular path and the woman regarded her for a moment. "Then you must lance this pain like a boil."

Yes, that was right, as well.

The men came in and Water Blossom served them each a portion. Only when the men had finished did Water Blossom offer Sarah a share. Water Blossom ate last, taking what was left in the pot.

Sarah wanted to speak with Thomas. She needed to slay the dragons between them. But his eyelids drooped and he nodded beside the fire.

"Where should I set my bedroll?" he asked.

"We'll sleep close to the fire," said the trader.

Thomas nodded wearily and laid out both his and her bedroll. Then he drew off his boots and slipped between the blankets.

There would be no talk tonight.

The next morning she awoke beside Thomas, upon the dirt floor. The scent of earth hung heavy about them. She crept out to use the outhouse and found none. She discovered some privacy in the cottonwoods that lined the river.

Through the trees, Sarah spotted a flash of color and instantly dropped to her knees. She peered over the bare branches of the brush all about her and saw the familiar stripes of Water Blossom's blanket. Sarah found her stooped beside a narrow stream that she had not noted upon arrival yesterday. Water Blossom used the side of the wooden bucket to break the thin crust of ice that clung about the reeds.

Sarah moved closer.

"Good morning," said Sarah.

Water Blossom started and dropped her bucket. She recovered herself, and the bucket, quickly.

"A cold morning," said Water Blossom.

Sarah lifted the full bucket from the bank.

"I thought about what you said last night. I'm going to speak to Thomas today."

Water Blossom cast Sarah a dubious look, but said nothing. The woman was devilishly hard to speak with.

She sat on the bank and only then did Sarah note that Water Blossom had drawn off her footgear to retrieve the water. She brushed the grass and dirt from her pink wet feet and pulled on fur-lined moccasins. Then she cocked her head and listened. Sarah listened, as well, but all she heard was the nicker of horses.

"If you talk today, then go now."

Sarah's smile faded and the bucket slipped from her fingers. She lifted her skirts and dashed back through the tall grass.

Rounding the sod house, Sarah stopped dead in her tracks. There before her sat Thomas on his horse. Sarah eyed his saddlebags and bedroll and then Roubideaux, also mounted, with the reins of the packhorse in his hand.

"I was just coming to find you," said Thomas, but the nervous shifting of his eyes told another tale.

Sarah forgot all about slaying dragons as she ran forward to grasp his horse's reins.

"Where are you going?"

Thomas dismounted. "Pierre thinks it better if you stay here with Water Blossom."

"You are going without me?"

"It's not safe."

Panic seized her heart. She clung to his coat and tugged. He stroked her windblown hair.

"Do you know what will happen if I lose you, too?" she asked.

He met her gaze and she saw that he understood her. She wouldn't survive it. Thomas stared a moment longer and then his hand settled at the back of her head. She knew he meant to kiss her. She tipped her head in welcome as his lips descended. His warm mouth slashed across her chilled skin. His kiss was fierce and possessive. She melted against him, emitting a sound of pure satisfaction as he deepened the kiss. Her arms encircled him as she demanded more and his tongue flicked out to dance with hers.

At last he drew back. Reluctantly, she let him go. Still holding her draped across his arm, he turned to face Roubideaux.

"We're taking her."

He righted Sarah. Roubideaux removed his hat and slapped it on his thigh.

"We agreed."

Thomas said nothing, only stared in icy silence as Sarah's heart hammered in her chest.

Roubideaux waved his hat. "Oh, all right! I need my wife anyways." The woman in question appeared carrying both water buckets. "Saddle two more horses."

Water Blossom nodded.

Before Roubideaux could change his mind, the women were saddled and ready. They turned their mounts north toward Indian Territory.

Chapter Twenty-Three

The arduous journey north took two days. Water Blossom fastened a travois behind one of the mules, upon which were the skins to make a teepee and most of the trade goods. Each night Sarah helped erect the dwelling. She was astonished at how quickly the tripod of poles became a snug enclosure. The fire of buffalo chips smoked, but cast out the chill that riding forced into her bones.

Sarah longed for a few moments alone with Thomas, but Roubideaux seemed perpetually at his side and she found no opportunity to speak with him.

On the morning of the day after they left the trading post, riders appear on the horizon, headed in their direction. Sarah's heart beat with terror and hope as she recognized a party of Indians outnumbering them two to one.

Roubideaux turned toward Sarah.

"Cover your head and keep it covered."

Water Blossom drew alongside her, giving Sarah the great heavy buffalo robe she wore instead of a coat. She pulled the heavy hide up and over Sarah's head, dousing the flame of her hair.

Thomas's horse shifted nervously, as if sensing his master's unease.

Water Blossom came to the front beside her husband, as if displaying herself to the braves. The warriors halted out of range of their rifles and the two groups faced off for what seemed like hours to Sarah, who sat rigid in her saddle.

At last, two of the Indians approached. Water Blossom called out to them as they grew near and her hail was answered in kind.

Sarah strained to hear the words exchanged, even knowing she could not understand them. The tone seemed civilized, if not the language.

The warriors turned their horses and moved to the head of their group, escorting them to the others.

Sarah tried to reassure herself that these Indians would help them, but she could not keep her anxiety from making her breathing erratic. She recalled the last time a group this large had surrounded her party, offering friendship and then demanding bribes before butchering the men and stealing her child.

The cold metallic taste of fear filled her mouth. She was dizzy with it as her horse followed along at the back of the group.

At midday, they crossed a river and then followed its meandering course. Sarah noted the frost gathering on the reeds and the fragile layer of ice clinging to their stems in the quiet eddies where the shallow water touched the bank.

She glanced ahead at Water Blossom, who rode without coat or cloak, and felt guilty for accepting her robe. She reached into her pack, nearly losing the heavy hide as she retrieved the coat Thomas had bought for his daughter. She handed it to Water Blossom, who accepted the offering, nodding her thanks.

As they rode, Sarah tried to picture her reunion with Lucie. They would hug and cry and rock back and forth in each other's arms. She could almost smell the fragrance of Lucie's hair as she conjured her daughter in her mind. Had she grown? She was a beanstalk reaching for the sky when the Indians took her.

Did she get enough to eat?

The day grew colder as gray clouds swept in. Sarah stared at the sky, deciding it was too cold to rain. By midafternoon the

first snowflakes arrived. These were not the gentle perfect cas-
cade of her memories of snowfall in Illinois. These were ice crystals flung by a savage wind. Sarah pulled the robe close about
her face and ducked her chin to her chest. A glance at her horse
showed her mount's freckled head also hanging as he blinked
his long lashes against the assault of ice.

Because of her posture, she did not see the village until they
passed the first teepees. Shocked at her inattention, she straightened to see shadowy forms of Indians standing in the icy wind
as their party passed. Sarah searched the draped Indians for her
daughter but saw no sign of her.

They were expected, it seemed, because no one made any
move to hinder their progress toward the heart of the village.

Roubideaux halted the riders and dismounted. From his pack
mule he retrieved ten knife blades and presented them to the lead
warrior of their escort.

With a nod of acceptance, the man led the other warriors
away. Sarah peeked out of the gap in her buffalo robe and saw
Thomas standing beside Roubideaux. Water Blossom was
speaking to two men.

Thomas came to stand beside Sarah, his head reaching her
thigh as she sat mounted above him. She dipped to hear him.

"We're going inside to speak with the chief."

Sarah made a move to dismount and Thomas held up a hand.

"Roubideaux, Water Blossom and I are going. You are to
stay here."

"Here on horseback?" she said, not quite believing she would
be left sitting in the snow.

"No, just outside that teepee."

Sarah gasped. "But why?"

"This is a gathering of men. Water Blossom is our translator,
so she is permitted."

Sarah did not argue. She only slipped stiffly from her horse
and stood beside Thomas. She opened the hood enough to reveal her face to him and then she kissed him.

"Be careful," she said.

He seemed speechless and only nodded. Was he shocked by the kiss or by her compliance?

She did not know.

Thomas followed Roubideaux, his boots crunching in the new layer of snow. He paused at a large teepee decorated with two green waving lines running around the base.

This was the home of Two Rivers, chief of the Sweetwater tribe. Roubideaux stooped to enter and Thomas grasped his arm.

"Is Sarah safe out there alone?"

"She's Two Rivers's guest. Nothing will happen to her while she's with us."

Thomas glanced back to see Sarah settle on the icy ground beside the teepee. He drew a deep breath and followed Roubideaux into the open gap. Air, warmed by the fire, carried the scent of wood smoke and tobacco to him as he entered the old warrior's tent.

Three men waited within. Thomas straightened and sat where Roubideaux indicated. Behind them, Water Blossom lowered the burden of trade goods she carried and closed the tent flap.

Thomas sat stiffly on the ground as gifts were presented to Two Rivers. The chief accepted a red Hudson's Bay blanket, casting it over his shoulders and nodding his approval. He passed an ivory pipe head to the man on his right and a two headed axe blade to the serious young warrior on his left.

Roubideaux spoke in what Thomas thought was passable Sioux. Then he pointed at Thomas and spoke again. The chief nodded, but the young one's eyes narrowed as he was introduced. Thomas held his gaze until the warrior looked away.

Roubideaux turned to Thomas. "The one on the right is the chief's son. Don't know about the one on the left. He's young to be on the chief's war council, but he's tied up in this some-how."

The scouts had given them no information on white captives and Thomas was anxious to hear what the trader had learned, but he waited in tense silence as Water Blossom took over, her light lilting voice carrying a respectful tone. Thomas listened to the exchange, wishing he had spent more time at the fort learning from the translator so he could understand the meaning of their words.

Roubideaux spoke to him again. "Two Rivers wants to trade but says they have no white captives. He's putting me in a spot. I'm not going to call him a liar, not and live to tell of it."

"But the boy said they have my daughter."

"They might have traded her off."

Thomas wondered what to do and his eyes settled on the young buck with the poker face. For the first time, he noted the eagle feathers tied in his hair and a thought struck him.

"Water Blossom, what's that fellow's name?"

She asked and then repeated his name. "Eagle Dancer."

Eagle Dancer—where had he heard that before? The boy! He'd said the warrior holding Lucie was called Eagle Dancer. The same man? Thomas fixed his stare upon the man. Yes. It explained his presence here and his sour expression.

He turned to Roubideaux. "Tell them I'm the girl's father, this girl." He flipped open the photo for the warriors to see.

The buck's poker face slipped as his eyes rounded in recognition.

"Tell Two Rivers that the boy called Sky Fox saw my girl with Eagle Dancer. They have my girl and I want her back."

Thomas pinned his glare on Eagle Dancer, who lifted his chin and said not one word. The chief was talking now. Roubideaux translated in a low whisper.

"He says they got the girl, but she ain't no captive on account of Eagle Dancer married her. He calls her part of his tribe." Roubideaux put a hand on Thomas's shoulder. "I'm sorry."

The rage swallowed Thomas whole. He sprang to his feet and lunged for the man who had defiled his daughter. Roubideaux was quicker and leapt to his feet and threw himself at Thomas. They landed against the tent poles with Thomas on his back.

"You'll get us killed," said Roubideaux, gripping Thomas's lapels. "Now sit down or, so help me, I'll gaff you myself."

Thomas's ears rang with his fury, but he sat.

Roubideaux spoke in apologetic tones as he motioned to Thomas. Water Blossom cast Thomas a meaningful glance and pressed her palm toward the floor as if urging calm.

Thomas breathed heavily through his nose, trying not to look at the man across the fire who had taken his little girl. The weight of the gun at his hip seemed heavier than usual, as if the cold steel called for justice.

But if he acted, they would surely kill them and Lucie would remain a captive. Or worse. She might end up like Alice French.

Water Blossom leaned close and held his hand.

"Your daughter is alive. She is here. This is good."

Thomas nodded mechanically. Yes, she was alive. He tried to focus on that and not the fury that beat against his ribs like an eagle swooping to strike.

Oh, dear God, what would Sarah say?

The chief pointed at Thomas and spoke.

"He wants to know if you will take a trade for the girl. It's the custom for the groom to buy his bride from her family. Eagle Dancer offers ten buffalo hides and four horses for your daughter."

Thomas gritted his teeth. "Tell the son of a bitch that I'll take his hide and my daughter."

Roubideaux rubbed his neck. "It's a good offer."

Thomas stared incredulously at Roubideaux.

"She's not for sale."

"You sure? She has laid with this young buck. She might be carrying his child."

Thomas felt sick to his stomach.

"White folks don't take kindly to girls who been through what your gal has. Be lucky to find her a husband at all. Might be best to leave her here where she's wanted."

"No."

"We could tell your gal she's dead. She wouldn't have to know."

Thomas considered the suggestion for the time it took to draw a breath.

"I want her back."

Roubideaux shook his head in disgust, as if he was being unreasonable. Then he continued to speak to the chief for some time and did not translate. At last he rose.

"We're going."

"What happened?" asked Thomas as he stood.

"Two Rivers won't trade away a man's wife. He says we can stay and trade, but not for Lucie. He offers one night's hospitality and then we gotta go. Better than we deserve after you attacked them."

"What about Lucie?"

"You best put that behind you, son. They ain't giving her up. Far as they're concerned, she's part of the family."

Thomas stared at the stony faces of the three men across the fire. He'd never felt so impotent in his life. Without adequate manpower, he could not force them to give up Lucie and they would not accept a ransom.

"Tell them that this girl does not belong to the Sioux. She belongs with her mother. What they have done is wrong."

"I ain't saying that. We're lucky to keep our scalps after your little stunt."

Thomas stood his ground.

"They're past listening—just like you." Roubideaux grabbed Thomas's arm and shoved him out of the tent.

"Dear God, what will I tell Sarah?" He hadn't realized he'd spoken aloud until Roubideaux answered his question.

"If you've a brain in your head, you'll tell her the girl died of fever."

Thomas straightened and glanced about. "Where is Sarah?"

"She wait in a teepee for us," said Water Blossom.

"What about Lucie?" he asked.

"They will keep her under guard until we leave. You will not see her."

The snow had stopped and the air now hung still and bitter cold. A boy waited to take them to a teepee.

"Might better leave tonight." Roubideaux tugged at his bushy beard. "I don't fancy them changing their minds and stealing my horses."

Water Blossom scowled, her voice full of indignation. "You are a guest. They do not steal from you."

Thomas thought that they had already stolen a precious gift. Would he never see the face of his daughter? He ducked into the teepee the boy indicated. He thought he could not feel worse until he saw Sarah rising to her feet, a look of hope pinned on her worried face.

Thomas bowed his head.

Chapter Twenty-Four

Sarah could not contain her grief and sobbed in Thomas's arms much of the night. To come so close to her daughter and not to see her. Her heart was breaking.

Lucie lived, but as a captive bride to a savage. How could fate be so cruel?

Roubideaux and Water Blossom sat silent across the fire as Sarah wailed. Finally, Water Blossom laid out their bedding, and she and her husband disappeared beneath a buffalo robe.

Thomas stroked Sarah's head as she wept softly.

"I'm sorry, Sarah," he whispered.

The knife in her heart twisted. This man was sorry. After all she had done, he had regrets.

"Oh, Thomas, are we to lose Lucie, too?"

He sighed, his breath fanning her cheeks. "She's alive. We might still be able to get to her. But tomorrow, you're going to have to leave her behind."

Sarah clung to him and pinched her eyes shut. "I'd give anything to bring her home."

"We'll bring her home. Just give it a little more time."

"She doesn't have any boots."

Thomas's strong arms held her. "The young buck will provide those things, until we have her back."

"Do they know about the army? Did you tell them they have orders to kill all hostiles harboring captives?"

"No. I didn't. He might decide killing us is a good way to be sure the army doesn't know about Lucie."

There was wisdom in this. How she envied his cool calculation.

"I can't think like that. Even now you don't lose your head."

He smiled. "Back in the tent, with the chief, I nearly killed that young buck that took Lucie."

"What?"

"Roubideaux stopped me. Just so you know, I don't always use my head."

"You're lucky they didn't kill you."

"Roubideaux said the same."

The teepee grew silent again. Thomas poked at the red coals with a stick.

She had waited several days for the right time or a moment's privacy to speak to him and had found neither. She was through waiting for the perfect opportunity. For all she knew, Two Rivers would murder them all in their beds. Water Blossom had assured them they were protected as guests, but Sarah had no confidence in these people's honor.

"I've been doing a great deal of thinking and I want to apologize to you, Thomas, for all the pain I've caused."

He could not have looked more stunned if she had lifted a burning log and struck him in the forehead.

"Sarah?"

"I shouldn't have married him. I'm so sorry, Thomas."

"You thought I was dead." He used reason again.

"But it didn't stop me from loving you. Can you forgive me?"

"I forgive you, Sarah." His hand reached out, bridging the gap between them. Fingers entwined. "I just can't forgive myself."

She inched closer, nearly holding her breath. "For what?"

"Leaving you, taking Hyatt." His gaze became unfocused.

"What happened?"

He nodded, as if expecting that it was past time to tell her.

"He wanted to tag along. Always tagged along. Back when we were kids, I'd throw rocks at him so he'd go home. But he had his teeth around the bit this time. He wouldn't turn back. Pa was against him going and Ma, well, she couldn't see giving up her baby. They tried, too, but nothing they said dissuaded him."

She stroked his shoulders, feeling the tension there, building with each breath.

"We were crossing the desert when the Navajo attacked." He looked in her eyes. "You've seen enough dying, Sarah. I don't want to burden you."

"You will tell me this time, Thomas. Tell me all of it."

Words poured out of him like seawater from a drowning man.

"I hid him in the wagon as we faced them. But there were too many. I killed one and two more came at me. I couldn't fire fast enough. They dragged me from the wagon and hit me with one of their clubs. I couldn't see past the blood. I heard Hyatt screaming and smelled the smoke." He grasped Sarah's hand. "They burned the wagon, Sarah. They burned it with Hyatt still inside."

He saw the horror of that day reflected in Sarah's face.

"I couldn't see, but I heard him calling. 'Thomas, help me. Help me.'" His shoulders sagged as Hyatt's long ago screams still rang in his ears.

"I blacked out."

He glanced to Sarah to see her taking it in, the horror, the guilt and finally the twisting remorse that held him to this day. He didn't see the cruelty of fate, only his own mistakes and all the things he might have done to avert this tragedy.

His voice cracked as he spoke. "Ma made me promise to look after him."

"Thomas, you couldn't stop it. You couldn't save him."

"I wish it had been me."

"Then no one could help me save our daughter."

That brought him back to her again.

"But we haven't saved her."

"We will."

He looked at her, perhaps rattled by the confidence in her tone. She wondered how he had survived what had killed so many.

"How did you escape?"

"I didn't, just blacked out. Next I knew I was lying on a U.S. Army cot, burned and blind."

"Blind!" Sarah gripped his arm.

He pushed back the hair from his forehead, showing the thin white scar that snaked across his temple. She had not seen it against the graying hair.

"After a month, Doc said I'd likely be blind my whole miserable life."

She gasped. "Oh, Thomas." How horrible for him. Alone and without his sight. Why hadn't he written? This thought germinated another that rooted. The idea grew into a mighty oak of certainty.

"That's when you wrote Samuel."

He nodded and then reached for her, burying his face in the crook of her neck. She thought she heard a ragged cry. She stroked his head and cooed. At last his breathing returned to normal.

His face shone wet with tears.

She held her breath a moment, gathering strength for what she had to say.

"Thomas, this wasn't your fault. None of it, not Hyatt following or me following. Hyatt would forgive you. And as for what Samuel did, it was wrong—so wrong."

"I think it's what I deserved."

She gripped his chin and looked into his eyes. "No, Thomas. It's not. We deserved a chance. We deserved the truth and both of us deserve forgiveness."

He looped an arm around her shoulder and sighed wearily. "Maybe so, maybe so."

He lay back, drawing her beneath the buffalo robes. Their bodies entwined like honeysuckle about a climbing rose.

She felt at ease beside him once more. She wondered if she should tell him that she still loved him, but hesitated, fearing to lose this tender moment.

Tomorrow, she promised. She would tell him then.

"We won't give up, Sarah," whispered Thomas. "Not ever."

Sarah breathed in the scent of Thomas and the buffalo hide, allowing herself to draw comfort from his presence. Perhaps the chief would change his mind and return her daughter. Perhaps.

Sarah's eyes drifted closed and her breathing grew heavy.

Someone shook her shoulder. Sarah blinked up at Water Blossom. "We must go ready the horses."

Sarah sat up, pushing her tangled hair from her eyes. Morning had caught her unawares. She glanced about to see that Thomas had left their bed.

The hope that seemed so bright last night shivered in the cold dawn of the Sioux camp.

"Keep your robe up over your hair," reminded Water Blossom as they made their way to the horse corral.

Sarah tugged her hat down low and tied her muffler about her head and face.

As they approached the penned animals, a woman stepped before Water Blossom. The two engaged in conversation. The tone seemed civilized, but Sarah saw her friend's eyes widen at the woman's words.

Water Blossom motioned to the woman, who looked to be somewhat older than Sarah.

"This is Yellow Bird, the mother of Eagle Dancer," she said.

Sarah shook her head in confusion.

Water Blossom's eyes rounded meaningfully. "The warrior who has wed your daughter."

Sarah's attention snapped to the woman again as Water Blossom continued.

"She says your daughter has cast an evil spell on the heart of her son."

Her friend turned back to the woman and Sarah stood on tiptoe as she strained to understand their words. At last Water Blossom translated.

"She says she will take me to your daughter. She wants her gone from the village."

"We will take her away," said Sarah.

Water Blossom shook her head. "I have said that. She says that we cannot. The sentries will never let us pass and her son will know of her deceit."

Sarah's mind reeled at the thought of seeing Lucie.

"We must sneak her away."

Water Blossom spoke to the woman and then to Sarah. "She says the chief has posted guards at your daughter's teepee until after we leave. But she wants the girl gone and says she will kill her if she does not go."

Sarah took a step toward the woman, reaching for her knife. Water Blossom slipped between them, as the mother of her enemy backed away.

"This will not help," said Water Blossom.

Then the idea came to Sarah. All at once and completely formed, the solution sprang from her mind like Athena from Zeus.

"We could both go. Once inside, Lucie can take my robes and leave in my place."

Water Blossom stared in astonishment. When she found her tongue she said, "Your daughter would not wish to leave you behind."

Her hope burst, for Sarah believed this was true. Then she knew what must be done. Could she do it? Did she have the strength to come so close and not speak to her child?

Yes. To save Lucie, she could do anything.

"I won't let her see me. You bring my clothing to her and tell her you've come for her. Don't mention me. Tell her to keep silent and take my place in line."

Water Blossom looked doubtful.

"It will work." Sarah motioned to their accomplice. "Tell her."

Water Blossom did and the woman nodded. The women waited as she gathered her things from the teepee. Sarah collected the necessary garments and added the new coat Thomas had purchased for Lucie.

"Will she not recognize the robes of her mother?" asked Water Blossom.

Sarah looked at the traveling dress, muffler and coat that Thomas had provided. "These are new. She has not seen them."

Water Blossom accepted the clothing and spoke to the other woman. In a moment they were off, following Yellow Bird.

They stopped as Yellow Bird spoke to the trader's wife.

Water Blossom nodded and then turned to Sarah. "Do not show your face to the guards as we enter. This way, three women go in and three women come out. Your daughter must not see you. Once we are away, the sentries will leave and Yellow Bird has promised me she will lead you from the village and put you on our trail."

Sarah nodded, caring only to get Lucie safely away. "Yes. Where is Lucie?"

"She waits in the teepee just ahead."

Sarah's heart squeezed with joy. She was so close. Would this work?

She stiffened her spine against the uncertainty. It had to.

Sarah's heart ached as she recalled that she could not speak to her child or kiss her goodbye. Sarah exhaled against the pain tearing through her.

She had little faith that Yellow Bird would lead her to safety. But if Lucie could escape, it would be worth the sacrifice. Thomas would care for Lucie now.

"Are you ready?" asked Water Blossom.

Sarah nodded. "If something happens, tell Lucie I love her and see that she gets to Thomas."

"This I will do." Water Blossom smiled and Sarah lifted the robe to cover her head.

Water Blossom clasped her hand and led her along.

Through the small opening in her robe, she spied two sentries beside a small teepee. One stood as they approached.

Yellow Bird spoke and they waved them in.

Sarah lowered her head, ducked into the tent and sat, clutching the robe with all her might. It took all her will not to toss the hide back and seize her child.

She heard Yellow Bird speak, then a familiar voice replied in Sioux.

Lucie!

Sarah started to rise and then forced herself back down. There was a rustling sound. Sarah lifted her gaze from the trampled grass to stare at her daughter's bare legs and new moccasins. Next, Lucie's tattered dress fell about her ankles. More rustling followed and a brief exchange of words. At last Water Blossom touched Sarah's shoulder.

"We go," she whispered.

Sarah lifted her head in time to see Lucie dressed in her mother's clothing, with the muffler wrapped about her head. Water Blossom draped a buffalo robe about Lucie's shoulders and glanced back, lifting a hand in silent farewell.

Tears sprang from Water Blossom's eyes.

A choking sob rose in Sarah's throat, but she made no sound as Lucie turned. Sarah lowered her head before their eyes could meet. There was a rush of cold air and the thump of the wood frame as the hide flap fell closed.

Sarah straightened.

She was alone.

Chapter Twenty-Five

Thomas glanced back once more to find Sarah still riding behind Water Blossom, her head lowered so it nearly reached her saddle horn. She seemed the picture of grief and misery. He had tried to speak to her earlier but Water Blossom had interceded, telling him that Sarah had requested that he leave her in peace until she chose to speak to him.

He knew it was hard for her to abandon Lucie, but they had ridden most of the morning and still she sat dejected, staring at her saddle horn. He gritted his teeth and tried to turn away, but found he could no longer honor her request. He laid the reins across his horse's neck, bringing him about.

Water Blossom eyed him as he passed but did not move to hinder him. He had little time to consider the worry in her eyes before he drew next to Sarah.

She seemed smaller, frailer from her burden. He waited for her to note his appearance but when she did not, he spoke.

"Sarah?"

Her chin lifted and Sarah's eyes met his, but the face was that of a stranger. He gasped in horror as he stared. Then recognition dawned. He knew this face that so resembled his own.

His daughter drew back the pink muffler covering her head

and her strawberry blond hair shone bright in the gray morning. What had Sarah said when he asked if the child was his? Something like, "Wait until you see her, Thomas. You'll know."

And so he did.

He smiled at his daughter, the girl he had only imagined.

"Lucie?"

She nodded.

He reached out to stroke her cheek and the muffler fell to her throat, revealing the ugly blue marks upon her chin. He recoiled before he could stop himself and saw the shame in his daughter's eyes.

Anger pulsed in his veins as he recognized the marks the savages had drawn upon his little girl's pretty face. The urge to kill someone nearly blinded him.

His jaw locked in rage as he looked about for the enemy. It was then that he first realized Sarah was not here.

Thomas craned his head about, becoming frantic.

"Sarah!" he called. Then turned to his daughter, grasping her arm.

"Where is she? Where is your mother?"

Lucie stammered. "I—I don't know. I never saw her."

She followed the direction of his stare, back the way they had come across the frozen wasteland of prairie now dusted with snow. Overhead, low dark clouds swept in from the north.

He spurred his horse to Water Blossom's. The trader's wife did not wait for his question.

"She stayed behind so Lucie's captors would not see that we have stolen your daughter."

The surge of terror that ripped through him was unlike anything he had ever experienced. He thought his heart might burst from his fear.

Sarah was back there with the enemy. They would kill her, just like Alice French.

Thomas wheeled his horse about. "I'm going back."

"The ones who helped us promised to steal her from the village and set her on our path."

Thomas shouted to Roubideaux. "Take them to the trading post."

Roubideaux's face turned red as he glared from Lucie to his wife. "Damn the post. Those Sioux figure out this double cross, they'll be on us like a pack of wolves. We're making for Laramie. Come along if you don't like dying."

Thomas turned to Lucie. "Follow them. Don't fall behind."

Lucie nodded and then lifted the soft muffler up to hide her chin as the stranger spurred his horse, retracing their path at a gallop. He had looked at her as if he knew her and he called her by name. He said her mother was there. She didn't understand what was happening.

"Move out," shouted the grizzled old man.

Lucie lifted her gaze to the billowing clouds and tightened her buffalo robe about her shoulders. She had never had a robe of her own, and she intended not to lose this one. The Indian woman with the kind face, riding before her, had also given her a dress, a wool coat and the pink scarf.

Lucie's spotted horse needed no urging to follow, responding before she had time to lift the reins. The pretty Appaloosa had more freckles than she did.

Lucie smiled at that. It didn't last. Soon her brow wrinkled in confusion again.

For so long she had dreamed of rescue and could scarcely credit that she was now away. After months of waiting, her retrieval had happened with a suddenness she did not understand.

Yellow Bird shouting at her as she changed from the tattered cotton into a fine blue dress. A strange woman draped her head with the pink scarf and then a buffalo robe. She had kept the calf-high moccasins Eagle Dancer had given her as a wedding gift.

And who was the other woman, the shrouded one who had stood silent and apart?

The hairs on Lucie's neck prickled as she mulled over what

had just happened. The strange man looking so stunned to see her. What had he said? Where is your mother? His look of panic haunted her.

With a shake of her shoulders, she cast off the vague dread. She was away, miles and miles away. This leader, with the beard, would take her to her mother, then she would get her answers—if they got away.

She glanced over her shoulder for signs of pursuit. The sound she heard was not a war cry but only the rising wind shrieking over the prairie like a banshee. Next came the ice, like stinging shards of glass, pelting her exposed hands and face. She withdrew further beneath the robe and huddled as the gale lifted her skirts, sending a blast of frigid air all the way up her bloomers.

They rode on, as the storm grew fierce. She fought not to lose sight of the mule whose travois scrapped along the icy path. By now Eagle Dancer would have noticed her absence and set out in pursuit. He would be so angry. Lucie's heart pounded in her throat.

Even her husband could not find her in this storm. She was half-grateful for the savage wind that turned her surroundings into a rolling sea of white, until she remembered the man and his wild gallop north.

As her feet grew numb and her bottom throbbed from the long ride, she began to worry less about capture and more about being lost in the storm.

Did the man know where he was going? She could barely see the line of horses, let alone the trail.

When the horse before her stopped, her mount dutifully halted before she could draw back the reins. Her gelding's head hung as if he were too weary to lift it and ice crystals coated his long lashes. Only his pricked ears told Lucie he was alert.

Why had they stopped? It took a moment for her eyes to discern the building. A house?

Her breathing quickened as she tried to recall when she had last seen a sod house. It seemed a lifetime.

The woman dismounted and motioned for her to follow. But she seemed rooted in place, disbelieving her own eyes. Her lip began to quiver as a tiny choked sound emerged from her strangled throat. Was this real? Had she reached freedom at last?

Her gaze remained fixed upon the sod structure, afraid somehow that should she glance away or even blink, the vision might be torn away from her once more.

A tiny seed of hope rooted in her heart. What if her mother was waiting for her just behind those doors?

With renewed energy she threw her leg across her saddle, ignoring the sting of tears that wetted her numb face.

She groaned as she slid to the ground, but her mount gave a sigh of relief. She followed the others, leading her gelding to the barn.

As she crossed the threshold the howl of the gale changed. She no longer felt the wind buffeting her. Now it wailed like a stubborn child denied entrance.

She stood trembling in the darkness. The sweet familiar scent of hay filled her nostrils. A flame sparked as the man struck a match and lit a lantern hanging by a wire from an overhead beam.

"Get the door," he shouted.

Lucie, now used to jumping to fulfill an order, dropped the reins and dashed back to slide the door along its rollers. When she had finished, she leaned against the solid planking, panting. Her breath came in little white puffs of vapor. The man now balled his fists at his sides. Lucie recognized the mutinous rage twisting his features and glanced about the enclosure in search of a place to escape.

When she glanced back she saw he stood before the Indian woman.

"Do you know what you've done?" he shouted. "They'll be on us as soon as they realize you've stolen her. They'll kill us all!"

She made no reply as he loomed over her. Lucie eyed a wicked-looking pitchfork and inched closer to the weapon. The ogre spewed twin streams of white vapor from his flaring nostrils over his frosted beard. He seemed, to her, a fire-breathing dragon.

"Answer me!" he shouted.

She didn't.

"Unsaddle these horses." He stormed out the door leaving Lucie alone with the silent Indian.

The woman exchanged the bridles for harnesses on the horses and faced the storm once more to remove the travois and collect both mules. Lucie forked hay into the crib for the animals. It took more time to drag the travois into the enclosure. Next, they stacked the supplies against the wall.

The Indian finished by chopping the ice from the large barrel to reach the water beneath. She filled the horses' buckets and then straightened, motioning to the door. Together they rolled the barrier aside and then closed it once more. The woman grasped Lucie's hand and pulled her along.

When Lucie glanced forward she could not see the house. Terrified of being lost in this sea of white, she reached to clasp the hand of the woman who held her wrist. Together, they stood paralyzed in the blinding storm. Lucie's heart seemed to stop as the snow swirled and then, there it was, just ahead and to the right. They ran now, dashing headlong for the safety of the sod structure until they touched the rough clods of earth. Only then did Lucie draw a breath.

On the leeward side of the house, the snow did not blind them. She noted the small shuttered window and, at last, the front door. The woman fumbled for the handle, lifting the latch.

The man turned toward the door as they entered, then returned to the business of tending his new fire.

Lucie looked around.

Empty wooden crates filled the shelves along the sod walls. Perhaps in the early fall this was a trading post, but now it seemed a cold, dusty shell. More empty crates, once holding liquor, lay stacked behind the door.

The woman moved forward to relieve the man of the fire tending and he sat on a low stool, his hands outstretched to the flame. Lucie crept forward, lured by the promise of warmth, yet wary of the man. He did not want her here.

The trader muttered.

"Never be welcome again. You've ruined us, you know that. Burned our bridges for good and all."

Lucie hung in the shadows as the woman chopped ice from the water barrel and set the chunks in a black kettle. Lucie huddled in her robe as the woman sliced potatoes and added barley to the pot, and then set it over the stove. After the man ate, the woman offered Lucie a bowl. Lucie nodded at the kindness. She had not eaten for so long.

Nothing ever tasted as good as the hot meal. It warmed her inside and out. When she had finished, the woman set aside her bowl to refill Lucie's. Lucie thanked her in Sioux.

The wind battered the roof, stealing through the crevices, and Lucie worried about the man who had ridden back. Perhaps the Indian thought the same thing, for she stared often toward the door.

"Are you taking me to my mother?"

The woman continued to stare toward the entrance. "Do you recall the third woman in the teepee?"

Lucie remembered the stooped figure clutching the robe about her face. She had denied the possibility that her heart whispered to her. Now, she recalled the dark woolen skirt of a white woman. The bowl slipped from Lucie's fingers and clattered to the floor, rolling in a lazy circle in the dirt. The woman's eyes reflected her sadness.

"She made me promise not to tell you until we were safely away. Yellow Bird said she would lead your mother from the village, but I do not trust her."

Lucie listened to the howling wind.

"They're out there in the storm."

Chapter Twenty-Six

Thomas planted his heels into his horse's sides.

He rode with his heart in his throat, barely able to draw a breath past the terror that threatened to consume him. To lose her again—he couldn't. He wouldn't.

He leaned over the horse's neck and pushed for greater speed. Snow swirled behind them as they galloped along.

Sarah was back here, somewhere.

His stomach clenched as he imagined what would happen when they found her in Lucie's place. How could she do this?

Didn't she know the danger?

But she did. Of course she understood that they would kill her, but she did it anyway—to save her child.

How would he save her?

He didn't know. Likely he couldn't, but that wouldn't stop him. Only death would stop him from reaching her this time.

His life without her had been a poor, wretched thing. The rich texture, bright colors and delicious tastes all died when he left her behind. He'd not do it again.

Not again.

He pressed low over the horse's withers, squinting against the blossoming storm. Visibility dropped and the wind howled, throwing ice crystals against his face like bits of sand. The un-broken downward grade told him the village was near. He saw a brown mass lying on the trail and registered only that some animal lay out in the open.

He galloped on, intent on his goal. It took several moments for his mind to register that a lone animal would never lie out in such a wind. He drew back on the reins, bringing his mount to a trot, then a walk and finally a stop. He planted a hand on the horse's rump to gaze back the way he had come. A prickling sensation crawled up his neck. Likely an elk had died and been left by his fellows.

He looked at the road ahead, but instead of proceeding on his course, he laid the reins across the horse's neck, bringing him about.

Blowing snow now coated even with the small, huddled form. He moved closer and saw it was no elk. A large tanned hide covered a body. Thomas clenched his jaw and swung down to the ground. Hope and fear stiffened his legs as he crept forward.

His winded horse stamped restlessly as Thomas gripped the hide and tore it away.

He released his held breath to the shrieking wind as he saw the moccasins, leggings and fringed dress. An Indian woman then, lost or abandoned in the storm. He did not know if he should be relieved or disappointed.

Perhaps she could be used as a bargaining chip. If she wasn't dead, he might be able to trade her for Sarah.

Her head still lay obscured by the hide in his hand. He gasped as bright auburn hair lifted in the gale wind.

"Sarah!"

Her head lolled as he drew her to him. No. Please don't let her be gone.

He stroked her pale cheek, finding her skin as cold as the snow upon which she rested. He pressed an ear to her chest and listened but could hear nothing above the whistling wind.

He thrust his hand down the front of her loose fitting hide dress. He could not feel a heartbeat, but her flesh radiated heat.

Heat. If she was warm, she might still live. He gathered her in the buffalo robe and carried her to his mount, draping her over the gelding's withers as he mounted behind her. Once astride he drew her up against him, gripping her tight with one hand as he gathered the reins with the other.

Then he turned away from the wind. Time seemed to freeze with the snow all about him. Ice formed on the hair at his neck as the storm pushed him along. The fort was too far. He would have to make for the trading post and pray they reached it before nightfall. He rode on, hoping the heat between them came from her body and not only his.

The sky darkened, though whether from the storm or the approaching night he could not tell. The blizzard grew in ferocity until it seemed a living thing.

The trail was no longer visible. Thomas could see nothing through the hailstorm of snow and ice. He had thought he could not be more frightened until he realized he might lose his way in this blizzard.

Sarah needed warmth, a fire and a blanket. If he could not find the trading post she would die. He paused for a moment, wondering if he still stood on the path. Uncertainty swirled within him like the blowing snow all around. Where was he?

How far to the post?

He could already have passed it by, come within feet of his destination and never known. What should he do—go forward, turn back?

At last, he pressed his heels to the sides of his tired horse. To stop was to die. He would walk to hell and back to save her. But how did he fight this vaporous, frozen enemy?

He had only the wind to guide him. The ice blasting against his back meant he still rode south, unless the wind had turned or he had drifted off the path.

Doubt billowed within him, but he urged his horse on. The

gelding's head drooped, radiating exhaustion. His mount looked done in, ready to lie down and die. He tried to pat the horse's neck and found his hand clumsy, as if refusing to obey his commands.

"Come on, Buck, take us home."

The minutes turned into hours and the cold stole away his strength. He could no longer grip the reins and his toes went dead as a block of wood. He fumbled to draw the buffalo robe tight about Sarah, afraid to look at her still, pale face.

How much longer could she last? Was she gone already?

He drew a breath past the panic.

Doubt dogged every step as he strained to see the trading post.

Something appeared in the field of white. Panic gave way to a silver strand of hope. Just ahead, he thought, a few more steps. But the wind roared and the shadows shifted showing him that nothing lay before him but the yawning jaws of the blizzard.

Again and again, he dared to hope and each time the illusion dissolved like a shadow over the moon.

He admitted, at last, that he could not save them. Only a miracle would bring them through this. With a sinking feeling, he accepted that he had missed the post and they now walked through a frozen nightmare.

He had never felt such bitter cold.

Should he stop? And do what, he asked himself? Hunker down and wait out the storm? What if it went on all night? They should forge on in hopes of shelter. To travel miles and miles astray as the storm stole his strength and killed his love seemed madness.

But if he stopped, here on the open prairie, with no shelter or fire, it would be to die.

He was not ready to die, yet, not when he had Sarah back in his arms. But death did not take only the willing.

And Lucie? Had she reached the fort?

He gazed down at the bundle in his arms, thinking he would not die without telling her.

"Sarah." He shook her and received no answer. His words slurred as he tried to tell her. "S-s-arah, I love you. Always have. Always will."

With his attention on her inert form, he did not see the dark shape looming in the storm. When he did, he forced back his hope. After so many disappointments, he was prepared to have this dying desire ripped away once more by the relentless wind.

His horse stopped. Thomas's breathing stopped. He lifted a hand as his horse impatiently pawed the icy ground. His fingers contacted the wall of a building.

He released his breath. The illusion did not disappear.

"Thank you, God."

Turning his weary horse, he rode along the wall, searching for the entrance. Instead, he came up against a split rail fence. He stared in confusion.

Was this the trading post or had he stumbled into some homesteader's barn?

It didn't matter. It was shelter.

He dragged his deadened foot from the stirrup, and slid it gracelessly down to the icy ground. There he found his legs unwilling to support him. A moment of stamping seemed to bring them back into service. He tied the horse's reins to the top rail and then took Sarah in his arms, praying all the while that she would move or speak. Instead, she lay still as death. He hurried to the fence and slipped between the two rails, sliding into the corral. On the leeward side of the barn, he still could see nothing through the snow blowing over the roof as he crept along the wall toward the corner of the building. He soon located a door large enough to allow livestock to pass.

Shifting Sarah to his side he grasped the latch, rolling back the door a few feet. Quickly, he stepped into the darkness.

A nicker of greeting told him he was in the company of horses. Groping along the wall, he came to a stall. He deposited Sarah against the wall and returned to his horse. It took some moments to locate the proper opening to the corral and to lead his grateful horse within.

Once inside the barn, his mount gave a groan of relief, shaking off the ice from his head. Thomas moved to relieve Buck of his saddle. Finally, he closed the door. The killing wind cried out in protest, beating against the wooden planks, seemingly bent on tearing away the meager protection to reach its prey.

Thomas finally found a kerosene lantern and a matchbox. Aware that hay-filled barns and fire were dangerous partners, he carefully lit the lamp, then gutted the match by licking his fingers and pressing them firmly over the flame. The orange glow of life filled him with hope. He raised the lamp and glanced about.

To his right he found hay, loosely pitched into a crib. At the end of the crib stood three burlap sacks of grain, the sweet smell of molasses reaching him as he delved into the upright bag. A narrow aisle separated the horses from their food. One communal stall held four horses that all regarded him with large curious eyes. He spotted Sarah's Appaloosa gelding and closed his eyes at the wave of relief. This was the trading post and Lucie had reached safety. His eyes flicked over Roubideaux's bay, Water Blossom's chestnut mare and the two mules. All here, all safe.

Roubideaux must have changed his mind, realized he couldn't make the fort and headed to the nearest shelter.

Sarah's gelding lowered his freckled neck to sniff at the bundle of hide that held Sarah. Thomas knelt by her side, drawing back the leather shield that had protected her from the worst of the wind. He pressed the palm of his hand across her cheek and mouth. For a moment he held his breath, and then he felt the gentle puff of air against the web between his thumb and first finger. Her breathing was shallow, but there. He wept with joy, but then dashed the sign of weakness away. He needed to get her warm.

He stared at the door. Beyond that lay the trading post, a bed, a fire and warm food. He reached to hoist Sarah and paused. Stories from the old timers at the goldfield stirred in his weary brain. What was it one prospector had said? They had found his brother dead in a drift not four feet from the front door. Disoriented in a blizzard while walking from the milk barn to his kitchen, a journey he'd made twice a day for his entire life.

Thomas lifted Sarah and carried her to the hay, resting her in this rough bed and adding the horses' blankets to her buffalo robe. Then he searched the barn for a rope, finding only one.

He turned to the door, sliding it back to admit the savage wind. He paused to tie the rope about the large corral post and the other end around his waist. Then he closed the door and stepped back. The barn disappeared. He was disoriented. Panic seized him and he ran back until he collided with the wall.

Flat against the frozen plank, he closed his eyes as he realized the miracle of finding this building at all. Thank God for his horse. Somehow the creature had managed to navigate blind, leading them to safety.

He pressed his back to the wall and pictured the layout of the post. Why hadn't he paid more attention?

The corral had been to the left and the trading post to the right. The corral had been behind the barn. That meant he needed to walk along the side wall and then cross the open ground between the structures.

He groped his way along the barn, reaching the front. He paused to draw an icy breath and then tugged at his lifeline. Certain that the knots would hold, he stepped out into the blizzard holding his arm over his face, trying to protect his skin from the stinging ice crystals in the lee of his elbow. A sharp tug told him he had reached the end of his line. He reached out, hoping to find the building just before him, but came up empty. He sidestepped to the right and still found nothing.

Likely the trading post lay a few feet before him. He fingered the knot and hesitated.

If he released it, he might find help. He might also find his death. He shouted, adding his voice to the howling wind. After a few moments he gave that up, again resting his fingers on the knot.

If he lost his way, he would leave Sarah alone in the barn. If he reached the post, he might still save her.

Chapter Twenty-Seven

The rope tugged at his middle. From the furthest point of his leash he thought he saw the trading post appear through the bands of snow. But did he believe enough to release the rope and step into the mouth of the gale?

If he did reach the post, how could he find his way back to her? He turned his head to look to the way he had come and saw the taut rope disappearing into the storm.

No. He would not risk it. They would make do in the barn.

His shoulders slumped as he returned, using the rope to guide him to her. He struggled to slide open the door. The wind seemed peevishly intent on ripping the wood from its hinges. He dug his toes into the earth and heaved, feeling the door roll into place at last.

He hooked a bolt that looked woefully inadequate for the task and then returned to Sarah.

She lay shivering in the buffalo robe, tucked into the bed of sweet hay. Exploring his surroundings, he found Roubideaux's supplies, blankets, steel blades and axe heads, beads, but no food. He gathered five blankets and laid them beside Sarah.

With a little effort he had the buffalo hide beneath her. The blankets he piled on top of her. At first she lay unmoving, then her shivering shook the makeshift bed.

Gradually other noises reached him. The horses munched their hay. Buck stood outside the stall and was trying to reach the hay in the crib. Thomas removed his bridle and opened the gate. Buck headed for the water, but soon returned for a helping of grain.

He scratched beneath the buckskin's black forelock. "You're a good horse, Buck. Thank you."

Outside the blizzard whistled at the joints and rafters, stealing into this small sanctuary.

With all the animals settled, he snuffed the lantern and groped his way back to Sarah.

He unbuttoned his coat and slipped out of his boots, then laid his hat on the hay. Sliding in beside her, he hugged Sarah, rubbing her back. He collected her hands and pressed them into the opening of his coat. Gradually, her tremors slowed until he could no longer hear the clacking of her teeth. Her breathing grew more regular.

"Sarah? Can you hear me?"

She nodded.

"You're safe now."

"L-L-Lu-see?"

He stroked her head. "Your horse is here. She made it."

She released a great breath and lifted her chin as if to see him in the dark.

"Take me to—to her."

"Yes, when the storm breaks."

He tucked her head beneath his chin and held her tight.

"You saved me," she whispered.

"That was a damned foolish thing to do." He tried and failed to sound stern. She nestled closer and he inhaled her scent. "Foolish and brave and grand."

"I knew you'd come back for me."

His breath caught, because for reasons he could not even fathom, she still had faith in him. She still believed.

"I'll always come back."

She murmured his name and curled within the circle of his embrace.

How had he ever thought to live without her? He'd not do it again. It had taken the horror of almost losing her to reveal his convictions. This was *his* woman. This stubborn, fiery, protective lioness was his mate. God help him, because he intended to tell her he loved her.

If she'd only give him the chance, he'd make a home for them all, the family she said she wanted. He started to picture the three of them together, but stopped, afraid that if he imagined his family strong and whole, some new cruel twist of fate would intervene to steal them once more.

Not this time, he vowed. The only one that could keep them apart now was Sarah. If she'd have him, he'd marry her. He intended to beg her to be his bride. And tomorrow, if the weather cleared, he would reunite his family.

He recalled seeing Sarah huddled on the frozen ground and shivered at the terrible memory. How he had found her in that storm, he could not say. It was God's own miracle. He rolled to his side and curled his body around her. She sighed and nestled deep into the cavity of his belly and hips. How perfectly they fit.

Here the howling wind could not reach them. They were safe in this shelter shared only by the horses that had carried them all to safety.

The desperate fright of finding Sarah and then riding through the terrible storm overtook him at last. Weariness pulled him into dreamless sleep as he nestled in the hay with his love. How long he slumbered, he did not know, nor could he say what brought him awake. His eyes snapped open and his senses came instantly alert. The darkness was not complete. Some light stole through the gaps in the rafters. Sarah shifted in her sleep and he forced himself to stillness.

He strained to hear what was amiss. The horses blew and

stomped as if impatient to be fed. They did not seem to sense any danger. Then he realized what was missing—the wind. The gale that had shaken the rafters through the night, wailing like a band of attacking Indians, now blew softly through the barn.

The storm had passed.

Thank God. He relaxed back into his bed.

Then he recalled his daughter and the Sioux. He sat up.

Sarah started awake.

"What?" she cried.

"The wind has died."

She blinked up at him and swept a strand of hair from her eyes. "That's good, isn't it?"

"Not if they come after us."

Now she was kneeling beside him, clutching his lapels.

"We have to get her away."

He drew back to stare at her, assessing her in the gloom. "How do you feel?"

"I'm fine, Thomas, fit to ride. Hurry."

He nodded, rising to his feet. They had not come all this way to lose their daughter now. He had hoped to have a moment alone with her to tell Sarah he still loved her with all his heart, but the desperation in her eyes urged him to action.

He forked hay to the crib as Sarah carried water to the horses. Then he threw back the bolt and slid the door open. The gray gloom of predawn greeted him with a blast of bitter cold air. The temperature must have dropped fifty degrees overnight and he guessed the thermometer now dipped well below freezing. Winter had arrived.

Sarah stepped around him and landed in hip deep snow, blown against the barn. Thomas stared at the drifts before them. Sarah moved to push on and he held her arm.

"Follow me."

Immediately, she fell in behind him, like the good little soldier she had become. He plowed forward, wading through snow that brushed his hips at times. His goal lay only ten feet away when the front door banged open and Roubideaux filled the opening.

"West!" he called. "I thought you were a goner."

"Still alive," he called.

Sarah poked her head out behind him.

"Lucie!" she called.

He thumbed over his shoulder. "Inside."

Sarah pushed at Thomas's back to hurry him.

Roubideaux raised a hand. "We best ready the horses."

Thomas nodded, breaking the rest of the trail and then allowing Sarah to slip past him onto the step.

"Lucie," she called.

From within the cabin came the trembling reply. "Mama?"

His daughter tore across the room and threw herself into her mother's outstretched arms.

"Mama!"

The two embraced, rocking side to side as they wept.

Thomas clenched his jaw against the squeezing pressure in his throat. Moisture clouded his vision as he moved to join his family.

Roubideaux stepped into the snow and grasped Thomas's upper arm. "West—the horses, or we're all gonna die."

Thomas cast them one last glance before turning to follow Roubideaux.

Behind him, Sarah clutched Lucie as if she meant to squeeze the life out of her. She could scarcely believe she held her child again after all the months of heartache and worry.

Lucie cried against her shoulder, seemingly only able to say, "Mama."

Sarah drew back first, because she needed the reassurance of her own eyes to see her daughter had survived her ordeal. She gripped Lucie's narrow shoulders, still clad in the coat Thomas had purchased. It hung upon her.

Sarah smiled as she lifted her gaze to Lucie's face, then the smile dropped from her lips. At first she thought it a trick of the light, some dreadful stain like berry juice. She lifted a thumb, trying to rub away the three inverted blue triangles that hung below Lucie's lower lip like fangs.

"Bruises," she muttered to herself as her rubbing did no good.

She met Lucie's round-eyed stare, noting the stiffness of her body and the grim expression on her face.

"Lucie, what have they done to you?" But she knew the instant Lucie could not hold her gaze. A chill rolled down her spine as she gripped her daughter's shoulders.

Lucie's chin sank to her chest. Her bluntly cut hair fell over her face and she used the palm of her hand to hide the ghastly marks scarring her chin. Sarah recognized the shame that consumed her daughter.

She dragged Lucie to her breast. "No, no, don't cry again. No more tears now. It's all right. It doesn't matter." But it did. There would be no new start, for wherever Lucie went these marks would brand her as a white captive. Sarah's heart ached with grief as she hugged her girl.

All the warnings of all the wretched men came back to her. Leave her there, she's better off dead.

"No." She hadn't meant to speak aloud.

Lucie's voice seemed strangled by her tears. "It's dreadful." She clutched her palm to her chin as she sobbed.

Sarah stroked her daughter's hair and whispered words of comfort as her heart broke. How could they do this to her child? She reined in her anger. It served no purpose now. She could not punish those who had abused her daughter, but how she wanted to.

Sarah drew away again in an effort to make Lucie meet her gaze. Lucie refused her gentle urging until Sarah clasped her hands to her daughter's face and lifted her chin.

"I'm sorry, Mama. So sorry."

"Now, what have you to be sorry for?"

Lucie shook her head. "That I didn't stay hidden like you told me. You told me, but I ran and they caught me."

"What?"

"I didn't stay put. I ran—I ran."

Sarah tried to absorb this. "I shouldn't have left you. I'm sorry, too."

"I know I should have killed myself when they captured me. But I was afraid to go to hell. Are you ashamed of me, Mama?"

Now Sarah could not rein in her anger. She shook her daughter hard. Lucie gasped in surprise. "Don't say that—not ever. How could you think to kill yourself when I told you I'd be back for you?"

Lucie said nothing.

"I'll *never* be ashamed of you, not now, not ever. You survived, Lucie, and I thank God for it."

"Mama." Lucie's lip trembled and her voice dropped to a whisper. "They did things to me."

Sarah's spine straightened. "It's all right now."

Lucie's eyes told her it would never be all right.

Sarah fingered the blunt ends of Lucie's hair, now cut at her shoulder, making the waves of red-gold seem fuller.

"They cut your hair."

Lucie sniffed and her gaze dropped again.

Sarah wrapped an arm about her daughter and squeezed. "I'm so glad to have you back."

The astonishment in her daughter's face nearly broke her heart.

"Button up your coat," said Sarah. "We're going."

Only then did Sarah note that Water Blossom stood in the shadows of the room, silently watching their reunion.

Sarah turned to her friend. "The storm is broken."

"How did you survive?"

"Thomas found me. We reached the barn."

Water Blossom nodded and lifted her husband's saddlebags.

Sarah moved awkwardly forward and hugged Water Blossom, who stood stiff and still through this ordeal. Sarah drew back. "Thank you for saving my daughter."

A smile flickered on the woman's lips and she nodded.

"I'll never forget this. You will forever have my gratitude."

Water Blossom shouldered the bag. "She not saved yet."

Sarah drew a great breath as her surroundings returned.

Roubideaux shouted from the yard. "Get a move on!"

Water Blossom hurried out the door.

Sarah looped an arm over Lucie's shoulders and urged her toward her Appaloosa, whose reins Thomas held.

He moved to the horse's side and clasped his hands, holding them low before him as a foothold. "You two ride double. Sarah first."

She placed her boot in the palms of his hands and swung up. Lucie followed. Lucie barely had time to clasp her arms about her mother when the trader set his heels to his horse without a backward glance.

Roubideaux took point with one of one of the pack mules in tow. Next came Water Blossom, leading the second mule, which was carrying far more goods than her husband's mule. Sarah pressed her heels into the Appaloosa's sides and they fell in behind the second mule. Next came Thomas guarding their backs.

Sarah glanced past him in search of a Sioux war party.

She looked back often throughout the day.

Thomas and Roubideaux alternated breaking the trail. Most places on the windswept prairie had less than a foot of snow, but in the valleys and on some hillsides, the drifts reached the horses's bellies. The trader's pack mules, heavy laden, became more resistant to moving forward and needed constant urging.

The morning turned to afternoon and the winter sun did not warm Sarah in the least. She was grateful for Lucie's slender body pressed to her back as they managed to generate some warmth between them. The bone-chilling wind continued to blow, lifting the powdery snow into temporary whiteouts. It was because of these swirling scattered squalls that she did not see anything amiss.

Thomas called forward to them. "Nearly there."

Sarah squinted but could see nothing to reassure her that safety lay near at hand.

"Over that rise." Thomas pointed to the unbroken snow on the hill before them.

To Sarah, it looked like every other knoll, until she noted gray smoke rising into the cloudy sky.

Her heart leapt with hope as she cast one last look back to check for pursuit. She did not credit her eyes at first. Sarah peered hard into the swirling snow at the dark shapes. They might be buffalo or elk. Lucie turned back as well, and gasped.

Sarah shouted, "Thomas!"

He lifted up on his stirrups as he turned, his gaze following the direction of her extended arm. He swore.

"Roubideaux! Indians!"

The trader, now in the lead, whipped his horse, dragging on his pack animal's bridle as his mount sprang into action. The pack mule shied and reared.

"Drop him," shouted Thomas.

"No!" called the trader, stubbornly gripping the lead line to his goods.

"You damn fool! You'll kill us all!" Thomas broke from the line, passing Sarah and Water Blossom. "Sarah, take the lead."

She did, setting her heels into her poor Freckles's sides. Sarah glanced back to see their unburdened pursuers closing the gap. Thomas followed them, his rifle drawn as he aimed at the charging warriors. Behind him the trader and his wife, still clinging to the mules' lead lines, fell farther behind.

Roubideaux let go first, abandoning Water Blossom.

"Let go, Water Blossom," called Sarah, but did not know if her friend could hear. Behind them, the Sioux drew close enough for Sarah to see the red and blue war paint on the lead pony's forelegs.

"Go," yelled Thomas, waving at Sarah.

She turned forward, focusing all her energy on reaching the safety of the fort. She kicked her mount as the crack of his rifle sounded behind her.

Roubideaux drew even with Sarah, making no effort to protect them as he lunged by. Arrows protruded from his saddle cantle.

Sarah kicked and Freckles lurched after him. She topped the hill, seeing the parapets of the fort rising from the frozen ground. Soldiers on the catwalk returned fire and she thought she heard a bugle blast beyond the wind whistling by her ears.

Her sturdy horse easily caught up to the trader's on the flat, stretching their lead as the main gate swung open before them. His horse stumbled twice under the burden of the heavy man. Sarah realized that Roubideaux's mount was weary from breaking trail much of the day. A cold blade of fear struck as she remembered that Thomas's horse had done the same.

She glanced back to see Thomas and Water Blossom still in the rear, but neither had fallen behind. It seemed as if he could have passed her but would not, and she realized that he acted as a human shield between them and their pursuers.

She hurried her horse, bounding ahead of the trader as Lucie lay across her like a second skin. Her daughter's back stood unprotected and that realization caused Sarah to lean further over the horse's neck to make them a smaller target.

Now they reached the well-packed trail of the wood-cutting details.

The cry of the Sioux reached her with the crack of rifle fire. When the first arrow whizzed past her head, she thought she mistook it, until a second hummed by, disappearing into the snow.

Before her, the gates yawned.

Chapter Twenty-Eight

"Faster!" shouted Thomas, seeming to be just behind her now.

Sarah kicked her horse and leaned low against his bobbing neck.

"Come on, boy," she urged.

The trader cleared the gate. Her horse lunged to the safety of the yard and she turned to see Thomas come next, followed by Water Blossom and one of the unattended mules.

Gunshots popped as the soldiers from the catwalk returned fire. The howl of the warriors echoed in Sarah's head as the gate swung shut securing their escape.

Horses and riders panted, sending white vapor into the air. Sarah gazed up at their saviors on the catwalk, still defending this patch of earth. Sarah turned to Lucie, who sat straight behind her, a hand to her chest as she stared in disbelief at the closed gate. Her daughter looked frightened, but unharmed.

Next, her attention moved to Thomas. His eyes met hers and he nudged his horse forward.

"We made it." Thomas reached out and clasped her hand.

She gripped him fiercely as joy and relief rushed through her.

"Thank God," she whispered.

From somewhere above them on a catwalk came a familiar voice.

"West!"

His hand slipped away. Major Brennan motioned with undisguised irritation. "Get up here. You too, Roubideaux!"

Thomas dismounted. He stood beside Sarah, resting an open palm proprietarily upon her thigh. "Will you be all right?"

She nodded, clasping his hand for a moment. "We'll be fine."

He gave her a winning smile and then hurried away.

Corporal Abby trotted across the yard and took hold of Freckles's reins. "You two are to report to your quarters."

Sarah lifted a brow at the order and Abby hastened to explain. "It's for your safety, Mrs. West. Major's orders."

Sarah nodded. Lucie slid down first and she followed, stifling a groan at the stiffness that gripped her back. Her daughter huddled close and Sarah noted Corporal Abby staring slack jawed at Lucie.

"Anything else, corporal?"

Abby straightened and his eyes shifted nervously. "No, ma'am."

"Well, dismissed then." She shooed him with both hands and he made an abrupt about-face, leading Freckles toward the stables.

Sarah glanced at Lucie, surprised that her daughter's head now topped her shoulder. She was a young lady and she had been a bride. Her heart ached at all her child had endured. She clasped Lucie's hand and was about to set off when she saw Water Blossom, alone in the yard, looking nervous as a fox before the hounds. Above them, rifle fire repeated. Answering shots continued beyond the walls. How must she feel? Outside her people fought, inside her husband stood upon the walls beside the soldiers.

"Water Blossom, come with me."

She led them to her room, tying her friend's horse and mule outside. From the quarters adjoining hers, she saw Chastity Corbit gawking through her window. It was then Sarah realized she still wore a buckskin dress and moccasins. The three of them must have made quite a sight, but there was no excusing Chastity's rude stare or undisguised irk.

No love lost as far as Sarah was concerned. This woman had

wasted no time telling the camp when Thomas had spent the night. Gossipy little witch.

If not for the gunfire, she's likely venture out to spread the news that Lucie had been found.

She and Lucie had been the target of much cruel treatment back in Illinois as a result of Thomas's disappearance, her hasty marriage and the baby that came too soon for anyone who could count. The whispers, the assessing stares, how well she recalled the women's brutality.

Lucie looked so frail. Sarah's heart grew heavy as she considered the burden she could not carry for her daughter.

For Lucie, rejoining society might be more difficult than surviving her captivity.

Sarah opened the door to her quarters and had not even got the stove going when a knock sounded at the door.

Sarah found Mrs. Corbit standing with hand raised, prepared to knock again.

"Mrs. West. I'd like a word."

Sarah stiffened, waiting.

"I know you are just returned, but I note that you have Indians in there." She pointed into Sarah's quarters. "Perhaps you are unaware that Indians are not permitted to reside overnight within these walls."

"She is the trader's wife."

Corbit's condescending tone revealed that this information failed to sway her and, in fact, gave her the verification she needed. "As you know, I am in a family way. Indians are attacking our walls at this very moment. I cannot be worried about savages at my own doorstep."

Sarah's gaze narrowed, thinking Water Blossom was worth ten of Mrs. Corbit. "I doubt you will be bothered."

"I must insist. I am prepared to go to my husband with this." She waved her hand toward her door and noticed Lucie standing with the shawl draped over her head.

"Is that one the trader's wife?"

Sarah bristled. "That one is my daughter."

Mrs. Corbit was rendered speechless. She only gaped, her eyes bulging like a catfish's. Sarah slammed the door in her face.

Water Blossom stood beside the door, her buffalo robe drawn up as she prepared to leave. "I go."

"Please don't."

"Yes," she nodded, without making eye contact. "I go."

Sarah grasped her friend and hugged her. "You saved my daughter and I'll never be able to repay you for that. Please don't let that stupid woman drive you off."

Water Blossom hugged her in return and then drew back.

"We two are friends. But my people and your people do not understand this, because they cannot see past their hate. They do not know a mother's heart. We can be friends here." She pointed to her heart. "But not here." She motioned to the world around them.

Sarah bowed her head, recognizing the truth of this.

Water Blossom turned to Lucie and touched her cheek, speaking in Sioux. Then she lifted her robe over her head and stepped out into the cold.

"What did she say?"

"Long life, good health and happiness always."

Sarah drew her child close and hugged her tight. "I want those things for you, too, baby."

For a long time Sarah and Lucie clung together, while gunfire popped outside with regularity. At last Lucie drew back. Sarah felt suddenly awkward. This was new. Never in her life had she felt ill at ease with her child.

Lucie clasped her hands before her and bowed her head. "I knew you'd find me, Mama. I knew."

Sarah looped an arm around her shoulders and guided her to a chair beside the stove.

"And so we did." Sarah beamed at Lucie. "I have something for you."

Lucie's expression brightened. Sarah retrieved the quilt and held out her offering.

Her daughter opened her arms to accept the gift, her fingers danced over the familiar fabrics, touching her pinafore and then the kitchen curtains before finally settling on the denim of Samuel's work shirt. Tears rolled down her cheeks.

"A memory quilt," she whispered.

"Something of the old, as we face the new."

Lucie clutched the quilt and then her mother. "I love it. Thank you, Mama."

Sarah wrapped her arms about her child, so grateful to have her back once more. At last they drew apart. Lucie spread the quilt upon the bed to admire the pattern.

"Flowers on a winter's day."

Sarah stared out at the sea of flower baskets she'd made for Lucie.

Lucie was crying now. "They burned your Ohio star quilt."

"What?"

"The blue Ohio star. They stole it and later they burned it. It was all I had of you." Lucie wiped at her tears. "But now I have this."

"And we have each other." Sarah clasped her daughter's hand.

Lucie tried for a smile and failed. "I just wish…"

"What?"

"That you could have found me sooner." Lucie motioned to her chin.

"It doesn't matter." Sarah's stomach hurt, because it so obviously did matter. "You're home now."

Lucie lifted her troubled eyes. "Home? Home to what? What is to become of me now, Mama?"

"Home to me." Sarah held her daughter's stare, forbidding herself to look away. "We haven't had a chance to talk yet. I want to hear about your…everything."

Lucie retreated to the chair and dragged the quilt about her shoulders. She stared at her feet, her cheeks aflame.

Sarah hesitated. They had not spoken about what had happened, but they must. And they must address this new distance between them. This, above all else, troubled Sarah the most.

"I love you," said Sarah.

Her daughter echoed her words without looking up.

The knock at the door startled them both. Outside, Sarah found Corporal Abby.

"Mrs. West, they asked me to tell you that the Indians have withdrawn. It's safe to come out. Supper's on in the mess."

Sarah hesitated looking back at Lucie, who cowered beneath her new quilt. The soldiers would gawk, the women would whisper. Sarah straightened her spine.

"I think we'll eat in our room."

"I could fetch you something," offered the young soldier.

"Thank you."

He stepped away and Sarah closed the door and breathed a sigh of relief. The next knock came so quickly after the first that she thought Abby had forgotten something but when the door swung open, she found Thomas standing before her, hat in hand. He rocked to his toes to look past her at Lucie and smiled.

"May I come in?" She hesitated and his smile dissolved. "Sarah?"

"Not tonight, Thomas. She needs rest."

He stayed rooted to the spot, his frown deepening by the moment. She grabbed her coat and stepped out onto the porch with him, grasping his elbow and drawing him to the end of the covered porch. There she stopped to face him.

"How is my daughter?"

She sucked in a little breath at his question and glanced nervously about. "Hush now."

She turned to see if anyone had heard him, but saw no one.

"Don't you hush me." He gritted the words out between clenched teeth.

Sarah lowered her voice. "She doesn't know yet, Thomas."

He scowled, raising his voice. "Why the hell not?"

She glanced toward the heavens praying for patience.

"In the last few months she's been ripped from her home, seen her father buried on the trail, been captured by Indians, married to a warrior and now thrust back into civilization. She's fragile as an unfired pot. I don't think she can take another shock right now."

Thomas glowered. "She hasn't lost her father."

Sarah gave him a hard look. "Thomas, your brother was the only father she has ever known. Of course, he was her father."

"Well, so am I." He dug in his heels. "And if you don't tell her, I will."

"Give me until tomorrow." She grasped his lapel. "Please, Thomas."

He pressed his lips into a thin line.

She stroked the lambskin sheathing his broad shoulders. "I think I know my own daughter."

"Our daughter," he corrected.

"Yes."

He sighed, hesitating for the time it took to stare at her closed door, and then he tugged his hat on his head and strode into the twilight, alone.

Sarah returned to Lucie with a heavy heart. They slept together in the narrow bed that night. The next day, they ventured out for the first time. Mrs. Fairfield and Mrs. Douglas spotted them before they had even crossed the yard and changed course to intercept.

The last thing Lucie needed was to be forced into the company of busybodies.

The two crunched through the snow, stopping before her. Mrs. Fairchild and Mrs. Douglas both forced smiles.

"Welcome back, Sarah," said Mrs. Fairfield.

"Thank you." Her throat felt tight and the cold seemed to freeze her forced smile.

Mrs. Douglas rocked nervously and Mrs. Fairfield tried again to steer the conversation.

"This must be Lucie."

Sarah nodded, her attention flicking from one woman to the next, searching for hidden agenda.

"Well, we are so happy to meet you at last." Mrs. Douglas beamed. "We heard of your return and have arranged a little gathering in the officers' mess to welcome Miss Lucie home."

Sarah had to give Mrs. Douglas credit. Her eyes never ventured down to stare at the marks on Lucie's chin. But that didn't mean they had to suffer the company of a room full of busybodies.

Sarah saw the hopeful look in Lucie's eyes and paused before refusing outright. Lucie must get back to living among women like these. Sarah eyed them suspiciously, not trusting that they wouldn't take this opportunity to force Lucie to relive her ordeal.

Lucie waited, deferring to her mother, but the hope shone clearly in her eyes.

"My daughter has endured a great deal. I hope you will comply with my wishes and not discuss her ordeal with her."

"Why, certainly," said Mrs. Fairfield, too quickly for Sarah's liking.

"Very well then. I thank you both for your concern over my daughter's welfare."

It seemed every woman in the fort had risen early to greet Lucie. On the surface they were cordial, but Sarah watched them when they were not speaking directly to her child and noted the bowed heads and whispers. She caught Mrs. Corbit rubbing her chin as she studied Lucie.

Sarah scowled, feeling like a guard dog ordered not to bite. She scanned the room once more and saw the only male welcomed to this gathering of hens. The boy, the one Water Blossom called Sky Fox, approached Lucie.

Mrs. Douglas made introductions. It was clear from the expression on Lucie's face that she recognized him, despite his new attire and cropped hair. He spoke to her in Sioux, quite shocking the assemblage. His words made Lucie laugh.

"What did he say?" asked Mrs. Fairfield.

Lucie smiled. "He said that we are two sides of the Medicine Wheel. He is an Indian who looks like a white boy, and I am a white girl who looks like an Indian."

Mrs. Douglas gasped. "He didn't." She wagged a finger at the boy who was now stuffing a large wedge of cake in his mouth.

Sarah changed the subject. "This boy told us where to find you."

Lucie nodded. "He told me that, too."

Sarah stood vigil beside Lucie until she begged for a moment of privacy to use the outhouse. Even then Sarah was uncomfortable with her out of her sight. When Lucie returned her face was flushed and Sarah felt certain something had happened. Sarah met her by the door and drew her aside.

"When can we leave this place?" asked Lucie.

"Right now." Sarah turned to make her farewells.

"I mean this fort."

Sarah hesitated. That brought another question. Where would they go? She had hoped that Thomas would see fit to extend his protection to his daughter and no doubt he would, but where did Sarah fit in? She even dreamed that he might ask her to marry him. She would—if he'd have her.

Lucie's eyes pleaded, but she remained mute, waiting.

"Why do you ask?"

She shrugged, lowering her eyes. When she spoke, her voice was so low that, Sarah had to lean in to hear her.

"A soldier—he called me the white squaw."

The surge of anger nearly took Sarah off her feet. She grabbed Lucie and spun her. "Who did?"

Lucie looked frightened. "I don't know his name. Please, Mama. Don't say anything."

"I most certainly will."

Lucie pushed at her mother's hands, seeking her release. Sarah complied.

"Can we not just go?"

"Of course." Sarah made their excuses.

Out in the yard, they walked side by side, their shoes crunching in the snow. How could they spend the winter here with all these men? She must get Lucie to a safe place. But where in the world was safe? Anywhere they went, men would say cruel things and women would gawk and whisper. It would be the same in any city or town they chose. Sarah blinked back the tears. Lucie had enough to deal with without her mother falling to pieces when she needed her most.

Sarah reached to grasp Lucie's hand and her daughter flinched. What had they done to her child?

They mounted the walkway and Lucie settled in one of the chairs beside their room. Sarah took the other.

"Lucie, honey, what happened between you and that warrior?"

Lucie's chin sank to her chest and her face reddened.

"I don't want to speak of him."

Sarah reached a hand out again and then faltered. Her arm dropped back to her side.

"But you can tell me anything."

Lucie cast her an incredulous look.

"Honey, if he hurt you or—or…" How did she say rape? The word stuck in her throat like an eggshell. "You can tell me."

Lucie knotted her hands in her lap. "I'm all right."

But she wasn't, she so obviously wasn't. What if she carried his child? The thought took the wind right out of Sarah. Should she ask, or wait and watch for the bloody rags that would provide the answer?

"Lucie, sweetheart, I have to know. I'm your mother."

Lucie's lips remained firmly sealed.

Sarah sat in shock. Never had there been secrets between them. She didn't understand Lucie's refusal to confide in her. How could she help her daughter if she did not know what had befallen her?

"I just want to leave the prairie. I hate it here."

Sarah nodded. "Yes. As soon as it can be arranged."

But even as she promised, she knew the impossibility of the task. Snow had fallen. The wagon trains had all gone. Traveling season had ended months ago and they were likely stuck here until spring.

"To Illinois," said Lucie. "I want to go home."

Sarah paused. There was no home there to return to, no farm, no family. What Lucie longed for was the safety of a time and place forever lost.

What would Lucie's friends think of her now?

The answer made Sarah shiver.

Lucie gave her a cautious stare. Her gaunt face and haunted expression made her look like a stray dog—no, a whipped one. Sarah bit her lip. Where was the confident child she had raised? It broke her heart to see the changes wrought by her captivity.

"Sweetheart, we can't." Sarah reached to clasp Lucie's hand.

Lucie drew away and her shoulders shook as she sobbed.

Sarah's mouth dropped open, as she stood speechless. It was natural for Lucie to want the security of home. But well she knew, that ship had sailed. The fact that Lucie didn't seem to understand this frightened Sarah.

What did she really know about what her child had endured to survive?

And Lucie would tell her nothing.

She gnawed at her cheek as she considered what to do.

Thomas drew on his leather coat. He planned to find Sarah and insist she let him see his child. Their argument, last evening, frightened him. He was joyful to have Lucie safe, but now recognized that Sarah had no further use for him. Sarah's need of him ended the minute they crossed into Fort Laramie.

Over these months together, there were times when he was sure she still loved him. Now, uncertainty plagued him. He had known her since he was ten. But still, he couldn't read what she was thinking.

He'd been patient, had pretended the child was his brother's, but he was through hiding. He was the girl's father. Last night, she insisted that Lucie was too bereft from her ordeal to be burdened.

He had honored her wishes and not slept one wink. Today he'd take matters into his own hands. His daughter had survived what many could not. That alone proved her to be clever and resilient, not to mention as stubborn as her parents.

The girl would know the truth.

As he crossed the street, he glanced toward Sarah's old room. There on the porch sat Sarah and Lucie. He made his way toward them.

Sarah did not note his approach. She had eyes only for Lucie and judging from her concerned expression, there was some issue at hand. Lucie huddled in her seat.

Thomas walked slowly past the blacksmith. Was his child crying?

She lifted her head now and he saw her face.

He drank in the sight of his child. True, she was too thin, but time would change that. The blue marks on her chin posed more difficulty. Thomas had to work to keep his smile in place as rage swept through him again at the sight of them. How he longed to get his hands on the cowardly bastard who'd marked her. He'd break his neck for a start.

Lucie saw Thomas now. Her eyes grew cautious at his approach and his smile gleaned none in return. Her eyes looked red.

Sarah followed the direction of Lucie's gaze, her expression somber.

Thomas wondered what Lucie saw as she looked at him. Did she see hair color that exactly matched hers or the long tapered nose and oval face that told of common blood?

Anyone who looked at her would recognize she was his child. But would she?

He cleared his throat and extended his hand. *Hello, Lucie, I am your father.*

"Hello again, Lucie."

This was not the way he wanted this meeting to go, with this strained awkwardness pressing upon them, but he pushed on.

Sarah obviously felt the same. His hand remained extended before him. At last, Lucie reached out and grasped it. Her small hand warmed his palm.

"I'm Thomas West."

"Thomas, please," said Sarah. There was no concern for him in her voice, just concern about what he might do. She was right to be worried.

He would not be distracted. He released his daughter's hand, wishing he could hold her in his arms. But he did not want to frighten the girl. He was yet a stranger to her.

Sarah moved to flank her child, her hands pressed one to the other as she glared daggers at him.

"Thomas, this is not the time."

He gave her a cold smile. "So you keep telling me."

"Mama, who is he?"

She drew a breath and motioned toward him. "This is Samuel's younger brother."

Lucie grasped his hand again. His heart clenched. She had Sarah's eyes.

Her voice was breathless with excitement. "I did not even know Father had a brother. Why, this is wonderful."

Thomas stood thunderstruck. Samuel had never mentioned his brothers—either of his brothers—to Lucie? Moments stretched and Lucie faltered, drawing back her hand. His blood turned to ice. He was uncertain. Perhaps Sarah did know best. His daughter looked fragile as a reed in winter. A stiff blow might break her.

Lucie clapped her hands in excitement as she sprang to her feet. "Then you are my uncle."

"Sarah?" he said, giving her a chance to set things right.

Instead, she gave him a look of utter fury. Not one drop of

compassion flickered in her eyes. She kept her narrowing gaze upon him as she spoke to Lucie.

"That's right," she said.

Thomas's insides twisted. She could not have hurt him more if she had drawn a blade and sliced him in two. He gaped as she gave him a cold shake of her head.

He extended his hands, seeking her permission to claim his child.

"Sarah, please," he whispered. "Tell her."

Lucie, meanwhile, now clasped his arm, holding him like a new toy.

"Tell me what?"

"Lucie, go inside," said Sarah.

Thomas wanted nothing more than to escape, like some wounded animal.

"Don't bother," he said. "I'm leaving."

He was leaving. Just as soon as he could make arrangements, for he could not bear to stay.

He turned tail and retreated, ignoring the wave of dizziness. He recognized the sensation for this was the second time Sarah had broken his heart.

He swallowed back the lump in his throat. There was no question now that she did not want him or any part of the future he had dreamed they would share.

He had lost Sarah again, and with her, went his daughter—this stranger of his flesh.

He gripped his hands across his middle as if afraid his guts might spill out on the street.

Chapter Twenty-Nine

Somehow Thomas made it to the barracks that had been his home for several months.

A terrible, devastating wave of grief flooded him. Lucie calling him uncle and Sarah waving him off as if he was some beggar in the street. The look of venom she gave him told him everything he needed to know about how she felt.

She didn't love him, didn't want him to have any part of their daughter. He knew he'd made mistakes, but he thought he had mended some of the fences in their quest to find Lucie.

How had he ever thought to earn redemption? He couldn't, not now or ever. He sat hunched on his bunk, curling around the pain. She knew what he wanted and was hell bent on not giving it to him.

Someone nearby cleared his throat.

Thomas glanced in the direction of the sound. Corporal Abby stood before him, pinning him with a concerned gaze.

"Get you anything, sir?"

Thomas knew what must be done. Sarah didn't want him, but Lucie was still his responsibility.

"You got an attorney in this fort?"

"We have the former professor."

Thomas pushed up onto one elbow. "Fetch him and tell the stable master to ready my horse."

"Going somewhere, sir?"

He nodded.

Abby did not move from the spot and Thomas glared.

"Your pardon, Mr. West. But it ain't safe to head out alone. The Sioux will pick you off like a stray buffalo calf."

Thomas said nothing.

Abby rubbed his chapped knuckles over one of his bushy sideburns. "There's a mule skinner heading out Friday, at first light with full guard. Only two days, and you'd have an escort. If you don't mind me saying, sir."

"I'll bear it in mind."

Abby waited another moment as if weighing the option of more discussion. He gave up and headed out the door.

Thomas spent his time stuffing his belongings into his saddlebags and gathering his bedroll. He'd see about grub at the store.

He wondered if she would miss him. Likely she'd be well rid of him. He'd thought from the beginning that some fences couldn't be mended. But for a time there, he'd forgotten and cultivated hope.

He forgave her and she said she forgave him. He guessed that was all he could expect. But his love for her had not died. He had carried it with him everywhere he went, like a thorn embedded deep in his flesh.

He wondered if this was how Samuel had felt all those years, loving a woman who did not love him back.

He bowed his head and prayed to God to care for his older brother. Tell him I don't hold it against him, Lord. Any man alive would fight to keep Sarah.

The door clicked open and he lifted his head. Thomas stared at John Corbit. The man was thin to the point of emaciation, and his captain's coat hung off him. Beneath his arm he clutched a portable writer's desk.

"Mr. West? Corporal Abby said you sent for me."

Thomas shook his hand, recognizing the man whose room adjoined Sarah's.

"I understand you seek an attorney. I'm the closest you'll find here in the wilderness. I'm the requisitions officer, but I took some law at Brown University prior to enlisting."

"I need papers drawn up. Can you do that?"

"Should not be difficult. What exactly do you require?"

Thomas explained his needs and the man set the desk on his lap and unfastened the latch. In a moment he had the ink open and his nib poised over a blank page. Together, they worked out the details.

When he had finished, Thomas offered to pay him, but Corbit refused.

"I'll see these delivered in the morning," said Corbit.

"I'm obliged."

Thomas hoisted his saddlebags and bedroll, walking with Corbit as far as the fort store.

"Well, West, Godspeed. I hope you reach North Platte Station."

"Thanks again, Captain."

"I'll see to these." He patted the breast pocket.

The men shook hands and Thomas headed into the store. He quickly bought the supplies he needed for the journey.

Back on the road, he could not keep from glancing toward Sarah's room. The light of a lantern glowed from within and smoke rose from the chimney. He sighed in despair and turned away.

Thomas reached the stable to find Buck dozing as he rested a hind foot.

"He's had a double helping of grain and I packed a pound of oats for your ride."

Thomas tossed the stable master a coin.

"Brennan know you're heading out alone?" asked the man.

Thomas swung up into the saddle.

"I'm not in the army, yet."

He gripped the reins and ducked under the entrance, making for the gate.

The sentries gave him a quizzical look. "Only party out is firewood—off to the left by the river."

Thomas nodded as he rode from the safety of the walls. He hoped that for just once in his life he'd done the right thing by giving Sarah what she wanted. But damn, he had never felt so low.

"Sarah."

It was out of his mouth before he could stop it. He clamped his lips together, resisting the urge to ride back to her.

He set his jaw.

If she had no use for him, perhaps the Union Army could set him a task. He planned to enlist as soon as he got east and see just what it was that drew nearly every able-bodied man from the Western frontier.

Sarah watched her girl, now reading the Bible by lantern light. Remorse crept over her. Thomas had a right to claim his daughter. She couldn't keep him from doing so, nor did she want to. But his timing had been bad, with Lucie weeping and begging to go home.

All Sarah's efforts to open a dialog with her daughter had failed. Lucie seemed determined to pretend that the months of her absence had never happened.

But they had. One needed only to look at her to see.

Ignoring this wall of silence seemed wrong. Sarah drew in a long breath and prepared to try again.

She was about to ask Lucie to put down the book when her daughter pressed her hands together, making the leaves thud as they collided.

"Mama, what is between you and my uncle? What did he want you to tell me?"

Sarah felt herself swallow before answering. How would

Lucie feel about her mother after she learned what kind of a woman she really was? Sarah stared down from the pedestal upon which Lucie had placed her and found herself dizzy from the height.

"I don't know where to start."

Lucie set the Bible aside. "You held his hand in the yard."

"He is family."

"But the way you looked at him."

A prickling unease crept like a centipede up her spine. Her daughter was too perceptive.

"How?"

"As if you adore him." Lucie rubbed her nose. "I wouldn't fault you."

"Wouldn't you?" Sarah steadied herself. Lucie had opened the subject. The time had come. Perhaps if she shared her secrets, Lucie might feel inclined to do the same.

Her daughter leaned forward in her chair as if afraid to miss a word.

"I hardly know where to begin." Sarah gave a halfhearted smile. "I fell in love with Thomas before you were born."

Lucie's eyes rounded.

"Did Papa know?"

She nodded. "Thomas went to California for gold. I wanted to go, too, but he wouldn't take me. He said it was too dangerous."

Lucie nodded her approval at this. She looked so much like Thomas that Sarah had to smile.

"I see you agree. I did not. I tried to stop him from leaving me."

"How?"

Sarah gave her daughter a long look, wishing she knew how her Lucie would respond to this next bit of information.

"I seduced him."

Lucie gave a little gasp that sounded like a hiccup as she plastered both hands over her mouth.

"It didn't work. He left anyway."

"Did you marry Father out of spite?"

"No. I married Samuel after a false report that Thomas had died and because I was pregnant."

Lucie's brow wrinkled. She did not understand. Even with the evidence of her own face, which so closely resembled his, she did not see.

"I was pregnant with you."

Lucie paled. "But—but," she stammered, "he's my uncle."

Sarah shook her head. "No. Samuel was your uncle."

Tears sprang to Lucie's eyes. Sarah felt as though a knife was twisting in her heart. "I'm sorry I never told you. I was trying to protect you."

"Does he know?"

"Yes."

Lucie sat still and silent for several moments, while Sarah waited for her daughter to abandon her, too. But she did not.

"Do you still love him?"

"Very much."

"Does he love you?"

"I don't know, but I know he loves you."

Her daughter shook her head. "He doesn't even know me. He doesn't know what I've done, what has happened."

"It doesn't matter to either of us. We love you no matter what you have done, no matter what has been done *to* you."

Lucie sprang to her feet and ran to her mother, who swept her into her arms. Hugging and rocking, the two embraced.

"I thought if you knew, if you knew…" Lucie wept.

"Shhh. We love you, Lucie. You are our little girl."

For a time Sarah just held her child tight as tears rolled down their cheeks. Finally Lucie drew back.

"I've been so afraid."

"But you're safe now."

Lucie sniffed and Sarah withdrew a handkerchief from her sleeve, offering it to her. Lucie wiped her red nose.

"I know I embarrass you, now. I'm so sorry. I tried to fight them, but they held me and then I tried to wash it off, but it— it…"

Sarah grasped her daughter's chin and lifted her face so she could see it. "What on earth would make you think you embarrass me?"

"You don't want me out of the room. You don't want me to talk to the officers' wives."

Sarah gasped. Is that what she thought? Good heavens, it had never occurred to her that Lucie would think she was ashamed of her. "I was trying to protect you."

Her eyes rounded in confusion. "From what?"

"From those nasty biddies and their wicked tongues and those awful soldiers with their cruel jokes."

Lucie's mouth rounded in a little *O*. "I thought I humiliated you."

"Oh, my sweet Lord." Sarah grasped her daughter's hands and stared into her beautiful eyes. "Never. I just didn't want you hurt any more. Do you understand?"

Lucie nodded. "But Mama, the warrior who married me, he—he had his way with me."

"I feared as much. Are you carrying his child?"

Lucie dropped her gaze. "No."

"I'm so sorry for what you have endured."

Her daughter looked up with a quizzical expression and waited a moment as if for Sarah to continue when she didn't, Lucie said, "That's all? I was afraid that when you heard what he did to me you wouldn't want me anymore."

Sarah's heart broke all over again. She drew her down beside her on the bed. They sat side by side upon the memory quilt with Lucie tucked beneath her mother's arm.

"You listen to me, Lucie Marie West. None of that was your fault and nothing you could do will ever, ever change how much I love you."

Lucie smiled.

"I have a confession to make," said Sarah.

Lucie drew back, her brow etched with concern.

"I have been afraid of what you would think of me once you learned the truth."

"What?" The shocked expression suddenly made her fears seem foolish. "But that's ridiculous."

"Still, I was afraid you would despise me for deceiving you."

Lucie straightened and a familiar stubborn expression blanketed her expression. "Never."

They sat in silence for a moment, the awkwardness and uncertainty now replaced with understanding.

"I'm so glad you told me," said Lucie. "You always seemed so confident, so perfect. I used to try to be just like you, but now…" She sighed. "I can't be like you, not after what happened. Knowing you had failings, well, it gives me hope."

Sarah didn't know what to say. She'd never felt perfect—far, far from it. But she had tried to keep up a front. Now she saw that this façade had made her daughter feel lacking. Without even intending to, she had caused Lucie grief.

"Mama? I'd like to see Thomas, I mean, my father."

Sarah recalled their last encounter and she sprang to her feet. Her daughter now looked concerned.

"What is it?"

"Thomas. I've made a dreadful mistake. I—I have to go."

"But it's late."

Sarah snatched her coat. "I don't care. I must find him."

She ran out into the night, heading straight for the barracks. There she found several soldiers, but no Thomas. A corporal said he had not seen him.

Next she tried the mess hall, but found it locked for the night. The catwalk?

She hesitated before the ladder. The sentry descended before her.

"I'm looking for Mr. West."

"He ain't up there."

"Do you know where I might find him?"

The man gave her a confused look. "Ma'am?"

What was wrong with the man?

"Have you seen him?"

"He's gone."

She stared hard at the soldier's astonished face, her voice sharp with fear. "Gone where?"

"He left when I came on watch. Headed out alone with night falling. Damn foolish, considering the current situation. Maybe the Sioux are all sitting in their winter camp, but there's always raiders, aren't there?" He glanced back toward the gate, now firmly bolted against the night. "Hope he makes it. The cause needs more men like him."

Sarah stood gaping. "The cause?"

"Didn't you hear? He's gone to join the Union Army."

Chapter Thirty

Sarah ran to the stables, certain the man was mistaken. How could he go without a word? Sarah's heart pounded within her chest as she reached the barn's interior. Like an arrow, she flew to the stall where he stabled his buckskin gelding and found it empty.

She fell hard on outstretched hands, her palms scraping against the rough-hewn planks of the stall's gate as she struggled to control the rising storm of panic swirling within her.

"No. He can't be gone."

She recalled the look of utter dejection upon his face as he had tried to tell Lucie the truth and she'd waved him off as if he were a fly in her pudding.

"But I love him."

That hadn't stopped him from leaving the last time.

Sarah sank down, coming to rest on an upturned grain bucket. She pressed her hands over her eyes as her world turned black.

She'd lost him again.

Why had she denied him? He had the right to tell Lucie. She had been so caught up in what was best for Lucie, and with her own petty fears, that she had not considered Thomas's needs.

She had waited to tell him of her love and now it was too late.

Her shoulders shook with the force of her sobs. Someone tried to rouse her, but she pushed them off. Running footsteps signaled their retreat. She wrapped her arms about herself and rocked, bathed in misery.

"Mama?"

She lifted her gaze to find Lucie standing before her.

"Thomas has gone. He left us."

Sarah sprang to her feet and hurried to her horse. "I have to go after him. I have to tell him."

Lucie grabbed her mother's arm in a vice-like grip. "Mama. You can't go now. It's dark."

Sarah reached for her bridle and Lucie tugged it away.

"Mama! Do you even know where he's going?"

Sarah lowered her head and held the cry in her throat, where it burned like fire. Lucie's arm went about her mother's shoulders.

"In the morning, we'll all go. We'll get an escort." Expertly, she relieved Sarah of the bridle. Then she steered her toward the door. "We'll go see the commanding officer. Perhaps they know where he was bound. They can use the telegraph and send a message ahead."

The telegraph, yes, they could do that. Lucie took her elbow and led her along.

Sarah glanced back at her horse, which regarded her over the top of the planking. Urgency tugged as she walked in the wrong direction.

"We need supplies," said Lucie.

Sarah tore her gaze from her mount as Lucie's words sank in. Yes, supplies, they needed those.

She became aware again out in the yard at the door to Brennan's office. What was she playing at? She could not go off willy-nilly. But what about Thomas?

Oh, dear God, it hurt in her heart. She pressed a hand to her chest as if to stanch the invisible wound there.

Lucie guided her into the commander's office. But instead of

Brennan, a tall captain entered. He had obtained such height that he had to turn his head slightly to one side in order to pass through the door frame. She recognized John Corbit.

"Mrs. West, I'm currently in possession of articles that belong to your daughter."

Sarah's brow wrinkled. "My daughter?"

"From her father."

Sarah turned to see how Lucie took this news and found her on her feet, waiting with an expectant look upon her face.

Lucie turned to Sarah. "Perhaps he left us a letter."

Corbit reached into his coat pocket.

"This purse contains some six hundred dollars in coin and notes."

He pressed the leather bag into Lucie's trembling hand. Both women's mouths dropped open at the sight of such riches. Sarah's stomach twisted, for she knew what this meant. It was Thomas's way of caring for his girl in his absence. In that moment, Sarah understood that he was never coming back. She held her breath as the requisitions officer reached inside his breast pocket.

"These papers transfer ownership of a hardware store, private residence, bank accounts, and a parcel of some four hundred twenty-three acres of land in Bakersfield, California, to Lucie West, as witnessed by myself and Dr. Perry."

"What?" Now Sarah was on her feet.

Corbit turned to her. "He gives her all his holdings and funds adequate to travel to said properties."

"But what about him?" asked Sarah.

"I should say the Union Army will provide for his needs, such as they are."

Sarah had a sudden vision of a blue uniform with gold buttons, then a splash of blood and a Union-issued casket.

"No. We must stop him before it's too late."

"I'd say there's no chance of that. He seemed determined and completely in control of his faculties." Corbit extended the packet to Lucie.

She turned to her mother and Sarah nodded.

"Thank you," she said.

"At your service." Corbit gave an awkward bow.

Sarah needed to find Thomas and explain that she was the stupidest, most ungrateful woman in the world. He had no reason to forgive her, but at least she would tell him the truth. She loved him with the whole of her imperfect heart.

"Where is he bound?" she asked.

"East, to Illinois. Plans to enlist with the cavalry. Excellent choice really, for a gentleman."

"So he would go first to North Platte Station. Can I telegraph ahead?"

"Normally, yes. But the bloody Sioux cut the line again."

Sarah accepted this setback with bitter disappointment.

"You are the supply officer. Do you have any wagons heading there tomorrow?"

"Supply wagon goes out every Friday."

Two days. Sarah cursed in silence. "Couldn't your man depart a day early?"

Corbit looked about to refuse. Lucie stepped forward and grasped his arm.

"Please, sir. I wish to thank my father."

The young man's face flushed as his broad hand trembled. Sarah had never thought to use female wiles upon the man and was so shocked by Lucie's masterful appeal that she was nearly as speechless as Corbit.

"Yes, yes. I'll arrange it. I'll speak to my mule skinner. Tomorrow, at daybreak."

Lucie released Corbit's arm and smiled at her mother. Sarah felt a spark of hope. Perhaps they could still catch him.

That night was one of the worst of Sarah's life. She would doze and then wake, searching the dark window for some flicker of morning light. At last the blackness ebbed, giving over by slow degrees to a cold winter's day. She sat upon her bed, her head aching from fatigue and her heart heavy as lead.

She did not know what Thomas would say if she caught him. But one thing she knew with certainty—if she did not catch him, she would never see him again.

He had half a day's head start and rode unencumbered by wagons, and unprotected by the militia. She offered a prayer for his safety.

She changed into her traveling clothes and slipped into her boots. Next, she turned to the washstand and began her morning ablutions. She was just setting the cord at the end of her braid when Lucie's image appeared in the mirror. Her daughter sat on her side of the bed, with shoulders slumped and eyes pinched shut.

Lucie stripped off her nightdress. It was only then that Sarah saw the marks circling her daughter's upper arms.

Lucie's head popped through the neck of her shift a moment later. She noted her mother's regard fixed on the tattoos and lifted her arm to give her a better view.

"Did it hurt?" asked Sarah. She did not really expect an answer.

"Yes. They used a needle to force the charcoal paste beneath the skin. As soon as they turned me loose, I scrubbed my face until it bled, hoping I could wash out the stain, but…" She lifted her hand to her face and shrugged. "As you see."

"Why did they do it?"

"The marks show I belong to the Bittersweet tribe—or did."

"Like a brand?" Sarah was horrified, but she kept her outrage in check. For once, Lucie seemed willing to speak of her time in captivity, and Sarah would not jeopardize that with an outburst.

"Not really, no. Many women chose to wear such marks, not just the slaves. They don't see them as ugly. In fact, some women think they enhance their beauty."

Such strange people, thought Sarah.

Lucie reached for her dress and stepped into it. In a moment, the mark on her arms were hidden once more. If only the one upon her chin could be so easily disguised.

"Do you think I'm ugly now, Mama?"

Sarah hesitated, choosing her words with care. Her first impulse was to deny that anything had changed. But that was a lie and Sarah no longer chose to delude herself or her daughter. If Sarah wanted honesty, she best begin with herself.

"When I first saw the marks, I was furious. I wanted to get my hands on the one who had done this to my child. Now, I worry how people will react when they see them. I think it will make your life harder."

Lucie nodded her acceptance at this.

"I wish I could protect you from cruel, stupid comments. But I can't."

Lucie sat upon the bed and Sarah perched beside her, draping an arm about her daughter's narrow shoulders.

"It doesn't change how I feel about you. You're still my baby, even though you're a young lady now."

Her daughter tucked her head on her mother's shoulder. "Do you think we'll catch him?"

Apprehension prickled in Sarah.

"I hope so."

Together they packed their gear. Lucie rolled her new quilt inside her buffalo robe and insisted Sarah take a robe as well. They headed for the mess hall. The cook had the fire stoked and a pot of oatmeal as big as a washtub awaited them. They finished their bowls in short order.

As they left the mess hall, they retraced their steps past the room Sarah had occupied these many months. Before the door to the left stood Mrs. Corbit clutching her crying baby. It seemed this woman spent much of each night in the cold as her husband slept in peace.

"My husband tells me you are now a wealthy woman, Miss Lucie. Rather odd, considering you are but Mr. West's niece." She did not sound the least bit happy for Lucie. "I am further told that despite Mr. West's provisions, you are chasing after him like two dogs after a fox. I wonder why?"

Sarah stepped between her daughter and the condescending busybody. "Well then, Mrs. Corbit, I shall enlighten you. Thomas is Lucie's father."

Mrs. Corbit gasped. Sarah took pleasure in the look of shock upon the woman's narrow face.

"Mrs. West! You are not the woman I judged you to be!"

Sarah smiled. "And for that I thank God. Good day, Mrs. Corbit."

With that dismissal she left the slack-jawed gossip to chew her own cud. Sarah breathed deeply of the crisp morning air.

"Mother? You're smiling."

"Am I? Perhaps because I feel truly liberated for the first time in my life. How I ever let myself be controlled by such narrow-minded little hypocrites, I'll never know."

"But she'll talk."

Sarah grinned. "Let her."

"Is this because we're leaving?"

She paused and Lucie did, as well. "No child. This is because I have finally come to my senses. For years I let women like that keep me down and make me feel unworthy. I gave all my power to little ninnies like her, God forgive me."

"But not anymore?"

"Lucie, there's no pleasing such people. From now on I will live my life as *I* see fit, and you should, too."

Off they went again, reaching the stables. There they found four bleary-eyed soldiers loading a wagon. Before them stood a team of eight mules jangling their traces as they waited.

Beside them checking each harness was a wiry little man, gray as a winter morning except for his green coat, which bore the distinctive indigo horizontal stripe of a Hudson's Bay blanket. He looked old and tough as shoe leather and seemed unable to extend his left knee as he hobbled up the line of mules.

"Good morning," said Sarah.

He glanced up, showing watery blue eyes, one of which had begun to cloud.

"You the reason I'm up before the damn birds a full day early?"

"Guilty," she said.

He gave a guffaw. "I'm Duke VanTongeren." He waved a hand at his mules. "And this here is Sam and Blue up front, then Duffles and Maria, Meade and Sickles right here and last is Reynolds and General Grant."

Sarah recognized the names of the leaders of the Union Army and their commanding officer. She stared at General Grant, a brown mule with enormous ears and a white bristly chin. He lacked his cigar.

"You named your mules after generals?"

VanTongeren nodded sagely. "Just the ones in the back. You always find the generals in the back."

She smiled. "I see."

"I'll be loaded in a jiffy. You best saddle up." He glanced about. "Two of you? You understand my job is to carry the goods and my mules. We hit trouble and I see to Sam and Blue first."

"Understood."

Brennan made his appearance. Circles darkened his eyes, but his smile was unmistakable. Sarah had never seen it before.

"Ah, Mrs. West. So you are leaving our company at last."

Sarah tried not to scowl, but couldn't manage it. The man was positively gleeful to see her back.

"Thank you for you kindnesses," said Sarah, finding her gratitude did not cost her as dearly as she feared.

"I am happy to see your daughter restored and I am providing a full escort for you and your, ah, child." He extended his hand. "Best wishes to you both."

He could not withdraw quickly enough. She smiled at his light step. The man seemed about to break into a jig. Well, she could hardly blame him. They had butted heads from the first meeting and Sarah was happy to leave his questionable hospitality.

They went into the stables and found Corporal Abby there.

"Major Brennan says that Lucie is to have one of his horses."

Sarah's smile slipped. It was an act of kindness she had never expected.

"I picked this here bay. He's gentle and smart. Well broke, too."

"Thank you, Corporal. Please thank the major, as well."

He tipped his hat and left them with their horses all saddled. They mounted and took their assigned places before the wagon. Before them, two columns of three soldiers led the way and behind VanTongeren rode ten more soldiers. Brennan had seen well to their protection.

Her horse blew white vapor as she waited for the gate to open. Finally, the men before them set out and the parade was in motion. The trail between the two forts had been traveled many times since the blizzard and the light dusting of snow that had fallen overnight did not hamper their steady progress. Still, their journey seemed painfully slow. The heavy wheels of the box wagon creaked on the snow as they rolled over trodden ground. By midday Sarah regretted her decision to wait for an escort, until she recalled the last time she'd traveled with Lucie. She bit back her discontent as the wagon wheel again sank into a soft spot just off the narrow trail, requiring the men to dismount to heave and strain before setting them in motion once more.

That first night they slept at a relay station and the second in a sod cabin. On the third night, Sarah was especially glad for the buffalo robe Lucie had insisted she bring, because they slept right on the snow. A trading post was a welcome sight the following night. The fifth morning, Sarah grew anxious. They should arrive today and she feared Thomas had already come and gone.

As the day progressed, the light snow grew heavier. White fluffy flakes stuck to Sarah's coat and accumulated on the brim of her hat. It was the kind of snow she'd anticipated as a child, a good packing snow. But now the sticky surface clung to the wagon wheels.

Corbit called the break and dismounted to chip the ice from the rims.

"How much farther to the fort?" asked Sarah.

"Only a mile or two, but it will likely take the rest of the day."

Sarah lifted her gaze to the trail, already vanishing beneath the fast falling snow. If she ventured out without an escort, she could reach the fort in less than an hour, if she could follow the trail and if there were no raiders waiting to pick off unprotected riders.

She sighed away her frustration, releasing it in a puffy white breath.

"The snow will keep him from leaving," said Lucie.

Sarah turned to her daughter. Lucie was always perceptive, a trait that had likely helped her survive among the Sioux. She had another quality that Sarah lacked—patience.

Sarah drew comfort from her daughter's observation.

"I hope you are right."

"We'll find him there. But what will you do then?"

No secrets, she thought, and told Lucie the truth.

"I plan to get down on my knees and beg his forgiveness. I'm going to tell him that I have loved him with all my heart since I was ten and I cannot bear to lose him again. I'll plead with him to come to California with us and leave the war to younger men." Sarah swallowed, drawing up courage to tell her daughter all of it. "Then I'm going to ask him to marry me."

Lucie's eyes rounded. "*You're* going to ask?"

Sarah nodded.

"Shouldn't you wait for him to ask?"

"I've waited for fourteen years to marry this man and I'll not wait another minute." She fussed with her scarf. "If he'll have me."

How she wished she could turn back time. A small voice in her head scoffed. Turn it back to when? To the day she refused to allow Thomas to tell Lucie the truth, before Lucie's capture, before Samuel's death, before Samuel cast Thomas aside or before she learned he lived? There was no going back. Only this moment existed—this one chance to finally make things right, if Thomas's heart was big enough to give their love one last try.

Chapter Thirty-One

Thomas stood by the window in the narrow, crowded barracks staring out at the accumulating snow. He cursed. He had hoped to continue east today, alone if necessary. But there would be no traveling in such a snow. Already nearly a foot blanketed the grounds before the barracks.

What did it matter, today, tomorrow? Soon he'd be miles away from her.

Oh, Sarah, how I wish I could have made you love me again.

He breathed a great sigh, fogging the pane of glass before him. For Sarah, the waters were too dangerous for a second swim. He understood that. For years he had protected his own heart, avoiding anyone who came too close. He wrote her name in the condensation upon the glass and then roughly rubbed it with the side of his fist, causing the glass to squeak.

He wished she'd never come back. At least then he had the comfort of believing her a faithless woman. But now he knew the truth and he knew about Lucie.

Not only had he lost Sarah, but he had lost the child he had only just found. Sarah would see to her care. She was ferocious as a mother. He could not think of anyone better suited to help Lucie come to terms with her terrible ordeal. But for a time he'd begun to believe there was a place for him in their world—that he would share in the joy of raising her, seeing her wed. Perhaps even live to see a grandchild come into this world.

Now, he had nothing but her memory—and the photo. He patted the coat pocket where Lucie's image remained. He would carry it with him into battle. Perhaps there, he could be of some use. In his present mood, killing men seemed to be all he was fit for.

He glanced out at the barren landscape before him. Snow piled up on everything, including the men hurrying between buildings.

He heard the sentry shout. The door swung open as a young sergeant stepped in. The snow on his boots slid away leaving blobs of melting slush in his wake.

"I need four men to unload a wagon."

The men instantly dropped eye contact, suddenly very busy with polishing buttons or boots.

"Johansen, Taylor, Mackey."

The men groaned and rose to their feet.

"And…" The room seemed to hold its breath. The sergeant smiled, taking his time before finally zeroing in on his fourth. "Nichols."

The man stepped into the boot he had only just snatched off the floor for polishing, leaving an unplayed hand of cards before him as he donned his coat and waited for the others.

"What wagon? Mule skinner's not due 'til tomorrow," muttered Johansen, stooping behind Thomas and peeking out the window.

Thomas turned to see steam rising off the backs of eight lathered mules behind a party of soldiers.

"Who's that?" Taylor pointed. "Looks like…looks like women."

The men stampeded to the window.

"Two of them!"

Thomas turned to see the object of the mêlée and started. He should have known.

Sarah was dismounting her freckled horse. Every man at the window caught a nice flash of ankle before her skirts dropped into place. A flick of her head sent the long auburn braid swinging to her back.

A collective "ooh" rose from the men.

His chest tightened at the sight of her and he could not seem to draw a proper breath.

"Pretty," said a man behind him.

"Wish she'd take off that damned hat," said another.

"I wish she'd take off her damned dress."

Thomas leapt to his feet and gave a mighty shove, sending this last man rolling to his back. He turned to face the others.

"That's my girl." She wasn't, of course, but damned if he'd listen to these men as they ogled her.

The soldiers muttered and lifted their hands in gestures of surrender as they withdrew.

"Well, what about the other one?" said Taylor, pointing a dirty finger at Lucie. "Can't have both of them, can you?"

Thomas leaned down to within inches.

"My daughter."

Taylor's eyes widened and he backed away, retrieved his coat and darted out the door.

Thomas, now alone at the window, returned his attention to Sarah. This was what he had hoped to avoid. He couldn't bear to see her again, knowing she didn't want him.

Why had she come?

Not after him, that was certain. Suddenly he knew. Of course. Damn the man. Hadn't Corbit given Lucie the paper and the purse?

That would explain why Sarah pursued him. His heavy heart still beat as he rose. Apparently, seeing her again had not killed him, as he'd feared. Best get the misunderstanding settled immediately.

He drew on his sheepskin coat and headed out into the snow. Lucie stood beside her mother. Thomas drank in the sight of her, trying to memorize every detail to keep locked safely in his heart.

Sarah spoke to Paul Johansen—asking for Thomas's location, no doubt. He waited for the man to point.

"Sarah."

She turned at the sound of his voice, standing still in the falling snow. Their gazes locked. She looked as disquieted as he felt. He took the first step.

"Papa!"

He was so focused on Sarah that he did not notice Lucie, but now he turned as she bounded forward, sending clumps of snow flying behind her.

Had she just called him—

"Papa!"

She said it again—looking straight at him this time. Her arms spread wide as she dashed the last few steps and launched herself into his arms.

He glanced at Sarah to see a gloved hand before her mouth as he folded Lucie into his arms. He closed his burning eyes, but could not stop the tears.

"Mama told me everything. I'm so happy."

Happy? He couldn't credit his ears, but he still held his daughter tight.

She drew back and he let her go. Lucie bounced up and down before him. "We caught you. Mama's been so worried."

He turned to Sarah, finding her still pinned to the spot, her horse's reins clutched tight in one gloved hand.

Lucie cried, "It's true, isn't it? You *are* my papa."

He stroked her bright hair and smiled.

"Mama has something to say to you." Lucie turned to her mother, waiting. Sarah stood stiff as an icicle. "Don't you?" prompted Lucie.

Sarah drew a great breath and then dropped the reins. She seemed to be wading through hip-deep water as she lifted one leg and then another, making slow progress toward them. He'd seen men approach a hangman's noose with greater enthusiasm. Sarah had something terrible to tell him. He felt it in his bones and saw it in her wide, frightened eyes.

Black dread settled in his gut.

"Didn't Corbit deliver the papers?"

She stood just before him now. Lucie shifted to settle her hand in the crook of his elbow. Could his daughter feel him tremble? He prayed not.

At last Sarah spoke. "He did."

"And the purse?"

Sarah nodded, her rapid breath sending out white puffs of steam like a locomotive.

He stared in bewilderment. Lucie had the papers and the money. Why were they here?

"Tell him, Mama. Tell him what you said to me."

"I—I." Sarah dropped her chin, showing him nothing but the crown of her wide black hat.

Lucie sighed dramatically and flapped her free arm. She frowned at her mother and then gazed up at Thomas.

"She loves you. She rode five days through the snow to tell you that she loves you. She said she would ask you to marry her."

Thomas's trepidation turned to utter flabbergasted confusion.

"What?"

His ears must be deceiving him. He reached, grasping Sarah's chin and forcing her gaze to his.

"Sarah? Is it true?"

Tears filled her eyes as she nodded.

Lucie clapped her hands. "I told you."

"But I thought…" That was when he noted their audience. The soldiers and mule skinner stood in rapt silence. Sarah hated a scene.

He motioned to the others. "Sarah, would you like some privacy?"

She straightened, standing tall. "Hang them. I have something to say."

"What?" He could not keep the astonishment from his voice. What had come over her?

"I don't give a fig anymore what people think. I do not need their approval to love you."

He held his breath, hardly believing his ears.

"Thomas, I'm a foolish woman. I should have known that any daughter of yours was strong enough to hear the truth. I've told her everything, including that I never stopped loving you."

Thomas's mouth gaped. Everything he wanted in the world stood within his grasp.

He reached for them both and held them tight.

Lucie's head popped up. "Will you marry her?"

Thomas released Lucie to grip Sarah's shoulders.

"Is this what you want?"

She smiled radiantly up at him. "Since I was ten."

"Well, I'll be."

Sarah tugged at his jacket.

"Forgive me?"

In answer, he lowered his mouth, claiming hers, tasting the sweetness he never thought to know again.

Her tension melted as he deepened the contact until she draped over his arm. He drew back, grinning. The men stomped their feet, howling and whistling.

She flushed, casting a glance at Lucie. Thomas found his daughter smiling as if addled.

Sarah raised her voice to be heard above the caterwaul of whoops.

"Thomas," Sarah said, "Will you marry me?"

"Yes, Sarah, I will."

Lucie gave a cry and clasped her arms about his chest. The men in the snow clapped. Thomas noted the mule skinner wiping his cheeks on a large red bandanna with his arm slung around the neck of one of the lead mules.

Thomas drew Sarah beneath his left arm and gathered Lucie in his right, turning to the men. "Look at my fine family!"

Sarah lifted her hands to her cheeks to dash away the tears of joy.

Chapter Thirty-Two

The night before their wedding, Thomas came to Sarah's door.

"You asked him?" she said.

Thomas nodded.

"And?"

"He looked as if he'd faint dead away."

She laughed at this. Sarah would never forget the look of horror on Major Brennan's face when she'd ridden back through the gates of Fort Laramie. She had turned into the proverbial bad penny that kept turning up.

"He asked me twice if it was some trick before he accepted. Said he'd be honored."

"Perhaps he feels that giving me away is the best way to be rid of me."

Thomas laughed. "You are the first bride he has walked down the aisle."

"Oh, I doubt that, with all the wagon trains streaming through here."

"He said you would be his first. Never thought to have the honor, he said, as he is a confirmed bachelor."

Sarah's smile turned nostalgic. "I hadn't thought of that. I only meant to try and mend fences. A way to show I hold him no grudge."

"Well, he's tickled. Said he'll have his buttons polished 'til they shine like gold nuggets."

"That's fine. And I spoke to the chaplain. He's expecting us midmorning."

"I'll be ready."

He gripped her hand, wanting to ask a question, but afraid to broach this sensitive subject.

She sensed his unease and sharpened her gaze. "What?"

"I was just wondering if you—that is, we—might still have children."

Her alluring smile took his breath away.

"Is that what you want?"

He nodded. "I'd like to hold a baby in my arms and be there when our child crawls and walks and knocks over the milk pail."

Sarah's eyes filled with tears.

"All the things you missed. I'm so sorry, Thomas."

"No, no more regrets. From here we move forward together."

He lifted her hand to his lips and placed a kiss there.

"I love you, Thomas. Now and always."

"Now and always," he echoed.

Thomas woke on his wedding day and sprang from bed to peer up at the sky. The gray clouds continued to menace, but no snow fell.

The bugler sounded first call and the men in their bunks groaned loudly or cursed. Thomas made his way to the washroom, where he nicked his neck in his rush to be done shaving and had to dab at the geyser he'd released until the blood finally clotted.

"Haste makes waste," he muttered.

An old artillery gunner limped into the room. The man had been here since the fort's inception and showed no ambition to ever leave. His rough hand clapped Thomas heavily on the back.

"Still time to retreat. I can have a horse saddled for you quicker than greased lightning."

Thomas smiled and shook his head.

"Guess I'll make a stand."

"I'd rather face a war party than one angry female." He gave his full mustache a stroke.

"Ever married?" asked Thomas

He rolled his eyes. "Why do you think I'm out here? If I got to take orders, at least I takes them from a man."

Thomas grinned as the man limped off muttering, "No living with that woman and no release except the grave."

Thomas grinned. "Sorry for your troubles."

The man turned, still scowling. "I reckon a few years of matrimony will knock that silly grin off your face."

"Then you should wish me luck."

"Luck? Ha! You'll surely need it."

Thomas grabbed his towel and headed back into the barracks. Reveille sounded as he drew on his trousers. All about him, men scrambled to finish dressing and prepare for morning roll call.

Thomas took his time. He was to meet Sarah in the chapel after drill call.

He wished he had something fine to wear. Instead, he drew on a clean cotton shirt and leather vest. He donned his coat and hat, stepping out to meet the day.

He tromped over the well-worn path from the barracks to the mess hall. Here at Fort Laramie, the officers had a separate mess and Thomas had been invited to make use of it today. He was happy to see several of the officers' wives already on hand.

Their conversation stopped the moment he entered.

Mrs. Fairfield smiled winningly and nodded.

"How is the groom this fine morning?" she asked, her apple cheeks glowing bright.

"Well, thank you."

"No cold feet?" asked Mrs. Douglas, the wife of the second in command.

"None."

"Well, that's a mercy," said Mrs. Fairfield. She rose and approached him with an assessing look. "You look very handsome in green, Mr. West. I do believe it suits you."

"Thank you." He shifted beneath their scrutiny. "Have you seen Sarah yet?"

"I have, but you shan't," said Mrs. Douglas, sounding shocked. "It's bad luck to see the bride before the service."

"Well, I'll take all the luck I can get." He took a seat. "I wish I had a fine black coat." He accepted a cup of coffee from a private. "But mostly I wish I could give Sarah a wedding gown. It's a pity she has none."

Mrs. Douglas giggled and Mrs. Fairfield jabbed her in the ribs.

"Yes, a pity," said Mrs. Fairfield. "Though I am certain she will still take your breath away. She is such a handsome woman."

"Beautiful," corrected Thomas.

"Just so." Mrs. Douglas rose. "Well, we'd best be off. We are in charge of refreshments."

Thomas stood as the women departed. Following her first encounter with them, after the attack, Sarah had given them only the barest civility. She had attended none of their functions, refusing all invitations. When Lucie returned she had guarded her daughter like a mother hen. But all that had changed upon their return from North Platte station. Sarah seemed more outgoing, confident. The women had responded to her change in attitude immediately, except for Mrs. Corbit. She seemed stiff as a corpse. Ah, well, he thought, no sense in trying to please everyone.

After breakfast, Thomas checked on the horses. It was there he heard the sick call, alerting him that the time for the wedding approached. This time he planned to arrive early, if you could call fourteen years late early.

He found several guests already in the pews. The mule skinner, VanTongeren, sat on the bride's side of the church dressed in fringed buckskin that he'd beaten clean of the worst of the dust. He'd stuck a hawk feather in his matted hair.

Thomas's side of the church held several officers, including Captain Corbit, minus his wife.

Thomas moved to his place in the front of the church.

The chaplain smiled and then turned back to the altar, arranging the candles.

Drill call sounded and Sarah did not appear. As the minutes ticked by, Thomas began to fidget.

The doors finally swung open and in stepped the bugler. He stood to the side and lifted his silver trumpet to his lips playing an ear-shattering rendition of the "Wedding March."

Thomas resisted the urge to stick his fingers into his ears as the doors opened again.

He drew in a sharp breath as Lucie stepped into view. Garbed in a pale blue dress, she no longer looked like a girl, but like the woman she was becoming. She held her tattooed chin high as she walked gracefully down the center aisle. Pride swelled in him like a spring rain.

Behind her, Thomas caught a glimpse of Sarah. He gasped. She stood in a shimmering ivory colored gown. The pale fabric contrasted with her rich auburn hair, making her appear to be the goddess of the harvest.

Escorting her with regal bearing, Major Brennan looked quite the dandy with his mustache freshly waxed and his hair shining like a wet beaver.

Lucie led the procession, stepping to the left when she reached the front door of the church. Soon, Sarah stood before him. Her braid was threaded with an ivory ribbon and wrapped to form a coronet about her head. Her smile drew his breath away.

Major Brennan bowed to Thomas and offered him Sarah's hand before taking his seat.

"You look beautiful," Thomas said, drawing her to her place beside him.

"Thanks to Mrs. Douglas and her hope chest. We are the same size."

Thomas absorbed this startling news. Had Sarah actually accepted something from the women she had once so despised? His Sarah *had* changed. Perhaps she no longer felt it necessary to slay all dragons, or perhaps she no longer saw all women as gossipy threats.

He tucked her hand into the crook of his arm and gave it a squeeze.

"Nervous?" he whispered.

"Only that the roof might collapse under the load of snow and prevent us from wedding."

He pressed her hand between his arm and body.

"No misfortunes this time and no escape for you."

Thomas turned to face the chaplain. The young captain did a bang-up job for a man more accustomed to comforting the sick and wounded. He rose to the occasion, offering verses and readings of joy and hope, ending with Corinthians chapter 13.

Thomas grinned until his face hurt. When it came time to say his vows, he could not get them out fast enough. Sarah stood straight and spoke her vows in a clear voice as sweet as an angel's chorus to Thomas's ear.

He offered a ring of silver with a pattern of lily of the valley. The blacksmith had fashioned it from a spoon of a sterling tea service Thomas had purchased as a wedding gift.

She gasped when he slipped the token on her finger.

"So lovely," she whispered.

Thomas wondered where she had placed the gold band Samuel had given her and then noted it upon Lucie's right hand, firmly on her middle finger.

Yes, that was right—a memento of Samuel for Lucie.

The chaplain granted Thomas permission to kiss his bride. He wanted to swoop down on her like a hawk on a chicken, but in respect to the witnesses he leaned forward and planted a modest kiss on her closed lips.

Best save the rest for behind closed doors, he thought.

"I now pronounce you man and wife," said the chaplain.

Thomas spun Sarah about and marched her up the aisle to the alcove. There they waited to greet their guests. Thomas shook more hands than a politician. He wished they'd just get on so he could have a moment alone with his bride.

He glanced at her. Sarah's cheeks glowed pink and her lips curled in a smile as she accepted best wishes from Mrs. Fairfield. Thomas glanced at the seemingly endless line and sighed.

Sarah cast him a look of mild reproach.

"Thomas?"

"Why don't they leave, already?"

Sarah's eyes twinkled. "Mrs. Fairfield has planned a reception and gone to great trouble to bake a cake in our honor."

Thomas slapped himself on the forehead. "I don't want cake."

Sarah giggled. "Yes, we all know what *you* want, but you shall be polite. Do you realize they had to use three Dutch ovens for the baking?"

Thomas accepted a proffered hand and shook mechanically.

"I don't care if they had to use the Dutchman himself."

Sarah accepted hearty congratulations from the bugler, then turned to her new husband.

"Thomas West, you've waited fourteen years, I should think—"

"—you'd understand my impatience."

The last guest, the mule skinner, offered his hand to Thomas and planted a smacking loud kiss on Sarah's pink cheek. Finally, the chaplain gave his blessing to them both.

Sarah clasped the man's hand. "Pray for patience, Reverend, for my groom has none."

The holy man looked aghast. Thomas shifted his attention to his boots.

"When the good Lord said be fruitful and multiply, Mr. West, he meant after the wedding feast."

"Yes, sir," muttered Thomas.

Major Brennan offered his elbow to Lucie. The chaplain motioned to the door, waiting for Thomas and Sarah to exit before him. He ushered them across the street to the officers' mess, seeming to feel that they needed a shepherd to ensure they did not cut away from the herd.

Inside, red, white and blue bunting hung from the head table, now draped in a pristine white linen cloth. On a small table sat a lopsided two-tiered wedding cake dripping with white and pink icing.

Sarah looked so pleased that Thomas felt selfish to have almost made her miss her celebration. He threw himself into the moment, enduring the not-too-subtle jokes of the men and enjoying more congratulations from the women. Most touching of all was to see Lucie conversing with the very women Sarah had expected to shun her.

He held his bride's chair as Sarah took her seat and then he moved to his place beside her. Lucie and Major Brennan sat at the head table as well. Thomas stared out at his guests. Sarah had been right. This moment was not to be rushed.

The attendees settled into their chairs as their meals were brought directly to their table. Prime rib and mashed potatoes and baked beans with bacon, of course.

Sarah avoided the beans. "I'm afraid to stain the dress."

He avoided them, as well, but for completely different reasons.

He finished first and waited for the last of their guests to lay aside their forks. Thomas drummed his fingers on the table until Sarah rested her palm over his hand.

He stroked the satiny sleeve of the gown.

"Pretty," he said.

"You know what they say. Something old, something new, something borrowed, something blue and a tuppence in her shoe." She leaned in conspiratorially. "I had to use a penny." Sarah lifted her wine glass and took a tiny sip.

He watched her long throat arch for a moment as she swallowed and felt himself heat.

"The dress is borrowed and old. The new?" he asked.

She cast him a devilish smile that caused him to lean closer, inhaling the scent of lilacs and powder. "The new and the blue are both the same."

He surveyed her wardrobe.

"I don't see anything blue."

"That's because it's under the dress."

His brow knit in confusion.

She cocked her head and fed him another tidbit of information. "You gave them to me the day you bought me a 'proper coat.'"

Thomas shook his head.

"To hold up my silk stockings?"

Thomas slapped his hand on the table.

"The New York garters!"

Heads turned. Sarah pressed a finger to her lips and shushed him but he couldn't keep from grinning from ear to ear.

"You wore them?"

She laughed. "Yes, Thomas. Finally."

"Silk stockings, too?"

"Stockings, as well."

He rubbed his hands together in anticipation. "Well, hot damn."

Lucie leaned in. "Papa, p-lease!" She exaggerated her words. "You're embarrassing me."

Sarah tried for a chastising look but she giggled, completely ruining the effect.

"Shall we cut the cake?" she asked, rising.

"Oh, Mama, you have no bouquet to throw!"

Thomas had completely missed the lack. She'd carried a small prayer book, bound in white leather and no doubt borrowed, as well. Of course, she couldn't throw that or she'd raise a lump on some poor woman's head.

Again Thomas absorbed a pang of regret. Of course, there would be no fresh flowers for a winter bride.

"You deserve to be a spring bride, Sarah, with an armful of white roses."

"A spring bride." She scoffed. "You can't wait another ten minutes and you want to wait for the roses?"

He chuckled. "You're right. I just want everything perfect."

She squeezed his hand. "Don't fret, Thomas."

Lucie dabbed her eye. "I wish I had a proper wedding gift for you both."

Sarah took Lucie's hand and then captured Thomas's as well. "I have the only gift I ever wanted. We are a family at last."

* * * * *

MEDITERRANEAN NIGHTS

Join the guests and crew of **Alexandra's Dream,**
*the newest luxury ship to set sail on
the romantic Mediterranean, as they experience
the glamorous world of cruising.*

*A new Harlequin continuity series
begins in June 2007 with
FROM RUSSIA, WITH LOVE
by Ingrid Weaver*

*Marina Artamova books a cabin on the
luxurious cruise ship* **Alexandra's Dream,**
*when she finds out that her orphaned nephew
and his adoptive father are aboard.
She's determined to be reunited with the boy…
but the romantic ambience of the ship and
her undeniable attraction to a man
she considers her enemy
are about to interfere with her quest!*

Turn the page for a sneak preview!

Piraeus, Greece

"There she is, Stefan. *Alexandra's Dream.*" David Anderson squatted beside his new son and pointed at the dark blue hull that towered above the pier. The cruise ship was a majestic sight, twelve decks high and as long as a city block. A circle of silver and gold stars, the logo of the Liberty Cruise Line, gleamed from the swept-back smokestack. Like some legendary sea creature born for the water, the ship emanated power from every sleek curve—even at rest it held the promise of motion. "That's going to be our home for the next ten days."

The child beside him remained silent, his cheeks working in and out as he sucked furiously on his thumb. Hair so blond it appeared white ruffled against his forehead in the harbor breeze. The baby-sweet scent unique to the very young mingled with the tang of the sea.

"Ship," David said. "Uh, *parakhod.*"

From beneath his bangs, Stefan looked at the *Alexandra's Dream.* Although he didn't release his thumb, the corners of his mouth tightened with the beginning of a smile.

David grinned. That was Stefan's first smile this afternoon, one of only two since they had left the orphanage yesterday. It was probably because of the boat—according to the orphanage staff, the boy loved boats, which was the main reason David had decided to book this cruise. Then again, there was a strong possibility the smile could have been a reaction to David's attempt at pocket-dictionary Russian. Whatever the cause, it was a good start.

The liaison from the adoption agency had claimed that Stefan had been taught some English, but David had yet to see evidence of it. David continued to speak, positive his son would understand his tone even if he couldn't grasp the words. "This is her maiden voyage. Her first trip, just like this is our first trip, and that makes it special." He motioned toward the stage that had been set up on the pier beneath the ship's bow. "That's why everyone's celebrating."

The ship's official christening ceremony had been held the day before and had been a closed affair, with only the cruise-line executives and VIP guests invited, but the stage hadn't yet been disassembled. Banners bearing the blue and white of the Greek flag of the ship's owner, as well as the Liberty circle-of-stars logo, draped the edges of the platform. In the center, a group of musicians and a dance troupe dressed in traditional white folk costumes performed for the benefit of the *Alexandra's Dream*'s first passengers. Their audience was in a festive mood, snapping their fingers in time to the music while the dancers twirled and wove through their steps.

David bobbed his head to the rhythm of the mandolins. They were playing a folk tune that seemed vaguely familiar, possibly from a movie he'd seen. He hummed a few notes. "Catchy melody, isn't it?"

Stefan turned his gaze on David. His eyes were a striking shade of blue, as cool and pale as a winter horizon and far too solemn for a child not yet five. Still, the smile that hovered at the corners of his mouth persisted. He moved his head with the music, mirroring David's motion.

David gave a silent cheer at the interaction. Hopefully, this cruise would provide countless opportunities for more. "Hey, good for you," he said. "Do you like the music?"

The child's eyes sparked. He withdrew his thumb with a pop. *"Moozika!"*

"Music. Right!" David held out his hand. "Come on, let's go closer so we can watch the dancers."

Stefan grasped David's hand quickly, as if he feared it would be withdrawn. In an instant his budding smile was replaced by a look close to panic.

Did he remember the car accident that had killed his parents? It would be a mercy if he didn't. As far as David knew, Stefan had never spoken of it to anyone. Whatever he had seen had made him run so far from the crash that the police hadn't found him until the next day. The event had traumatized him to the extent that he hadn't uttered a word until his fifth week at the orphanage. Even now he seldom talked.

David sat back on his heels and brushed the hair from Stefan's forehead. That solemn, too-old gaze locked with his, and for an instant, David felt as if he looked back in time at an image of himself thirty years ago.

He didn't need to speak the same language to understand exactly how this boy felt. He knew what it meant to be alone and powerless among strangers, trying to be brave and tough but wishing with every fiber of his being for a place to belong, to be safe, and most of all for someone to love him....

He knew in his heart he would be a good parent to Stefan. It was why he had never considered halting the adoption process after Ellie had left him. He hadn't balked when he'd learned of the recent claim by Stefan's spinster aunt, either; the absentee relative had shown up too late for her case to be considered. The adoption was meant to be. He and this child already shared a bond that went deeper than paperwork or legalities.

A seagull screeched overhead, making Stefan start and press closer to David.

"That's my boy," David murmured. He swallowed hard, struck by the simple truth of what he had just said.

That's my *boy*.

* * *

"I can't be patient, Rudolph. I'm not going to stand by and watch my nephew get ripped from his country and his roots to live on the other side of the world."

Rudolph hissed out a slow breath. "Marina, I don't like the sound of that. What are you planning?"

"I'm going to talk some sense into this American kidnapper."

"No. Absolutely not. No offence, but diplomacy is not your strong suit."

"Diplomacy be damned. Their ship's due to sail at five o'clock."

"Then you wouldn't have an opportunity to speak with him even if his lawyer agreed to a meeting."

"I'll have ten days of opportunities, Rudolph, since I plan to be on board that ship."

* * * * *

*Follow Marina and David as they
join forces to uncover the reason behind
little Stefan's unusual silence,
and the secret behind the death of his parents....*

Look for
FROM RUSSIA, WITH LOVE
by Ingrid Weaver
in stores June 2007.

HARLEQUIN®

Mediterranean NIGHTS™

Tycoon Elias Stamos is launching his newest luxury cruise ship from his home port in Greece. But someone from his past is eager to expose old secrets and to see the Stamos empire crumble.

Mediterranean Nights
launches in June 2007 with...

FROM RUSSIA, WITH LOVE
by *Ingrid Weaver*

Join the guests and crew of *Alexandra's Dream* as they are drawn into a world of glamour, romance and intrigue in this new 12-book series.

www.eHarlequin.com

MN1

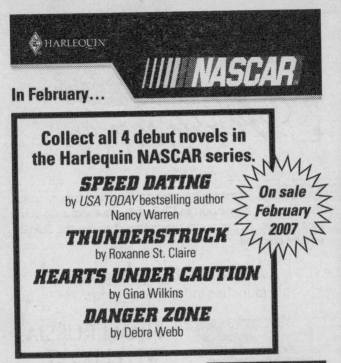

HARLEQUIN

///// NASCAR.

In February…

Collect all 4 debut novels in the Harlequin NASCAR series.

SPEED DATING
by *USA TODAY* bestselling author
Nancy Warren

THUNDERSTRUCK
by Roxanne St. Claire

HEARTS UNDER CAUTION
by Gina Wilkins

DANGER ZONE
by Debra Webb

On sale
February
2007

And in May don't miss…

Gabby, a gutsy female NASCAR driver,
can't believe her mother is harping at her
again. How many times does she have
to say it? She's not going to help run the
family's corporation. She's not shopping
for a husband of the right pedigree. And
there's no way she's giving up racing!

///// NASCAR

SPEED BUMPS
Ken Casper

SPEED BUMPS *is one of four
exciting Harlequin NASCAR books that
will go on sale in May.*

SEE COUPON INSIDE.

www.GetYourHeartRacing.com

NASCARMAY

Silhouette®

ROMANTIC
SUSPENSE

**Sparked by Danger,
Fueled by Passion.**

*This month and every month look for
four new heart-racing romances
set against a backdrop of suspense!*

Available in June 2007

Shelter from the Storm
by **RaeAnne Thayne**

A Little Bit Guilty
(Midnight Secrets miniseries)
by **Jenna Mills**

Mob Mistress
by **Sheri WhiteFeather**

A Serial Affair
by **Natalie Dunbar**

Available wherever you buy books!

Visit Silhouette Books at www.eHarlequin.com   SRS0507

HARLEQUIN®

Super Romance®

Acclaimed author
Brenda Novak
returns to Dundee, Idaho, with

COULDA BEEN A COWBOY

After gaining custody of his infant son,
professional athlete Tyson Garnier hopes to escape
the media and find some privacy in Dundee, Idaho.
He also finds Dakota Brown. But is she ready for the
potential drama that comes with him?

Also watch for:

BLAME IT ON THE DOG by Amy Frazier
(Singles...with Kids)

HIS PERFECT WOMAN by Kay Stockham

DAD FOR LIFE by Helen Brenna
(A Little Secret)

MR. IRRESISTIBLE by Karina Bliss

WANTED MAN by Ellen K. Hartman

Available June 2007 wherever Harlequin books are sold!

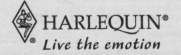

HARLEQUIN®
Live the emotion

www.eHarlequin.com   HSR0507

REQUEST YOUR FREE BOOKS!

 Harlequin® Historical
Historical Romantic Adventure!

2 FREE NOVELS PLUS 2 FREE GIFTS!

YES! Please send me 2 FREE Harlequin® Historical novels and my 2 FREE gifts. After receiving them, if I don't wish to receive any more books, I can return the shipping statement marked "cancel." If I don't cancel, I will receive 6 brand-new novels every month and be billed just $4.69 per book in the U.S., or $5.24 per book in Canada, plus 25¢ shipping and handling per book and applicable taxes, if any*. That's a savings of close to 15% off the cover price! I understand that accepting the 2 free books and gifts places me under no obligation to buy anything. I can always return a shipment and cancel at any time. Even if I never buy another book from Harlequin, the two free books and gifts are mine to keep forever.

246 HDN EEWW   349 HDN EEW9

Name _____ (PLEASE PRINT)

Address _____ Apt. #

City _____ State/Prov. _____ Zip/Postal Code

Signature (if under 18, a parent or guardian must sign)

Mail to the **Harlequin Reader Service®:**
IN U.S.A.: P.O. Box 1867, Buffalo, NY 14240-1867
IN CANADA: P.O. Box 609, Fort Erie, Ontario L2A 5X3

Not valid to current Harlequin Historical subscribers.

Want to try two free books from another line?
Call 1-800-873-8635 or visit www.morefreebooks.com.

* Terms and prices subject to change without notice. NY residents add applicable sales tax. Canadian residents will be charged applicable provincial taxes and GST. This offer is limited to one order per household. All orders subject to approval. Credit or debit balances in a customer's account(s) may be offset by any other outstanding balance owed by or to the customer. Please allow 4 to 6 weeks for delivery.

Your Privacy: Harlequin is committed to protecting your privacy. Our Privacy Policy is available online at www.eHarlequin.com or upon request from the Reader Service. From time to time we make our lists of customers available to reputable firms who may have a product or service of interest to you. If you would prefer we not share your name and address, please check here. ☐

HH07

ATHENA FORCE

Heart-pounding romance
and thrilling adventure.

A ruthless enemy rises against the women
of Athena Academy. In a global chess game
of vengeance, kidnapping and murder, every
move exposes potential enemies—and lovers.
This time the women must stand together...
before their world is ripped apart.

THIS NEW 12-BOOK SERIES
BEGINS WITH A BANG
IN AUGUST 2007 WITH

TRUST
by Rachel Caine

*Look for a new Athena Force adventure
each month wherever books are sold.*

www.eHarlequin.com   AFLAUNCH